Wessex Revisited

Love from Vesta

Wessex Revisited

Vesta Robson

authorHOUSE®

AuthorHouse™
1663 Liberty Drive
Bloomington, IN 47403
www.authorhouse.com
Phone: 1-800-839-8640

First published by AuthorHouse 10/28/2011

ISBN: 978-1-4567-8792-9 (sc)
ISBN: 978-1-4567-8793-6 (ebk)

Printed in the United States of America

Mrs Vesta Biddiscombe
8 Eden Lane, Gainford,
DARLINGTON DL2 3BG
United Kingdom.
Telephone +44 (0)1325730488
Email: vestabrian@tiscali.co.uk

CHAPTER ONE

A fine bone china coffee mug, thankfully less than half full, came hurtling across the room. Jim Coniscliffe jumped to his feet, dripping and ashen faced.

"What in the name of hell are you playing at, Clarrie?"

"No, you haven't a clue, have you? Sitting there with your nose in your infernal documents! I'm bloody fed up, that's what."

"What with for heaven's sake? Good job, lovely kids, comfortable home. Need I go on?"

"So that's what makes life worthwhile, does it? What about me and my needs?"

"Hang on, let me get this lot mopped up and then tell me about it."

"Don't patronise me, Jim. I'm not a child."

Jim went off into the kitchen to clean himself up whilst Clarissa sat seething in front of the raucous telly adverts. She stalked over to the set and almost punched it off.

"Hey, I was watching that!" Jim shouted from the kitchen. Clarissa lunged at the set and punched it back on, turning up the volume. She flung herself back into her chair and stared viciously at Jim who'd come back into the room.

He abruptly turned the set off again. "Come on Clarrie, what's eating you?"

"Well it's not 'my age' if that's what you're thinking, along with the doctor and every other male under the sun as far as I can make out. I want to do something with my life before I peg out."

"Well you're hardly likely to do that for a while, unless there's something you're not telling me. There isn't is there?"

"Yes there is something. I want to write, seriously I mean."

"Well what's stopping you?"

"Three kids, two elderly mothers, a dog, a job, endless chores and no stimulus! That's all!"

"What stimulus do you want?"

"Interesting, encouraging people. And where are those in this godforsaken neck of the woods?"

"Well surely you're stimulated with your job?"

"Oh please don't give me that crap, stimulating young minds and all that. If I could I'd get out tomorrow!"

"You can. I make enough to keep the wolf from the door."

"And the kids at Uni? Or had you forgotten Rob goes off to Birmingham in the near future? God knows what Tom's going to make of himself. Not a tycoon by the look of things. And then there'll be Jenny when you're almost about to draw your Old Age Pension. Don't talk balls Jim. Their 'conversation' was put a stop to by the said Jenny coming from Brownies, 'starving'.

"I'll see to her." Jim ushered his daughter into the kitchen, leaving Clarissa to feel ashamed of herself as she calmed down and thought over the past few weeks. Poor Jim. He couldn't stand rows and, truth to tell, because of his placid temperament her short fuse was not given much rein. This wasn't her first outburst by any means, though she'd not resorted to violence before. Her behaviour was becoming incomprehensible to herself, never mind anyone else.

Only a couple of weeks ago she'd just finished the weekly shop in her local supermarket and was standing in a reverie at the bookstall near the exit when the checkout girl's voice broke her contemplation.

"Mrs Coniscliffe, you've forgotten yer change, luv, AGAIN!"

Clarissa had been arrested by a rather more tasteful paperback than was usually on display. Its cover depicted a mediaeval walled garden in which disported a series of graceful maidens around an icily aloof and beautiful princess. To one side stood a handsome knight in an attitude of despairing devotion. Hunting dogs of lean, whippet-like proportions took their ease under carefully pruned umbrella trees. Flowers were scattered throughout in glowing abundance and a courtly musician serenaded the company on his lute.

"Forget yer head, luv, wouldn't yer? Only jokin'. Lost in a dream world was yer? Like me. Better than real one, Ah think." Tracy took in the paperback. "OO! Ah really like that. It's lovely in'it?" Clarissa thanked the girl and wearily pushed her bulging trolley out to her car. Tracy was right.

She was always forgetting things—Jenny from school, the dog's dinner, washing left mouldering in the machine. The list was endless.

"Mum . . . . MUM"

"Do you have to shout like that Jenny?"

"Well, why don't you answer?"

"Sorry I was miles away. What is it?"

"Have you done my Angel's wings yet? We're practising with them tomorrow."

"Oh lord, I've forgotten all about them. Sorry darling."

"Oh ma." Jenny was copying her two elder brothers here and this always infuriated her mother. "You're hopeless. I asked you ages ago."

"Jenny, I've said I'm sorry. I'm very busy you know. Please don't speak to me in that tone of voice and don't call me 'ma'.

"The boys do."

"Well, they shouldn't. Now off to bed with you. I'll see you have your wings in the morning." Jenny flounced out of the room.

When the house had settled down after bedtime and the clearing up of the debris of the evening meal, and demolishing a pile of marking, Clarissa settled down to the Angel's wings. Handicraft wasn't Clarissa's forte and she scared Jim off by her colourful language. At last well after midnight, stitching, her mind wandered off onto the topic of earlier in the evening. What in the world was she doing hunched over this unwieldy mountain of material, wounding her fingers, not to mention her pride (Jenny's wings would not win a prize as usual!), pouring Eng Lang 'n' Lit into unwilling receptacles and generally realising that life as she would like it had passed her by? This vague feeling that she'd like to write covered up a vast well of dissatisfaction together with a niggling sense of guilt that, as Jim had implied, with her comfortable existence she ought to feel well fulfilled.

Packing up Jenny's wings for the next day, she suddenly remembered that she simply had to do some preparation for her sixth form lesson. She took up the set text 'The Return of the Native' by Thomas Hardy. The class was currently analysing the main female character, Eustacia Vye, whose desire to live in the emotionally charged world of romantic love, rather than face up to the unyielding demands of the real, brought tragedy to all around her and ultimately to herself. One critic said of Eustacia it never entered her head to pick up a piece of embroidery to while away her hours of idleness. A knight in shining armour to whisk her off to the land of excitement, intensity and endless ecstasy would be the only solution to her problems and she invested at least two of her male acquaintances on Egdon Heath with this task, to the destruction of them both.

As Clarissa made notes for the next day she felt, not for the first time, an inexplicable uneasiness as she recognised traits she shared with Eustacia. She longed for intensity of feeling in her life, something that engaged the core of her being. She wasn't a clodpole. She was sensitive, musical, attractive (many said 'beautiful'), with a good degree in English from Manchester University, yet life as she'd anticipated it as a young girl had somehow evaded her.

She'd come somewhere near it before the kids were born, holidaying in sundrenched Tuscany, ablaze with sunflowers and golden soil, wandering around the wonderful hill towns and then, in the evenings, sipping the local wine in the balmy evening air. Surely this was it at Haddon Hall or Hardwick?—those mansions in Derbyshire associated with love and elopement, wandering around in their lovely grounds and long galleries in the melancholy stillness of an early autumn afternoon; tramping around some grey and menacing castle on a snowy December day; Christmas Eve with its scents, carols and mulled wine.

But, alas, reality was returning to a sink full of dirty dishes, a burst pipe, a child's injury, a dishevelled bedroom and the garden full of dog mess waiting to be cleaned up. It had begun to dawn on her that perhaps one had to work hard for romance to become a reality. She would have to wash up those horrible dishes, pick up the dog dirt, scour the bedroom and then, perhaps, with the silken counterpane on the scented pillows and the soft glow of low lights, 'Romance' (as in Keats, Byron, Shelley, of course) would be grasped.

And the knight in shining armour? When she had first known Jim he had seemed a dynamic man, for a while Mandarin class in the Civil Service, often walking the corridors of power in Whitehall, working on some report or other requiring meetings with junior ministers and the like. She had met him at a party thrown by one of her flatmates, who worked at the BBC as a trainee broadcaster. She, as a mere trainee teacher in a tough comprehensive school, was flattered to be singled out by him and fell instantly in love with him and the prospects of an attractive lifestyle ahead. He wasn't goodlooking, but was very charming and witty, and fed her romantic notions with red roses and expensive candlelit dinners. After a whirlwind romance, they married and settled down in a comfortable flat in North London.

After their second son was born the dynamism seemed gradually to drain out of Jim. He was working on a very knotty project to do with a forthcoming Government bill and he was constantly under pressure and worn out. A visit to the doctor informed him starkly that he had a potentially fatal and ongoing condition and if he didn't get a less demanding job he couldn't answer for the consequences. Out of the mandarin class, he was obliged to go where his masters sent him and he and Clarissa found themselves on a new, somewhat featureless estate in Normington, a town in the north of England.

Jim soon found a calmer life style suited him admirably. He had time to join local groups and follow his hobbies, which were of a somewhat sedentary nature and entailed riffling through magazines and agendas of the local town council. Their daughter was born, rather as a mistake though she soon became the apple of their eye, and when she was old enough for school Clarissa took a part-time English post in a local comprehensive to buy the extras she felt might help towards the romantic setting she longed to live in.

Jim's dynamism had mellowed into even temperedness, apart from the ups and downs of his condition. He was dependable and comforting in his way but Clarissa had become a bit of a puzzle to him. He was mildly amused by her crushes on personable men who crossed her path and, if he was at all disturbed that he wasn't all in all to her, he was far too busy with his own interests to be seriously worried by her 'diversions' as he called them. He put up with her absentmindedness and put it down to her 'age', but he found her moodiness harder to take.

The two boys shrugged it off as the way mothers of a certain age *were* but Jenny, still at primary school, became very upset by her mother's uncertain temper. As she undressed wearily for bed in the spare room her mind went back to the evening of the supermarket incident. Jenny was a clever little girl and had no worries at school, so Clarissa and Jim were surprised to be called in for a special meeting with the class teacher. Apparently there had been a falling off in Jenny's standard of work and a lack of concentration. Recent portraits of 'Mum' depicted a bad tempered, negative female with grumpy-isms in the balloons coming out of her mouth. When Mrs Bench had queried these, Jenny had vehemently proclaimed that she 'hated Mummy.'

"Ordinarily I would have taken very little notice of such an incident, but considering the whole picture I decided to call you in for a chat. I certainly don't want to pry, but I thought you should know."

Throughout the whole proceedings Clarissa had said nothing, leaving Jim to make the right noises to Mrs Bench, but when they got home she burst into tears, fled up to the bedroom and locked the door behind her. A pale-faced Jenny peered round the kitchen door at Jim.

"What's the matter with Mummy? Is she poorly? Is it my fault?"

"No my darling it is NOT your fault and, yes, Mum is a little poorly, but honestly and truly it's not serious and nothing for you to worry about. The important thing I want to tell you is that Mummy loves you even though she sometimes is cross with you. And I love you too, very much."

As with tonight, Jim had spent the rest of that evening reassuring Jenny and getting her off to bed. If the older boys noticed their mother's absence they said nothing, though meaningful looks of a not very complimentary nature passed between them from time to time until they went out to their respective rendezvous. Rob the oldest boy was soon to go off to university and, the way his mother was behaving, his exit from the scene couldn't come soon enough for him. When they had had tiffs before, Jim had always been the one to open up communications and get things sorted out, but on this occasion he thought he'd leave Clarissa to 'stew' for a while. When she didn't put in an appearance next morning he got Jenny off to school complete with wings. Surprisingly also the boys were up and about, not malingering in bed as was their usual morning routine. Jim was on the point of leaving for the office when Clarissa came down.

"Look love—why don't you see your doctor—I'm sure you need a bit of help. Or at least ring Anna and have a chat. I must dash but I'll try to ring you before you go out to school this afternoon. Bye."

Left to herself, Clarissa felt dreadful. Guilt was the uppermost feeling. She knew she had been childish and unfair and she really was worried about Jenny. She daren't ring Anna who, though a very good friend, was a fiendishly down-to-earth person with no time for wallowing in feelings and would have declared that you simply had to take everything that life threw at you and get on with it. She rang Maria, a more 'sensitive' soul.

"Well I think you need a change," was Maria's response to Clarissa's call. "Why don't you take yourself off at half-term somewhere for a few days?"

"How can I? I can't leave Jenny too long with Jim. You know how he can be sometimes."

"Well I'll have Jenny. She'll be good company for Sally. I'll take them out and about."

"Oh Maria, would you? I've had my eye on a short course on Thomas Hardy in Dorset for some time now. I'd love to go but I think they'll be fully booked by now. It was advertised months ago."

"Ring up and find out and we'll take it from there."

"You're an angel Maria. It's a thought! I don't think Jim will mind. I've been such a pig lately that he'll be glad to see the back of me."

The course was indeed fully booked but Maria insisted that Clarissa take herself off anyway. Jim was all for her having a breather but the boys weren't so amenable. "How can you go running off, leaving Jenny the way she feels at present? She'll think you've gone away because of her! And what about Dad? Don't you think he needs a break?"

Her mother-in-law, who lived about forty miles north, too looked stoney-faced when approached, but didn't say anything. She never interfered in her son's business but was always willing to help when needed. Since her husband's death five years previously she prided herself on her independence and was intolerant of people 'giving in' to their feelings. Jim was determined that Clarissa should have a chance to recover from whatever was getting her down and it was none of his mother's business anyway.

CHAPTER TWO

In fact it wasn't easy getting away. Clarissa had to go through a series of 'boring, tedious' tasks—getting the dog looked after, leaving the house in a reasonable state, preparing meals to leave in the fridge, trying to get the boys to see her case a little more sympathetically and failing pretty completely, trying to convince Jenny that her trip was going to make mummy better and therefore nicer, letting her aged mother know her plans for the next few days—before she could set off on her visit to Hardy country to try to 'find' herself in the surroundings of Tess, Bathsheba, other Hardy heroines, and her alter ego, Eustacia. She planned to video the Dorsetshire countryside and the locations mentioned in the Hardy novels—that awful Flintcombe Ash where Tess struggled to survive, Egdon Heath, where the natives appeared and disappeared in the light and shadows cast by the bonfire on Rainbarrow summit and Eustacia queening it over all.

She was booked in at "The Greenwood Tree" in a village about eight miles east of Dorchester, which she'd picked out of the "Guide to literary and romantic accommodation", hoping it would give her the atmosphere she was looking for. Imagine her dismay then, when, on inspecting the bed she found not crisp, white, lavender scented cotton starchedness, but polycotton slipperiness in shocking pink. The telly stared bleakly from a plastic imitation wood table. A thick pot mug and two cling-filmed biscuits constituted "welcome" and a wonky dimplex radiator was all the warmth she could expect.

The 'Snug' promised better but disappointed even more. No yokels sucking on clay pipes on the settle in an enormous inglenook, but a fruit machine and wall-to-wall wraparound 'musak'—loud, but not loud enough to drown Sharon and Gavin bickering between gulping intakes of Marlborough lights. She rang home on her mobile but the call was barred over and over again, so she assumed the signal was poor from where she was. She rang from the pub's public phone to find the line engaged at the other end. By the time she got through she was tired and frustrated. She was assured by Jim that all was running smoothly, which ought to have calmed her, but curiously made her a little miffed. Apparently life at home could gZZo on quite well without her. "You enjoy yourself and don't worry about us", were Jim's signing-off words. She went to bed and writhed all night long in the slithery sheets.

Her first day's journeyings around Hardy locations took place in weather of a totally nondescript variety—grey, bland and uninspiring. No ominous clouds, no autumnal mellowness, no dramatic gales! Egdon Heath turned out to be bits of left-over scrubland, on the largest of which sprawled an army camp and firing range. Try as she would she could not conjure up the opening scenes of 'Return' with Eustacia outlined, goddess-like, against the fire-lit sky.

Woolbridge Manor, the scene of Tess' wedding night, was still there but scarcely a hundred yards from an unsightly railway crossing. Romance was still eluding her it seemed! She returned to the "Greenwood Tree"after a singularly disappointing day and went straight up to her unfriendly room. And here she slumped on the bed, wondering how on earth she was going to fill in the evenings? She glanced through the hotel brochure, scanned the untempting dinner menu, flicked through teletext to see if the box offered an option—it didn't—and finally, after a lukewarm shower in the bathroom along the corridor, she plucked up courage and went down to the so-called Snug for an early G&T. She ordered some sandwiches to take up to her room and opted for a novel and an early night.

The Snug was empty at such an early hour except for one other occupant—a man of about forty five utterly absorbed in a sheaf of printed papers which he kept annotating. On the reproduction mediaeval bar table at which he sat, a few assorted belongings were scattered—mobile 'phone, a newspaper and a pint of beer. Although ripe for amorous adventure, Clarissa was not forward and would no more have tried to attract the man's attention than fly to the moon, but there was no doubt about it, he was attractive in a way that appealed to her. He wasn't stunningly good looking or 'macho'; he wasn't particularly tall—slightly above her own height she guessed, though it was hard to tell from his seated position. He was wiry and agile-looking and his face was stern but sensitive. Just her type, Clarissa shamefacedly admitted to herself. She would drink up quickly and disappear to her room.

"Your sandwiches are ready, madam. Shall I send them up or will you take them with you?"

"Oh, I'll take them. It will save you the bother."

"No bother at all. It's all part of the service, but if you don't mind . . . You can use those stairs over there, they come out near your room."

Clarissa got up to go. As she walked towards the stairs trying to balance the plate of sandwiches, her novel and a handful of leaflets she'd picked up, she bumped into a stray bar stool and her plate tilted to one side causing one of the sandwiches to fall to the floor. The pub dog was instantly on the scene, so was Frank, the landlord, and the man had half stood up to come to her aid.

"Geroff, Strider"—this to the big black Labrador who by now held her sandwich tauntingly in its mouth. In a gulp the sandwich was gone and Strider was snaffling the remainder of her supper from the plate, which at this juncture was just about at the right level for opportunist dogs. Clarissa was all embarrassed apologies, the landlord and his wife apologetic and scolding the greedy Strider. The man continued to look concerned and slightly amused.

"Tell you what Mrs Coniscliffe, we'll send another lot up to your room in a few minutes. You go up and relax."

Clarissa, hot and flushed, mumbled her thanks and shot off up to her room as fast as possible. Would Bathsheba or Eustacia have appeared in such a clumsy light? She wasn't the stuff of romantic heroines and that was that. In her clinging polyester bed she decided that she would pack up and go home the next day.

* *

She was down for breakfast by eight thirty and found herself alone apart from a couple of business types on a table in the corner farthest away from her. There was no sign of the man from the evening before. She had her breakfast, collected her case from her bedroom and went to the reception desk to settle her bill. The landlord and his wife were surprised that she was going after having booked in for four nights and made some difficulties about what was owed. She agreed to the amount they asked for, although she felt they'd charged rather steeply considering she insisted that it was a family matter which had cut short her stay and therefore not really her fault.

She got into her car and set off. It was a much brighter morning weather-wise so, instead of going straight for the most direct route to the north, she decided to go into Dorchester to have a look around. After parking her car (with some difficulty for it was market day) she wandered fairly aimlessly until she came to the museum with its huge Hardy collection. By a fluke she managed to get into the Hardy archives (for she had not the requisite references) and spent two hours poring over interesting, but not entirely relevant to her purpose, documents.

She felt quite exhausted, so she decided she'd restore herself with a coffee and something to eat at the little refreshment bar overlooking the courtyard. There were only about five small tables and she secured the only empty one very near to the counter. She was aghast to see the man from the "Greenwood Tree" take his place in the short queue at the bar. She hoped to God he wouldn't see her. She still felt embarrassed from the incident in the Snug, almost as though he had guessed her thoughts about his attractiveness, never mind the demonstration of her clumsiness. She started to thumb through the leaflets and tried to avert her face.

"Do you mind if I sit here? The lady from the "Greenwood Tree"—if I'm not mistaken!"

Clarissa attempted to look surprised and indicated the empty seat opposite to her. She was flattered that he remembered her and this gave her courage to ask if he'd been into the documents room, knowing full well that he had. After various pleasantries about what they'd seen, the better weather and the surprisingly good coffee, he asked her if she was from the neighbourhood. She told him that she came from the North, was on a sort of Hardy quest, but it was all very airy-fairy and so far she felt she was wasting her time and was heading off home as soon as she left here.

"You haven't given yourself sufficient time to make such a decision and to have come so far. Seems a pity."

"Well it was a last minute decision to come and I'm afraid I didn't have time to prepare an itinerary or anything in advance, so I feel I'm floundering around somewhat."

"Have you any idea of what you want to do?"

"Write," she tentatively replied, "though I've no idea whether I've got any talent."

"Have you published anything?"

"Not really. A couple of poems in a local magazine. I wrote a bit at college and I run a students' creative course at the school where I teach part-time. That's all."

"And what precisely has Hardy to do with it?"

"Well I love his work and I thought a 'nose' around down here might 'inspire' me." She laughed self deprecatingly over the word 'inspire'. "Anyway what about you? Are you from these parts?"

"No. I'm from London."

"Holiday or business?"

"Before we go any further, let's introduce ourselves. I'm Sam Melsonby."

Clarissa gave her name and he smiled. "Could look good on a dust jacket! I'm here on business—I'm in films. Don't look impressed—I'm an actor, but not a star and you won't find my name anywhere near the top of the credits. I work with a few colleagues. We call ourselves "The Group". We specialise in educational films—writers, artists, musicians—that sort of thing; popularising I suppose, but I hope tastefully with not too many gimmicks. In fact, our next venture is to be some aspect of Hardy."

Clarissa was impressed. She couldn't help thinking that fate was somehow lending a hand here. Was Thomas Hardy bringing them together? Immediately she dismissed the thought as absurd. A film star was unlikely to find her a gift from the gods!

"Will you have an acting part in the film?"

"Not if we can get anybody better, but I've got a lot of general research to do before we even think of planning a film. I'm here to do that groundwork now. See what's feasible within the constraints of our budget and so on. We work on a shoe string!"

They chatted on quite easily, sharing their thoughts on T.H. and other more general matters. Clarissa looked at her watch and jumped up, trying to collect her belongings together without the disaster of the previous evening. "Goodness, I must be on my way—I want to get home before dark . . . ."

"Do you really have to go? I sort of got the impression, last night, that you were staying a few days?"

"Oh yes, I was booked in for four nights but, as I told you, I had such a fruitless day yesterday that I decided last night I would quit and I checked out this morning."

"As I say, what a pity to have come so far and achieved so little. Mind you, as I've already said, you haven't given yourself a chance. Tell you what, why don't we pool our brains and see if, together, we can make a bit of progress? If you would like to, that is?"

"There's nobody expecting me back home for three days, so that isn't a problem but I'm not sure. I'll feel a bit of a fool going back to the "Greenwood Tree" after spinning a yarn about being urgently required at home."

"Well, we'll find you somewhere else. In fact, I wouldn't mind another place myself. "The Greenwood Tree" has the virtue of being cheap, that's all."

It seemed that Dorchester and surroundings were popular this half-term and there was nowhere suitable available, so reluctantly they returned to the "Greenwood Tree". After another cock and bull story, some raised eyebrows, a pretence that her room might well have been taken when the girl was on duty that morning and a general implication that her erratic behaviour had caused considerable trouble, Clarissa was again ensconced in her bedroom, which curiously didn't seem quite so bleak now!

The Snug, too, took on a new aspect with an attractive companion to drink with and the meal afterwards was really quite passable. Clarissa was aware of her own attractions to men she met back home, teachers and village folk, but she awarded a degree of sophistication to Sam and she couldn't believe that she could attract such as he. And it was clear that he was gently flirting with her and presumably did find her an attractive woman. The food and wine heightened Clarissa's already dizzy level of excitement and she had to tone down the 'wonderful' time she was having when she rang home. The news that all was continuing to go well at home pleased Clarissa this time and helped to cancel out the niggling guilt she felt at so enjoying herself with her stimulating new companion.

CHAPTER THREE

So as not to arouse the suspicions of Frank and Lilly they kept to separate tables over breakfast, but they met in the car park and decided their movements for the day ahead. Sam had to attend a briefing with a colleague from London and that would take up the whole morning. They arranged to meet for a plan of campaign over lunch and Clarissa was to join Sam in the foyer of the Casterbridge Hotel around one o'clock. She parked her car at the top of the town. Clarissa felt focused already and did none of the meanderings of the previous day. She followed the outline of the Roman walls to get a general feel of the town and its Walks. On three sides were tree-lined paths and she stopped to admire the Elizabeth Frink sculptures and the Roman Town House. She took in the statue of Thomas Hardy at the Top o' Town and noted the Dorset County Library for future reference.

She still had time to see what she'd missed of the museum the day before and spent the next hour browsing through exhibits of local and ancient history making sure she did not miss the reconstruction of Hardy's study at Max Gate which was smaller than the photos in the leaflets and books suggested. She couldn't believe how concentrated her mind had become. Everything seemed possible to her now. The happiness of having someone to share her interest was something she hadn't known since University days and the fact that that 'someone' was an attractive man fuelled her sense of at last finding her purpose in life. Of course she realized that her thoughts were running too far ahead and, when Sam walked towards her after parting from an attractive woman about the same age as herself, she experienced both jealousy and confusion—jealousy for the obvious reason and confusion because again she felt as though Sam had divined her thoughts about him and found them both ridiculous and impossible.

She deliberately made no allusion to his colleague and adopted a distant and rather flippant attitude to cover her real feelings.

"Let me treat you to lunch in a rather good little French Bistro." Sam said. "I've patronised it a few times. It's nothing to look at but the food is excellent and doesn't require a mortgage to pay for it either. It's down on the river which isn't much at this point, but it's really very pleasant." He waved aside her protests at not being allowed to pay her share and they made their way to "L'eau à bouche" in the pleasant hazy sunshine.

It was a small, unpretentious place with red and white checked cloths on the tables, run by a French couple who had their placid smiling six month old baby boy, Tomas, in the dining room with them. The buildings in the terrace of which it was a part were the premises of artists and craftsmen of various sorts, many of them linked to the other side of the tiny river by little bridges. The menu promised delights and they were not disappointed. They both chose something simple which belied the skill required to produce it. Françine and Emile were both sophisticated and friendly. They clearly regarded Sam as a regular and without gush made sure he and his attractive companion wanted for nothing. The undoubted French ambience contributed to Clarissa's illusion that she was abroad and the north of England seemed on a different continent. They were both slightly whoozy with the wine and planning receded further and further down the agenda.

"There's a pleasant garden at the back with a few tables. Why don't we have a breather outside and then get down to some planning", Sam suggested.

Clarissa couldn't believe she wasn't in a dream—one of the fantasies she indulged in on dog walks. She was rapidly coming to the conclusion that a soul-mate had been lacking in her life and, dangerously, Sam was assuming that role for her. The sensuous warmth of the walled garden, the drone of the last wasps of the year, did nothing to dispel this illusion and Sam's attentions were, she was certain, not imagined. What had not been established as yet was, did either of them have a 'significant other'? Good wine and enjoyment of each other's company had divorced them from difficult reality and neither felt inclined to investigate anything so complicated on this perfect afternoon. They discussed their 'project' in a desultory way but, apart from deciding that 'The Return of the Native' might be worth considering, Clarissa left the bistro more enthralled with

Sam than with Thomas Hardy. Two strong French coffees countered the effects of the wine and Sam felt able to suggest a ride to Hardy's birthplace at Higher Bockhampton.

As they drove through the winding, high-hedged Dorset lanes, Clarissa stole glances at Sam's profile and his hands on the steering wheel. She still couldn't believe that such an attractive and accomplished man would seek her company. With all his contacts in London and the film world he must move in a milieu far above the level of sophistication to which she had been used for the last umpteen years. However, with the aid of the lovely afternoon weather and the glow afforded by good food and wine she knew she was creating a favourable impression. When they got out of the car to view the cottage he took her hand and smiled at her. "This is fun, isn't it?"

"Much better than my solo travels yesterday, that's for sure," she quipped, not wanting to give away the intensity of what she was really feeling. For quite some time they wandered without saying anything and then she felt a gentle pressure on her hand and, as she responded almost against her will, he said, "You must have an important somebody at home?"

"Yes," she replied simply, "and you?"

"There is somebody in London. Important? Yes, but less and less in an emotional sense, but still someone I care about."

"The person you parted from at lunch time?"

"Francesca? No, she's one of our group—publicity. She's lovely but we're colleagues only. No, I have a partner Esme. We've been together for five years but there are problems. Have you children?"

"Three. Two boys and a girl." She was reluctant to give their ages as this would give away her own age and she wasn't prepared for that yet.

"And partner?"

"Husband. I've been giving him a bad time lately. Oh nothing like that. We're terribly faithful," she laughed rather cynically. "But I've felt a bit restless lately and I've taken it out on him—moodiness and so on. Sounds pathetic, doesn't it? Anyway, I don't know why I'm telling you all this. Sorry."

"Please don't apologise. It seems we've both got problems. Tell you what, let's find somewhere for a cuppa. I'm feeling dry after the wine."

"We're not making much headway with our project, are we? We scarcely took in the Birthplace. But yes, I'd love some tea but it's my treat this time, though I realise I'll still be in your debt. By the way that was a delicious meal. I must do the same for you—tomorrow perhaps?"

"Tomorrow might be problematic. I may have to pop up to London with Francesca for an emergency meeting with the others. But I'll be back late tomorrow night or at the latest early the next morning."

Clarissa tried her hardest not to show her sharp disappointment. "You'll have to put me on some kind of a track with my researches. You see how helpless I am without you", she giggled.

"Good", he said quite seriously. "I think I want you to miss me."

They found a hotel which served afternoon tea and they found themselves alone in a vast lounge where they could talk without being overheard. "Tell me about this restlessness as you call it—that is, if you want to. If you think I'm prying please tell me. I'm interested, that's all."

"Oh, I just feel I could be doing something more fulfilling with my life."

"More fulfilling that being a mother and a teacher?"

"Yes that's what Jim—my husband—says. And of course I'm fulfilled in those ways, but I still feel I've missed out somehow. Perhaps it's a mid-life crisis or something. I'm sure I'm not the only woman who feels as I do."

"Most women would give a lot to have what you've got, I'm sure. And I'm not trying to say 'count your blessings' or anything like that. We can't help the way we feel. We all know we should be thankful compared to the poor two-thirds of the world, but how many of us are? We fortunate people have very high expectations."

"You're making me feel ashamed of myself already."

"Has your coming down here anything to do with your problem?"

"In a way, yes. Jim thought it might help if I had some time to myself. So this Hardy thing is a bit of an excuse, though I do want to do some research—posh word—on some aspect of Hardy as a stimulus to a bit of writing."

"You don't have much confidence in your powers as a writer, do you? It's a tough life, you realise—this writing lark!"

Clarissa did not answer for a minute. She had hoped her lack of confidence wouldn't be picked up, even though every word she uttered demonstrated it.

"Well, I expect I can toughen myself up, if I have to. At the moment I just need to get on and do it."

"How much do you want to write? Do you feel you absolutely must write above all else?"

"I love writing and I think I can do it. My problem is—have I anything to say that hasn't been said before—and much better? Have I an individual angle on anything? I don't know. I'm not writing to get published, though I know that's a defence against *not* being published. I just want to know whether I can create something structured—a sort of work of art if you like—and I would like to *say* something."

"What's wrong with just story-telling? We all love a good tale. Is it necessary to say something, as you put it?"

"What constitutes a good tale? Is it just a series of intriguing events or is there a point to these events other than keeping us reading on and being entertained? I'm not sure I'd be any good at that either, to tell you the truth. That certainly demands skills I'm not sure I have. Pretty hopeless aren't I?"

"Hm. I'd say you've a bit of sorting out to do in more ways than one."

Probably the wine as a lift to the spirits was wearing off and moroseness was setting in, but Clarissa suddenly felt close to tears. She was clearly transparent as a pretty ordinary mixed up, middle-aged woman who took herself too seriously. It hadn't taken this eminently attractive perceptive man long to sum her up and find her hopeless.

"I think I'll go home tomorrow and start the process. It's clear I'm not ready to impose myself on the unsuspecting public yet." She buried her face in her handbag so as not to let him see her upset. "Meanwhile we'd better getting back to the hotel."

Their journey back to the "The Greenwood Tree" was almost silent. Just before they got out of the car Sam turned to her and put his hand on her shoulder. "Have I spoken out of turn? I'm sorry. What right have I to voice an opinion about you after such a short time?"

"I expect you're expert at analysing people, especially someone as ordinary as me."

"Don't go home. And you're not ordinary. Confused? Yes. As I am. You must have realised by now that I find you a very attractive and interesting woman. *Interesting.*" He emphasized the word as she indulged in yet another display of self deprecation.

* *

They agreed to meet for a light supper snack later on in the evening. Sam had some work to do following his meeting of the morning and in preparation for London the next day. Clarissa was simply exhausted and in spite of an unsettling conflict of emotions she slept soundly until her alarm woke her to get ready to meet Sam in the Snug for a drink. She took pains with her appearance wearing a casual trouser suit and a skilfully draped scarf which complemented her dark hair and vivid blue eyes. The effect was not lost on Sam, who said simply "You look lovely."

The evening passed lightly without the 'charged emotions' of the afternoon. They discussed a possible approach to their project. They had decided that for one reason or another 'The Return of the Native' had been neglected and might bear some investigation as a topic for an educational film, as it was still on exam syllabuses. At the same time Clarissa might find something to stimulate her writing. A flexible plan was mapped out for Clarissa to follow the next day, but was by no means set down in tablets of stone. Frank brought sandwiches for them and they compared notes on holidays they'd had. Neither had travelled extensively, Sam because of the expenses incurred by the Group (though it was obvious that he was not living on the breadline as his comments about the Group tended to suggest) and Clarissa because of family constraints, but they had visited and loved many of the same places, They both had loved Tuscany and reminisced merrily until bedtime. It was when they came to say goodnight that Clarissa realised that, though she had successfully kept in check her feelings of intense attraction to Sam, they were there nevertheless and if Sam had suggested a shared bed she was not sure she would have resisted. As it was he kissed her gently on her forehead, touched her hand lightly and left her.

A feeling of rejection was added to her already mixed cocktail of emotions and again the shamefacedness that she could so easily have let herself get into this situation. She tossed and turned for an hour, when there was knock on her door. Her heart leapt, as she thought the impossible and feared it, but it was Lilly's voice from the other side. "Are you awake Mrs Coniscliffe? I'm sorry to trouble you, but there's a call for you. I thought I'd check first to see if you were awake. You can take the call in your room."

"Oh I'm so sorry Lilly. Thanks anyway."

It was Jim. "Where on earth have you been hiding yourself? I've tried your mobile umpteen times. You've obviously had it switched off."

"It's very late Jim. Is it something urgent? Is Jenny alright?"

"Yes, she's fine but you haven't exactly kept in touch. Maria thought you might have 'phoned to say goodnight."

"Well I haven't exactly been away for long and I'll be back the day after tomorrow."

"How are things going? Are you feeling any better?" Clarissa didn't know whether she was or not, but this was not something she could go into at this moment or with Jim. So she said she was and that she was sorry she hadn't kept better in touch, but the time had simply flown. "I'll bring her something nice back."

"Hm." was Jim's response. Clarissa knew Jim didn't approve of what sounded like trying to buy Jenny off.

"How are the boys?"

"Oh they're OK, as far as I can tell. I hardly ever see them. I think Tom's got a girlfriend."

"Tom? You sure? I can't believe it! Tom?"

"Well I think so, but it's not such a big deal. He's not getting married or anything."

"Well, well. Dark horse. Are you OK? Work and everything?"

"Fine, but I'll be glad to see you back."

Clarissa couldn't honestly say she was looking forward to being back, so she lied and said she was.

She felt troubled that Jim had rung so late and for no good reason. The fact that he was obviously missing her, and that Jenny was too, didn't make her feel as guilty as it perhaps should. She knew she wouldn't relish what would be expected of her on her first night home. Not that Jim was a demanding type, but he would be disappointed and wonder at her coolness. Was there a niggling doubt that the intense emotions she had always longed for weren't unalloyed satisfaction? Jealousy, feelings of rejection and of guilt were intriguing to read about in novels, but in reality? As she lay awake, turning things over in her mind, she wondered why she was feeling so disturbed. After all nothing had happened that she need be ashamed of. And nothing *need* happen.

Tomorrow she would pursue her own research and she may not even see Sam again. He had given no clear indication when he would be back.

And she would have to leave early on the day of her departure. These thoughts brought her no pleasant relief, however. She couldn't bear the thought of not seeing Sam before she left for home. She drifted off into a troubled sleep and woke feeling totally unfit for what she'd planned for the day.

CHAPTER FOUR

Sam had already left when Clarissa got downstairs. Over breakfast the thought occurred to her, again, to book out and go home. Only the thought of confronting Frank and Lily stopped her. She swallowed too many cups of awful Greenwood Tree coffee to galvanise her into activity, collected what she would need for the day (including her car which in her besottedness with Sam, she'd forgotten to pick up—Frank kindly ran her in to where it was parked at the top of the town). She set off towards Higher Bockhampton and Hardy's Birthplace, which some scholars think was the original for 'Blooms End', the home of Eustacia's husband, Clem Yoebright's place in the novel.

According to Hardy's sketch map of the novel's location, Bloom's End faced Mistover Knap, Eustacia's home high up on the Barrow, though there is doubt as to how near to geographic accuracy was the landscape in Hardy's imagination.

The morning was hazy but fine and promised to be warm later on. At the Birthplace Clarissa looked across the garden which, in summer, must have been a riot of colour, but at this late stage in the year looked rather tangled and a shade overgrown with filmy cobwebs cloaking the vegetation. She went to reception and enquired as to the chances of looking round that day. Unfortunately the first entry wasn't till eleven o'clock, an hour and a half away and she felt she would rather get on to other sites and, as she was returning home the next day, she would have to miss out on the trip. She looked round the garden, recorded it on camera and the exterior of the house. Then she walked in what she thought was the direction of Mistover Knap, but soon found herself in rather dense woodland with the footpath petering out here and there, so she gave this up as a bad job.

Getting back into her car she set out once more, this time to what was reputed to be the site of the 'Quiet Woman' inn on the road between

Dorchester and Tincleton—'Duck Dairy House'. Though pleasant enough in itself on a now warm and sunny morning she could capture little of the novel's atmosphere from the nineteen-thirties farm house, modern barns and ramshackle outhouses serving as commercial outlets for this and that. Nothing of the old inn trappings remained. She was beginning to think that without her 'Svengali' she could accomplish nothing. She swept her camcorder over the area for future reference and turned to go.

"Are you looking for something, lady?"

Clarissa turned round and thought she was seeing things. A bent old man complete with hat, smock and high leather boots was looking at her quizzically.

"Oh sorry. Am I trespassing? I'm looking for the site of the 'Quiet Woman Inn.' I was told it was somewhere here."

"Never were 'Quiet Woman'. 'Traveller's Rest', mebbee, and when my father drank in 'er 'twere 'The Duck'. You best get over to Halstock. 'Quiet Woman' be there, lady. Get a good sup there an' all, I tell ee."

She almost thanked him as Granfer Cantle in this 'time warp'. So far, he was the only approximation to what she hoped to find . . . . The Hardyesque!

"You live here, do you, Mr . . . ."

"Weatherstone. Not far, but you'll not see my patch easily. 'Tis hidden."

"Sounds intriguing. How long have you lived in your hidden home?"

"Nigh on a hundred year, man and boy. I s'pose you're doin' summat on Thomas, eh?"

"Well yes. I'm trying to get a new angle on some of his work, I suppose."

"I could give you an angle, lady, that I could." said Mr Weatherstone, somewhat enigmatically.

"Oh?"

"Yes, but I'm not speakin' out of turn, that I'm not."

"Did you know Thomas Hardy, then?"

"Might of, but I'm not speakin' out of turn."

"I don't want you to say anything if you don't want to, Mr Weatherstone."

"Will, that's what people call me. Would you like to see my house, lady? Most folk don't get a chance to see it, but you've got a pleasant way wi' yer and though I ain't sayin' nothing, a glance o' my 'ome might help yer wi' yer searches. T'was in 'is verses, did yer know that?"

Clarissa was inclined to take this with a pinch of salt, but he seemed a harmless enough character so she saw nothing wrong in going along with him, after ascertaining that it wasn't too far away and it was alright to leave her car where it was. It took them about fifteen minutes to walk at Will's pace, across the field on the other side of the road from Dairy House, to a deep pond surrounded by tall reeds. Skirting round the pond, which Will assured her was NOT 'Heedless William's Pond', as many folk "diggin' into Tom Hardy seemed to think—that's over by Higher Bock'ampton way—but a pond belonging to the Weatherstones for many a long year.

They came to what can only be described as a wooden shack, painted very dark green and blending in with the surrounding woodland. A few hens and a magnificent cockerel were pecking around and an ancient sheepdog lazed in the shadow of the overhanging roof timbers.

"Come in lady. I'll get ee a drink of elderflower cordial wi' a dash of zummat. Sit down and be comfortable."

As Will was out getting the drink Clarissa gazed around the simply furnished room. The wooden floor was bare except for a few homemade rugs scattered around. The chairs and table were from another era and again looked as though a craftsman in a small way had turned them out—rough-hewn, but corners smooth and shiny through time and use. Completely dominating the room and quite out of character in being elegant and ornate was a grandfather clock. Once again Clarissa experienced a literary time warp and looked behind her to see if there was a second 'rival' clock as in 'The Woodlanders' and was disappointed to see that there was not.

The drink Will served was delicious and the 'zummat' made it extremely potent so that for the second time in two days Clarisssa experienced drowsy effects and a sense of unreality. She hoped the drink would loosen Will's tongue, so she plied him with a few inoffensive questions to start with, hoping she could be bolder later on.

"Who built this house, Will?"

"Oh ma'am, don't ee flatter 'er by callin' 'er a 'ouse. 'Tis nothing but an oul' shack. I knows that, but it's been our 'ome for one an' a 'alf century. My granfer put 'er up when he was first married and my father and now me 'ave looked after 'er."

"Have you any one to carry on looking after her when you can no longer do so?"

"No, lady."

"You didn't marry then?"

"Yes ma'am. I were married once briefly."

"Did you wife die?"

"She left me." Clarissa was nonplussed and felt she could not pry. Will would have to *offer* any information on this topic. She murmured that she was sorry to hear that and sipped her cordial in silence. She put her glass down, thinking of the driving ahead. She was pulled in various directions. She would like to hear more should he offer it. She knew she ought to get on with looking at some more sites, but she didn't want him to think her unappreciative of his hospitality. Will decided the issue by saying "Don't you want to know why 'er left me?"

"Well, yes, if you think it's any of my business, but I don't want to be nosey."

"She ran off wi' an architect or a stonemason or zummat."

For one exciting moment she thought she'd hit on something researchers can only dream of—someone who knew . . . . , but then she realised that, though Hardy had begun his working life as a stonemason, he would have been a well-established writer when Will's wife 'ran off'.

"Anyways she's dead now," and Will fell into a seemingly unhappy reverie as he sighed from time to time. Clarissa said gently, "I must go now, Will, but I'll return some time if I may. "Thank you so much for your hospitality."

The afternoon had worn on and it was almost dark when she got back to her car, having been led slowly back by Will, who pressed her hand warmly and invited her to return and see him again soon. Before she drove off he vanished into the gathering gloom and all the way back to "The Greenwood Tree" she wondered if she were waking from a pleasant and fascinating dream. She was dying to tell Sam of her day's experiences and her prowess as a researcher and, though she half expected that he would not yet have returned from London, she was disappointed not to see his car in the car park or himself having a beer in the Snug. In her room she made some new notes and tried to put some order into those she'd covertly jotted down during her visit to Will.

CHAPTER FIVE

After a refreshing nap and a shower she once again paid special attention to her appearance for Sam and once again chastised herself for acting like a silly teenager. Was she serious about her researches or was she simply using them as an excuse for an affair? One thing was certain, she was well on the road to falling head over heels in love with Sam. Before going down to the Snug she rang home, where Jenny answered the 'phone.

"Jenny, I thought you were at Maria's. You're not in the house alone are you?"

"No, but Daddy's busy cooking the supper and he seems to be cross with Tom and I'm homesick and—oh when are you coming home, mummy?"

"Tomorrow, darling. Promise. Now get Daddy for me, please."

It was a minute or so before she heard Jim's voice. "Yes?" was his curt enquiry.

"Its *me,* Jim."

"I know. You'll have to be quick. It's chaos here and I'm trying to feed the kids."

"Jenny seems to think you're cross with Tom. What on earth's the matter?"

"It's too complicated to go into it now, but there are problems with his girl friend. You'll find out all tomorrow. I really must go now. Bye." And the phone was put down on her.

Clarissa was stunned and more confused than ever, but decided that she would only stew over things if she stayed in her room and besides, in spite of her guilt that Jim was dealing with problems alone at home, she desperately needed to see if Sam had returned. She went down to the Snug but, without Sam, who was nowhere in evidence, it struck her as soul-less as it had on her first night. Once again Sharon and Gavin were alternately battling it out over the top of the blaring music and snogging ostentatiously for the benefit of a group of giggling females at the bar. A gang of youths were applying themselves assiduously and noisily to the fruit machine and a tableful of birthday party-ers were blowing party-poppers in all directions. Clarissa pushed her way through the unyielding customers and tried to attract the attention of Lilly, unsuccessfully. Finally she mouthed her question—had she had any 'phone messages? Lilly shook her head and turned back to serve.

Clarissa couldn't stand the racket any longer and went up to her room to think. She decided that if Sam didn't contact her by nine o'clock she would pack up and set off for home that evening. She spent the time throwing things into her suitcase and tried to interest herself in "Weight, Sex and You" on the telly, whose message was unsurprisingly that the fatter you were, the less were your chances of good sex. Had she been at home she might have put pen to paper complaining of such unsuitable material before the Watershed, not to mention its political incorrectness. As it was, it merely served to fill up the emptiness of her own room and shut out the rowdiness from the bar. At five minutes past nine she checked the room to see if she'd left anything, picked up her luggage and went down to the bar to settle her account and check out. Dressed in her outdoor clothes and flourishing her credit card, she attracted Lilly's attention more easily this time, though Lilly was again astonished that Clarissa was leaving before her scheduled departure and at such a late hour. "For goodness sake drive carefully dear and take plenty of stops. It's raining quite hard. Why not leave it 'till morning?"

"No, I must get back as soon as I can. The problem I spoke of earlier has got worse. Anyway the traffic will be lighter at night. Goodbye, Lilly. Say goodbye to Frank for me." She almost ran out of the pub. When she got into her car she remembered that she'd meant to leave a note for Sam—something cool and business-like. She simply could not face Lilly again so she decided to sneak up to his room and slip the note under the door. "Sam, I've had to leave tonight—emergency at home. Research went very well. Met someone who met T.H, a Will Weatherstone who lives over the field from Duck Dairy Farm. You can contact me . . ." and she left her address and telephone number. As she slipped the note under the door she couldn't help thinking that T.H. would have approved but she feared that, in true Hardy fashion, it would doubtless contrive to go astray!

* *

Lilly was right. It was raining *very* hard. The winding, dark, country lanes were not easy to negotiate at the best of times but in the dark, with her headlights emphasising the rain driving into the windscreen, it was nightmarish. She had to battle on until she reached the major road which would ultimately lead her to the motorway and then she would take stock. She simply daren't stop on these deserted roads even though common sense told her that nobody in their right mind, however villainous or ghoulish, would be lurking for her on such a night. Even so at the speed she was forced to drive she was scared that some unsavoury character could easily force her to stop. She locked the doors and accelerated as much as she dared.

The radio did nothing to raise her spirits with one station already issuing severe weather warnings, another putting out a murder mystery play and Radio 3 broadcasting some modern composer's more than usually lugubrious 'Requiem'. By the time she reached the motorway it was well after midnight and she was tired and hungry. Much as she didn't relish the thought of being a lone woman in such a place at such an hour, she decided she would have to call in at an all night Service Area for a break.

Inside her small car she felt very vulnerable creeping around the enormous lorries parked up for the night. She got soaked running the short distance to the cafeteria building, where she fortified herself with soup, roll and a coffee. A scattering of customers mostly ignored her, except for one unsavoury individual who kept staring at her. She tried to ignore his gaze and was disconcerted when he got up just as she did and followed her to the exit. She thought she would throw him off by going into the 'ladies'. It was equally as scary and empty as the dining area and she wouldn't have been surprised to see her stalker walk in. She stayed about ten minutes or so tidying herself up and then ventured out.

He didn't seem to be around so she once again ran the short distance to her car and sped off towards the motorway slip road. It wasn't long before she was aware of a pickup van overtaking several cars and pulling in behind her. Each time she pulled out to overtake, the van did the same and pulled back in behind her, so she was left in no doubt that she *was* being stalked.

The rain was still pelting down, causing considerable surface water on the road and spray from other vehicles which prevented her from speeding off and outstripping her pursuer. She fumbled in her handbag for her mobile 'phone, her car veering dangerously on the waterlogged road. She wasn't used to phoning and driving at the same time so it took some time to dial 999. The only information she could give the police was the service area ten miles behind as a landmark and the registration of her car. All she could do was to drive on and hope a patrol car was somewhere not too far away. Her pursuer was now flashing his headlights at regular intervals so she was blinded both in front and behind. She didn't know how much longer she could tolerate the situation and was close to tears of despair, which didn't help at all.

The van suddenly drew out and started to drive parallel to her. The nearside window was lowered and the driver, a hooded youth, leered at her and started to shout at her. They must have driven a couple of miles like this, with motorists speeding by in the fast lane. Just as Clarissa was on the point of pulling on to the hard shoulder, she saw a police car speed up behind her, siren blaring. With difficulty they forced the driver to stop and Clarissa drew up behind him. She forced down the hysteria and flopped exhausted over the steering wheel.

"Are you alright, madam?"

"Yes, I think so, but scared to death."

"I'm afraid I'll have to ask you some questions." The policeman eased himself into the passenger seat, whilst his colleague dealt with the van driver in the police car. After Clarissa had answered the questions as best she could, the officers exchanged places.

"Our friend here says he was only trying to attract your attention to the fact that you had your fog light on—which indeed you have, madam."

"I'm afraid I can't accept that as an excuse for his reckless behaviour. He kept trying to make eye contact with me in the service area."

"He says you kept trying to get him to look at you. May I suggest it's a funny hour for a woman to be on her own in a place like that."

"You make it sound like a den of vice, officer. I'm on my way home—to an emergency as it happens—and feeling tired, I followed road safety advice and 'took a break' in a place especially designed for the purpose."

The officer insisted on knowing the ins and outs of her business and eventually, though not appearing too convinced of the veracity of what she told him, he took down her address and telephone number and said she was free to get on her way, but that she would be contacted in due course. Her 'stalker' was driven off in a police car; his van no doubt would be dealt with later. Left alone on the hard shoulder, Clarissa's held-back tears flowed freely. She sobbed partly from relief, partly in reaction to the ordeal she'd been through, but mostly from utter disbelief that she could be in such a humiliating situation—rejected by Sam, doubted by the police and heaven knows what by her family. Eventually commonsense somehow managed to prevail and goad her into action. She knew she couldn't sit there weeping on the hard shoulder of a motorway without attracting further unwelcome attention so she pulled herself together and set off once again.

The long remainder of the journey, though tedious, passed more or less uneventfully until she ran into the beginnings of the morning rush hour. Exhaustion dictated that she rest somewhere until the traffic peaked. She couldn't face another Service Area so she took the next slip road off and almost immediately found herself on comparatively quiet country roads and, though apprehensive of stopping anywhere, she looked for a suitable spot and turned off the engine. She made doubly sure that the doors were locked, and climbed into the back seat and lay down.

Clarissa was on the verge of sleep when a loud rumbling announced the presence of a huge farm vehicle looming over her. She had not thought carefully enough when she chose a field gate entrance for her forty winks. With a great deal of confused unlocking of doors, clambering out of the back into the front, searching for keys and jamming of gears, Clarissa eventually allowed the monster to get into the field. The driver glared at her as she drove off. It was pointless now trying to rest, so she decided to get back on the motorway and brave the rush hour. The rain was still coming down but not quite so heavily, enough, however, to slow the traffic to a crawl for much of the way.

When she reached home it was about nine thirty and nobody was in. Clarissa was hungry but too tired to cook anything and, after a glass of water, she went up to the bedroom and crashed out. When she woke up she looked at the clock and saw that it was eleven. She was sure she could smell toast and coffee but decided that it was hunger causing an olfactory hallucination. She pulled on her dressing gown and wandered downstairs into the kitchen.

There at the table sat a ravishingly beautiful Asian girl in a satin dressing gown!

"What in the wide world . . . ." Clarissa began. The girl jumped up, startled.

"Oh, Mrs Coniscliffe, I'm so sorry. Tom said you wouldn't be back until tonight."

"Would you mind telling me what's going on?"

At this point Tom walked in from the garden where he'd been putting out food for the cat.

"Mum, let me introduce you to Amy, a friend of mine. Amy, this is my mother."

The two women shook hands rather stiffly and Clarissa motioned to the girl to sit down again. She, herself, remained standing near to the Aga as she was feeling chill, probably the effects of her night's ordeal.

"We didn't expect you back this early in the day," Tom began.

"Hm. That's pretty obvious." Clarissa couldn't help running her eyes over Amy's state of 'déshabille.' The silence which followed was awkward, but only for Clarissa it seemed, for Tom and Amy recovered their sang-froid very quickly.

"Have some coffee, Mum. It's fresh and you look as if you could use some. Have you travelled all night?"

Without going into any details Clarissa gave a brief account of her night's travails and to Tom's further enquiry said that she'd had a fruitful trip and got some good ideas for research.

"What are you researching, Mrs Coniscliffe?" This from Amy.

On being told, Amy showed considerable interest and said that though 'Return' wasn't her favourite, she did like Hardy and thought it was a shame that he didn't seem to be in favour at present. Amy was reading Psychology and English at the local University.

Clarissa was puzzled how Tom could have met her as his pursuits were not at all academic. This was something she would follow up at a later date. Now she accepted Tom's offer of coffee and after asking how things had been at home she excused herself to shower and dress.

She sipped her coffee, sitting on the edge of the bed in a state of some confusion. Her head was whirling after the events of last night on the motorway and now Tom's romance, which was clearly at an advanced stage. Tom had always been a difficult lad with a mind of his own. He was extremely bright and could have got into the local private school on the results of a scholarship examination she insisted he sit, much against his will and the advice of his father. Tom refused to go on the grounds that both Clarissa and Jim were convinced Socialists and had set their faces against the private sector until Clarissa waived her principle in the case of the education of her own offspring.

At the comprehensive he survived on his wits and managed to get a string of good exam results with the minimum of effort. His 'A' level results could have got him into any prestigious university but again he refused to apply, maintaining he'd had enough of formal education and was going to try his luck in the *real* world. For months that seemed to involve lying in bed till lunch time and spending half the night goodness knows where—behind the bar at a pub it turned out—so how he had met someone like Amy, Clarissa couldn't imagine.

Once again Clarissa found that her firmly held moral and political views were in conflict with what she wanted for her own children. She had not considered the possibility of her children having black or Asian partners, though in principle she was not against it. Tom had never been a girl chaser and as far as she knew Amy was his first girl friend. She was beginning already to accuse Amy of being scheming and ensnaring her inexperienced Tom for her own selfish ends. With these thought she went into the shower but was abruptly summoned out of it again by Tom's shouting to her that she was wanted on the 'phone. Her thoughts flew to Sam and she raced out on to the landing to the upstairs one, bumping, en route, into Amy, clad only in a barely concealing towel, suggesting familiarity between the two women which Clarissa was certainly not wanting to encourage.

"Clarissa Coniscliffe?" The voice at the other end of the line wasn't Sam's, though it was male with a far from local accent. "This is Avon & Somerset CID here. About the events of last night. I think you ought to be ready to give evidence in a court case. Obviously we'll be in touch at a later date, but I want you to be prepared for that eventuality." On top of all her recent experience, the disappointment of the call's not being from Sam and the prospect of appearing in court caused a flood of tears. She was glad to hear the front door bang, signifying that Tom and Amy had gone.

She spent the day on automatic pilot, sorting out her case, washing and doing all the mundane jobs that follow a period away from home. She was dreading Jim's return from work but was quite relieved when he *did* arrive home, with Jenny, whom he'd picked up from Maria's, in tow. Clarissa ran with outstretched arms to Jenny and in spite of the child's coolness she hugged her almost feverishly. She responded to Jim's embrace rather less enthusiastically, but nevertheless experienced a warm affection towards him, which grew to something amounting to passion in the privacy of their bedroom later that night. Surprisingly Jim didn't seem as 'keen' as she'd expected and feared. They quietly discussed Tom and Amy.

"How on earth did he meet someone like Amy?" Clarissa enquired.

"Apparently she does some clerical work at the pub where Tom hangs out. Helps to pay for her uni fees or something. She's nice. I like her, but I've only met her once."

"Are they sleeping together?"

"Well they share a room when she stays over, but whether they share a bed I haven't presumed to enquire."

"I'm not at all happy about that," Clarissa said with a certain amount of truculence, "not with Jenny being around and all that. Anyway he hasn't known her five minutes. I hope he knows what he's doing. I don't want one of her bloodthirsty brothers or whatever round here making trouble."

"As far as I know she's an only child."

"That's worse. I bet her parents watch her like a hawk. There'll be trouble, you mark my words."

"I'm more concerned about Jenny. I didn't want to worry you but she had two bouts of what Maria could only describe as sleepwalking."

"What? What on earth do you mean? She often gets up to go to the toilet, but I can't imagine she sleepwalks."

"Well, try this for size. Apparently Maria heard noises about one o'clock in the morning and there was our Jenny sitting on the top stair moaning something about mummy leaving home and she knew it was all her fault. When Maria called out to her, Jenny took no notice, got up and walked downstairs and picked up the telephone."

"Did Maria speak to her?"

"She asked who she wanted to 'phone but Jenny didn't speak at all—but the next night, though she didn't walk, she was muttering about the doctor and mummy."

"I find this hard to believe. I think she was probably just wanting attention. You know what she's like, sometimes."

"Well it sounds like a pretty serious cry for attention, if you ask me."

"Why didn't you take her to the doctor's or bring her back here?"

"Oh come on, Clarrie. That's easier said than done with you away, my job, etc, etc. Anyway I thought I ought to consult you first."

"Does Tom know about this?"

"I did mention it to him and he said he wasn't at all surprised."

"Well that's nice, what did he mean by that?"

"You'd better ask him. He's more perceptive than we give him credit for, that lad. He may even have chatted to Jenny himself. I couldn't get anything out of her, though I didn't say Maria had seen her sleepwalking or whatever it was. I just asked her whether she was finding it difficult to sleep with you away and so on, but she said she was sleeping just like she usually did."

"Oh what a problem our kids are! We'd better take her to the doctor's tomorrow. I'd like you to come with me."

"Yes OK, though we don't want to frighten the girl by over-reacting. Let's get some sleep if we can. We're both tired."

CHAPTER SIX

The next evening Jim and Clarissa took Jenny to see the doctor who questioned them each privately. They didn't want Jenny to know that she'd been sleepwalking in case they frightened her and made the situation worse. The doctor questioned Jenny without mentioning the sleepwalking but tried to get from her what was troubling her. The child wasn't very forthcoming and he asked Clarissa (not in front of Jenny) if she would like some help from a child psychologist, though in his opinion at this stage, he didn't think it was necessary. Clarissa wasn't keen but said she would talk it over with Jim and come back to the doctor. The doctor said he was sure that the matter would soon be resolved with extra love and attention being given to Jenny, making clear he wasn't accusing the parents of being remiss in this area, but remarking that Jenny was clearly a sensitive child who quickly picked up disturbing vibes when all was not as she expected it to be.

Jenny's coolness towards Clarissa nevertheless continued and, whilst Clarissa was exasperated, thinking this to be attention-seeking behaviour, she wasn't unduly worried and was sure the child would 'come round' in due course. Clarissa made every effort to spend as much time as she could with Jenny and took her out on 'special' trips and arranged treats of all kinds so that gradually Jenny did 'come round' and seemed to be her old self again, but not entirely. She still seemed to prefer Jim's and even Tom's (not to mention Amy's) company to Clarissa's.

Clarissa still continued to be distant towards the Tom/Amy relationship, though she couldn't explain to herself or anyone else why. Clarissa had to admit Amy was a most impressive young woman, who continued to be friendly and courteous towards Clarissa in spite of the latter's coolness. However Tom didn't bring her round as often and she never spent the night. Things came to a bit of a head when she and Jim went along to a University Dramatic Society production of 'Romeo and Juliet', with a black student playing Romeo. They had seats next to Amy and her family and had drinks with them during the first interval. Everybody was raving about the excellent male lead and how the family feud was underlined by the lovers being from different cultures.

On being asked by Mrs Khatiri what she thought of the production, almost against her will Clarissa found herself saying that she wasn't convinced by the choice of a black Romeo and she thought it was just a gimmick on the part of the director. There was a shocked silence. Mr and Mrs Khatiri looked hurt. Jim muttered oil-on-troubled-waters type noises and Tom declared in no uncertain terms that it was time some people crawled out of the dark ages. Amy tried, calmly, to encourage Clarissa to justify her view which, she said, was a valid one. Clarissa knew she had clanged. She knew beforehand that she was going to. At the very lowest level, manners, if not diplomacy, informed her that her response was cackhanded. She realised that she would have to retract and started to do so, but Tom was already steering the Khatiris back to their seats. Needless to say Clarissa spent the second half of the play in an agony of something like remorse. She didn't see Tom for a week after that. He didn't come home to sleep and he didn't ring. He called one teatime to collect his things and informed his parents he was moving out.

"I'm not shacking up with Amy, if that's what you thinking. I've got a place where I can take her without her being insulted. I *might* in time tell dad my address." And with that he left.

"I really don't think we deserve this," said Clarissa after the door closed behind Tom. "What's it all about? Surely not that incident at the play!"

"Well you could have been more tactful—what you said about the black Romeo."

"Well I only meant that it would have been OK if the whole cast had been black."

"And where do you think they're going to get all black actors in a British University? Besides that's not the point. If you believe in equality then it shouldn't matter a monkey's curse what colour the actors are. I couldn't believe what I heard came from *you*."

"Please, Jim, speak to Tom and tell him I didn't mean to be offensive."

"Well, he's so angry I expect he'd put the 'phone down on me. And anyway we neither of us know where he is now. I'll pop round to the pub and have a word with him. But you'll have to come to terms with the fact that Tom and Amy are an 'item'."

Clarissa half-heartedly agreed. In fact Tom wasn't a lad to bear grudges and within a few days he came round to his parents' house and made it up with Clarissa. He was adamant, however, that he wasn't moving back in and in fact he was staying above the pub for a peppercorn rent and was happy with his independence.

As the weeks went by, Clarissa had so much on her mind that she was hardly aware that Sam hadn't got in touch. Jim's mother had to go into hospital for a minor operation. Things at school were hectic to say the least, with her in charge of the Christmas pageant. With all that Christmas entailed, there was plenty to keep Clarissa more than busy. She thought of Dorset with a mixture of nostalgia (she had thought that 'her' sort of life was beginning) and anger at herself, for being so naïve in thinking so. The incident on the motorway was just what she deserved and look what a nuisance that was going to be with a trial pending. She had already made a flying visit to Bristol to appear in the Magistrates' Court at the first hearing of the case. There was no time to let Sam know, even if she'd had the courage to arrange a meeting. She decided that this was her life, she was stuck with it and would have to make the best of it.

* *

It was one evening after a particularly fraught day, with hurried Christmas shopping thrown in for good measure, that Tom arrived announcing he was 'starving'. Jenny had two friends in to play who were also 'starving'. Clarissa was flying around the kitchen trying to satisfy the various dietry foibles of family and friends.

The 'phone rang. "Get that, please, someone. I've got my hands full here."

Tom took the call and came into the kitchen, where Clarissa was struggling with recalcitrant spaghetti. "It's for you, mum. Fellah called Sam,"

Clarissa went hot and cold but she tried to act as casually as she could and, wiping her hands, she went out into the hall and picked up the 'phone.

"Hello. Clarissa Coniscliffe here."

"Yes, that name *would* look good on a dust jacket. How are you?"

Summoning up an enthusiasm and confidence she certainly didn't possess, Clarissa replied brightly that she was fine.

"I'm sorry I haven't contacted you before now, but I've had problems both on the domestic and career fronts, to mention but two."

"I'm sorry to hear that. Do you want to talk? I'm willing to listen, but now isn't all that convenient. I can ring you back,"

"Would you? Late-ish on tonight? Say ten?"

Tom was all curiosity, but she managed to keep him at bay by saying the caller was to do with some writing project she had on. Tom didn't take her writing seriously so he soon lost interest, but, on leaving after his meal, he observed, "Sam, eh? Sexy name. Sexy voice!"

After Jenny was put to bed the evening dragged. Jim was out to a committee meeting and would most likely go on to the pub with the other members, which would just about give her time to squeeze in a call to Sam. At about ten minutes to ten it dawned on her that she hadn't Sam's number! What a fool! She tried 1471 but the number had been withheld! She was almost frantic with frustration. Would Sam ring again or would he assume her non-contact meant no opportunity and he wouldn't bother her again? Time now took wing and she realised that any minute now Jim would be home. She had given up hope when the 'phone rang and actually made her jump.

"Have you been running? You sound almost breathless!"

"Er, yes, I . . . was just putting the cat out and was in the garden. I stupidly forgot to ask you for your number earlier. I'm afraid we may have to make this short. Jim will be in any minute now. Sorry."

"You haven't changed. Still apologising. I should have given you my number when we were in Dorset, so it's me who's stupid. Anyway, it's great to hear you. To get to the point—when can we meet? I followed up your very good research, found out more *very* interesting facts from your old friend, and I think we could get going on our joint project. I need to talk to you—business—and I'd like you to meet the rest of our gang. So when can it be?"

Clarissa fumbled for a chair. She felt faint at the thought of meeting him again and the fact that he was still talking in terms of a joint project after a lapse of some weeks meant that he really meant it. She realised that to be taken seriously as a colleague she couldn't prevaricate, but she simply could not up and go with the way things were at home.

"You flatter me and I would love to meet your colleagues, but I must have time to make arrangements. I said I was fine but there *are* problems back here and I doubt if I can get away so soon after my last adventure. I think you'd better count me out."

"I'll do no such thing. Look, I know things are difficult for you with family, etc, but there are ways around things. You don't have to do all the travelling. We could meet somewhere near you or halfway or something. A lot of the stuff you could do at home anyway."

"What stuff?"

"Oh lord, I haven't even mentioned the fact that we'd like you to be one of our scriptwriters, or to be more precise our only scriptwriter—funds being what they are at present! In fact I'm jumping the gun. You'll probably refuse when you hear now much we can pay."

"But you don't know whether I'm up to the job. You haven't read any of my work. I'm probably crap—if you'll pardon the expression."

"That's true, but I can't see you not being up to our modest standards. Sorry that doesn't sound very flattering, but what I mean is that our audience is mainly school kids and it's how the material is presented that's important. As a teacher yourself you'll have a pretty good idea of what's required. Instinctively I know you're the right one for our particular job."

"Well I'm flabbergasted. I'd certainly love to have a go, but as I say it's going to be difficult and I don't want to let you down." Jim's key turned in the lock. "Look, Jim's just come in so I'll ring you sometime tomorrow, during the day."

"Sorry no can do—I'm tied up all day tomorrow. I'll ring you. Take care." And he was gone. Once again Clarissa felt deserted. Once again she'd have to wait for him to call and she'd only just reconciled herself to his not being a part of her life, as she'd fondly imagined in Dorset. Jim didn't comment on her preoccupation nor was he bothered by the fact that her enquiries about his evening were lukewarm. After twenty years of indifference to his committees and their doings there was nothing unusual about it tonight.

CHAPTER SEVEN

Talk about bombshells and bolts from the blue. Whether Clarissa was getting in touch with the more intense, emotional world she craved for was debateable, but certainly the future demands on her time promised to be far from boring and mundane. Following the first elated reaction to hearing from Sam after so many weeks' silence, panic set in, in a big way. Could she fit in trips away from her part-time job, the demands of family and all the rest? But more than that—was she up to the job? How could Sam put such faith in her? He hadn't even seen a sample of her writing. He was taking a ridiculous risk, yet he didn't seem the type who would let his heart rule his head. It was unreal and she felt that if she ignored it, it would just go away. She had always needed to be 'pursued', to feel that she was really needed. If Sam wanted her as a script writer, or anything else, he would come back to her again. Meanwhile she would get on with her life here.

Goodness knows there were problems enough to be dealt with, not least Jenny's continued dreams and hostile attitude to herself. She was not sleepwalking, but in her dream Clarissa always figured as some kind of ogre or tyrant. She was still upset, too, by her behaviour to Amy's family at the students' production. She had been rude and racist to lovely people and she still had difficulty in accepting Amy as a serious partner for Tom. She was ashamed she felt so. All her long-held socialist principles condemned her, as did Jim who couldn't see what the problem was. And herself and Jim. There was a rift developing between them. He didn't attempt now to pacify or please her as he used to. Committee work was taking up a great deal more of his time. What time he did spend at home was devoted to Jenny—helping with her homework, reading to her, taking her for walks with the dog and listening to her problems. The plain fact was that Clarissa felt isolated in her own family.

It was during one of Jim's infrequent nights in that the 'phone rang as Clarissa was putting Jenny to bed. Jim took the call and shouted up that it was for her. She picked up the upstairs 'phone. It was the Avon and Somerset Police.

"You'll be getting a letter from us, Mrs Conisclifffe, but this is to inform you in advance that you are being called as a witness in the case against Christian McKenzie."

"Oh dear," said Clarissa. "I suppose I do have to attend?"

"Most certainly you do, Madam. The case against the young man is far more serious than the incident on the Motorway. You will be given the details in the letter. The case is in two weeks' time and we thought you would like to know as soon as possible so you can make arrangements to come to Bristol."

"It's all terribly inconvenient. But if I must, I must. Thank you for letting me know personally."

There was no doubt it would be dreadfully inconvenient, but there might be the possibility of meeting Sam. She would ring him when she got an opportunity, though she was reluctant to do so, needing yet more reassurance. But damn it! She would!

Jim was curious to know who the call was from and, on being told, said he would go down with her to give her support. Maria or his mother would have Jenny. He was flabbergasted when she said she would prefer to go alone. She, who'd always needed him with her on occasions which demanded the confidence and practical know-how he possessed.

"I would really like to go with you," protested Jim. "I could do with a bit of a break and I've some holiday outstanding. This seems like a good opportunity."

"But you'll be hanging around on your own when I'm in court. There's no fun in that."

"I'll take myself off during the day and meet you in the evenings. It's ages since we had any time away together. It'll be liked a second honeymoon."

This was just the sentiment Clarissa did not want to hear at this juncture.

"I don't think we should leave Jenny without one of us being at home, the way she is at the moment."

Jim looked disappointed. It was clear he had his heart set on going with her. "Well, Tom will be around to keep an eye on her. She's close to Tom and wherever she stays he'll drop round to see her."

Clarissa still looked doubtful, seeing meetings with Sam fading into the distance. Jim went on. "I suppose we could take Jenny with us—yes, why not? It will mean time off school, but she'll easily catch up and the change away might do her some good too."

As it happened, the beginning of the trial coincided with an in-service day for Jenny's teachers, so it was settled that the three of them would go down the weekend before it started. At any other time a short holiday with Jim and Jenny would have delighted Clarissa, but now it meant it would be difficult to arrange a meeting with Sam & co. and if she didn't see them this time it would be difficult to get away again. Somehow she would have to send Jim and Jenny off on a day trip or something while she pushed in a meeting with her 'colleagues', as she supposed she must now call them. Of course, Sam might not be able to get down from London and the sooner she found that out the better. She was getting used to spending her days in a fever of anxiety, willing Sam to ring. Eventually just at the point when she had summoned up the courage to ring him, he rang.

After the usual pleasantries—Sam had rung about nothing in particular—Clarissa told him about their proposed trip down to Bristol for the trial. He was surprised and alarmed at the stalker incident and it was obvious that he was genuinely upset that she'd suffered such an ordeal on the way back from their special Dorset time together.

"I can't let you know just yet of my movements that week but if you give me your hotel number, I'll ring you there. I'd really love to see you and I'll bring an outline of our discussions so far and see what you think."

It was not at all satisfactory to leave things so much up in the air, but it seemed the best they could come up with. Once again, Clarissa was left in a state of anxiety. But this "I'd really love to see you again," made her heart race. Preparations for going proved easy now they were taking Jenny with them. The dog would be looked after by Tom and, no doubt, Amy. Jenny was thrilled to be going, particularly missing school!

The trial was due to start on the Tuesday and Clarissa had to report to a solicitor's office in Bridewell Lane on the Tuesday morning to be briefed by her legal representatives. Jim had organised a week off for himself and some time from school for Jenny. They travelled down to Bristol on the Friday evening and spent the weekend re-discovering Bath. Jenny was really taken with the Roman Baths and all the Jane Austen connections—being the daughter of an English teacher and still not put off by information offered by her parents, as she would be soon, she was familiar with the novelist's name and the titles of the novels.

The weather was cold but bright and, were it not for the ordeal ahead and the tension associated with the uncertainties of a meeting with Sam, Clarissa would have found the weekend enjoyable. Jim seemed very relaxed and, though affectionate in his approach to her, did not press for bedroom favours. Clarissa was grateful for this as she could not have responded, her mind being so taken up with Sam.

Jim and Jenny dropped her off at the solicitor's office at nine o'clock sharp on Tuesday morning. Clarissa was to contact them by mobile 'phone when she had finished and they would play the rest of the day by ear. She had to put all the thoughts of Sam out of her mind to concentrate on the details of the case. It seemed that her stalker was up on three charges, one of dangerous driving and the other two more serious, possessing and pushing drugs. Apparently the police had found drugs in his van when they stopped him on the motorway the night of Clarissa's ordeal. He was under the influence of drugs that night.

She was welcomed by her solicitor, Michael Baines, and was introduced to the prosecuting council, Harry Hetherington. If the police had made her feel the guilty party, these two made her feel more so. She was grilled mercilessly. Every statement she made was challenged, turned inside out and upside down, so that at the end she scarcely knew what had happened. She could quite see how wrongful confessions could be wrested out of suspects! By lunch time her head ached and her throat was sore with the endless repetitions she'd uttered. She decided not to meet Jim and Jenny for lunch and opted for a drink and a sandwich on her own as the best way to help her recover. She was forbidden, even if she'd wanted, to discuss the case and she wasn't up to being pleasantly chatty. So she rang Jim and arranged to be picked up outside Baines' office later on in the afternoon. She came across a pub, went in and ordered a beer and a sandwich. As she lunched, her mind reverted to Sam. She was troubled that Jim would be curious if a strange man rang and would see it as a shadow over their 'holiday'. So with her customary reluctance she rang his number in London. After a few rings a disembodied voice instructed her to do the usual. She did not want to leave a message so she tried his mobile number, again with no luck. She rang his home number again and left what she thought was a business-like message. "Clarissa Coniscliffe here. Please ring after eight tonight. It's to do with the script—rather urgent." She hoped a 'significant other' would not be suspicious, but she would have to leave Sam to deal with that problem. She couldn't go on a minute longer living in the uncertainty of if and when he would ring.

There were only a few loose ends to tie up at the solicitor's and by four o'clock she'd rung Jim to come for her. She collapsed on the bed and slept until it was time to get ready for the evening meal.

CHAPTER EIGHT

The three of them had a pleasant early dinner and about eight o'clock Jenny went off to bed and Jim and Clarissa had a long evening ahead of them. They went into the bar and settled down to their respective books with a drink as, although Jim had plenty to report about his day with Jenny, Clarissa was too uptight to engage in any kind of conversation and in any case was exhausted by the day's legal goings on. The trial was to begin the next morning at ten o'clock and she wanted an early night. She concentrated not at all on her novel and willed a message from Sam to come through. She'd arranged with reception to inform her of a call if it should come and she was furiously working on what story she would concoct for Jim. Just as she was giving up hope she was summoned to reception. Sam had called.

"Got your message, Clarissa. I can make it down to Bristol, but the thing is when?"

"Hello Sam. I suppose the safest time would be Friday night as the court sessions should be over. I don't think the trial will go on into next week, but of course I can't be sure at this stage."

"It would suit me if the trial did go into next week. It would give us a bit more time to discuss things, etc, but how would you be fixed?"

"Well, Jenny has to get back to school and Jim would have to take her back. I would have no problem in that case as it would be out of my hands."

"Tell you what, I'll come down for Friday night anyway and we'll take things from there."

"What on earth am I to tell Jim? I've hardly seen him this week—apart from the weekend—and he'll expect a grand finale to our so-called holiday."

"Well tell him the truth—that you've been head-hunted for scriptwriting and a golden opportunity has arisen for a preliminary discussion. I'm surprised you haven't told him yet. It's business, Clarissa."

Clarissa was taken aback by the matter-of-factness of his insistence on business. She knew she had been fantasising about the romantic angle. "I don't really know why I haven't said anything. Silly of me really, as Jim knows I've been looking for something stimulating to do. Yes, alright, come to the hotel and have dinner with us and I'll bring him up to date with events before you arrive—if I can. As you can imagine the trial has more than a little taken me over."

"I'm sure it has. I'm so sorry. I wish I could be there to hold your hand as it were. Until Friday then. I'll look forward to that."

Clarissa's feelings took another lurch. "I'm a fool" she told herself. "I'm a silly forty-two year old teenager." On Friday she would make it clear to Sam that she'd thought no more of their sentimental interlude in Dorset and it was business or nothing.

Jim was satisfied with her explanation that it was further details to do with the case (she couldn't face going into the Sam thing tonight) and they went to bed.

* *

Jim took her to the court and went off with Jenny, promising to come for her when she rang him. Jim would have liked to stay with her and she would have welcomed that, having heard tales of how intimidating these places can be, but it was no place to have children hanging about, even if it were allowed. It was an Edwardian building designed to chasten all who visited, defendant, plaintiff and witness alike. The walls were clad in dark green glossy tiles set into relief by narrow borders of dark brown tiles of the same no-nonsense variety. Around the walls were cold, hard benches on which people sat in poses of varying degrees of apathy. The only concession to humanity was a battered drinks machine. Most of the personnel looked grimfaced and impassive and took no notice of the people gathered there to have their fates decided.

There seemed to be some delay for it was well after ten thirty before Clarissa, who was the prosecution's first witness, was called into the court room. How she longed for one friendly face! There were few people in the public gallery as this was not a case likely to arouse much interest.

She looked at the defendant and was surprised to see that he was a black youth. She had not seen very clearly in the dark on the night of the offence. He certainly didn't look the frightening individual of her ordeal and her embellishing imagination. He was slight and, though doing his best to look cocky and casual, only succeeded in looking pathetic in his designer clothes bought to cut a dash in court. Clarissa looked straight at him, but he avoided eye contact with her whilst looking around defiantly.

Clarissa was questioned by both barristers in a straightforward way with none of the traps she expected to be deliberately laid for her by the defending Counsel. The questioning drew from her an accurate account of what happened that awful night, from her point of view, and in what seemed no time at all she had taken her place in the body of the court room to observe the trial's progress.

As the small procession of witnesses took the stand it became clear that the boy (for at 17 he was hardly more than that) had had the almost classic deprived childhood. Father disappeared, mother on the streets trying to make ends meet, bunking off school, bad company, drugs, stolen cars. His most serious offence was pushing drugs, for which there could be a statutory prison sentence. During the afternoon session a black woman came into the court and sat down where Clarissa had a clear view of her. It turned out that she was the boy's mother, who had attended to hear him questioned. She certainly did not look your typical prostitute—if such a being exists—being neatly and discreetly dressed and with a refined, if somewhat worn, face.

When her son went into the witness box, she looked anxious and never took her eyes off him as though willing him to say the right things. The defence made as good a case for leniency as was possibly in the circumstances, but the evidence stacked against the youth was pretty damning and the outcome could only be a verdict of guilty on all the counts of dangerous driving and peddling and being in possession of drugs. The Judge's summing up was balanced, but did nothing to sway the jury one way or the other. The jury went out to consider its verdict and were out all the rest of the afternoon without reaching a decision, which seemed odd considering the cut-and-dried nature of the case.

Proceedings were adjourned until the next day when the verdict would surely be delivered. Clarissa was depressed by the day's hearings. She certainly had not wanted to press charges, but that was out of convenience for herself. She had not expected to feel any degree of sympathy with her 'stalker', but as his short life history unfolded she was made more and more aware of the unfairness of life. This lad was younger than Tom and yet had been exposed to the worst that life could throw at him. And there were thousands like him whose aspirations reached no higher than the kicks which they could get out of stealing and poisoning their system with noxious substances. She was the guilty one she felt, who in spite of her high falutin' principles, did very little to try to change society or even let injustices trouble her much, except as the stuff of debate.

Clarissa rang Jim and Jenny was all questions in the back of the car.

"Did the Judge wear a red gown with fur, mum? Did he bang his hammer thing? Has the criminal gone to prison in a big van?"

The child's innocent questioning was natural enough, but it saddened Clarissa even more.

"We don't know yet, darling. I hope not."

"Why not mum, if he's a bad man?"

"I mustn't talk about the case, Jenny, until the trial's over. But I will tell you just this one thing. He did bad things, but he had a very unhappy life with a daddy who ran away and didn't care for him and I think that's what made him to do these dreadful things."

"Well, I'm sometimes unhappy, mum, but I don't do wicked things, do I?"

"Of course you don't, my little one, but you have a mummy and daddy who care about you and try to help you to do nice things. I promise to talk about everything with you when the case is over. Now before we go back to the hotel I would love a spin out in the country to get some fresh air, after being cooped in that place all day."

Jim decided to take Clarissa to the spot by the river he and Jenny had visited that morning. They walked along the river bank where Jenny appreciated another chance to feed the ducks and moor hens.

"You look all in," remarked Jim. "Was it awful?"

"Not for me particularly. It was all straightforward. But that poor kid! And his mother! What a life—we just have no idea of how the other half lives.

"It seems to have got to you. Will he be banged up, do you think?"

"It looks more than likely, I'm afraid. Though the jury is taking its time for a relatively uncomplicated case. Anyway enough of that. I've something to tell you which I should have told you before now."

"You're leaving me!" joked Jim.

"What did you say, daddy? Where's mum going?"

"Oh Jim! Daddy's only joking, darling. Take no notice. When I was in Dorset I met some people who are into making educational films and we got talking . . . and well, to cut a long story short, they asked me to join them as a script writer!"

"Why tell me now? It seems an odd time with all that's going on down here at this moment. Script writer, eh? Sounds exciting!"

"One of them is coming over to discuss some stuff with me tomorrow night. I've asked him to have dinner with us and meet you."

"That's a shame. I was hoping we could do something special tomorrow night as it's probably going to be our last night."

"Well the thing is, it seemed a good chance to get together. Meetings can't be that frequent because of the distance."

"Where does this group hang out? Dorset?"

"London."

"You're stuck out on a bit of a limb, then."

"Well most of the work I can do at home, but there will be the odd bit of travelling for conferences and so on."

"Well if you've arranged this thing tomorrow night, I suppose that's it. It would have been nice to be consulted."

Jim made no comment on 'him' and, after Clarissa apologised for upsetting his plans for a special evening, they halfheartedly joined Jenny in feeding the ducks and then returned to the hotel for a meal and bed.

CHAPTER NINE

Clarissa was in the court building at nine o'clock. The jury were already in session and most of those concerned with the case were sitting around chatting quietly or sipping whatever the drinks dispenser dispensed. Clarissa sat near the defendant's mother and couldn't help overhearing the conversation that went on in desultory fashion between her and a woman companion. His mother was of the opinion that a spell inside might do him good and bring him to his senses, but her friend disagreed, maintaining that prisons were universities of crime and said she was hoping for some lenient sentence involving some rehabilitation. They both agreed that fundamentally Christian was not a bad lad, but had bad friends who were always leading him astray. It seemed he had a talent for drawing and was always doodling in a cartoon style. "His art teacher said he could've got into Art College, but he never seemed to finish anything. I started the street game to put something away for him. The money's still there but I don't suppose it matters much now." Again Clarissa thought of Tom, who only had to snap his fingers and he could get into any university and was wasting his time bar-tending. She hoped along with Christian's mum's friend that Christian would be given a second chance.

The morning dragged by. Clarissa asked if she could slip out to buy a paper and whiled away the rest of the morning sipping a nondescript drink passing itself off as coffee and doing the crossword. They were told at just approaching noon that they were to be back for the afternoon session at two o'clock. Strictly speaking Clarissa was not obliged to attend, but as a significant witness she felt she ought to be there to see the outcome. She had come to have an emotional interest in the young man.

She went back to the pub she knew and ordered a sandwich and coffee. To begin with she had a glass of sherry as she felt she needed something to raise her spirits. She thought about them eating with Sam that evening.

It wasn't going to be easy. She really didn't want Jim and Sam to meet. She didn't want Sam to be part of her everyday humdrum existence. She wanted to keep him in that other, intense, area of her life where husbands, kids, chores, did not impinge. Could she hide the romantic feelings she had for Sam from Jim or would he guess that being Sam's scriptwriter wasn't all she dreamed about? She pulled herself up short. Hadn't she just decided that she would put all romantic thoughts out of her mind? After all Sam's last words—well almost his last—had been that theirs was a business arrangement. But then he'd added how much he was looking forward to seeing her and, in spite of everything, she was certainly looking forward to seeing him.

The jury was ready to come back into the court room and deliver its verdict. Christian's mother looked tense and all cockiness had gone from the defendant. Clarissa crossed her fingers and sent up a prayer to the god she didn't really believe in. As more or less predicted, the verdict was 'Guilty' on all counts. She found out afterwards that there had been a great deal of debate and soul searching in the Jury room. Yes, they'd all agreed the boy was guilty, but many had been reluctant to commit themselves, feeling that the odds had been stacked against him from the start. The cynical ones (or realists, as they chose to call themselves) maintained that this was always the excuse for criminal behaviour and what about those who'd had just as bad a start, but didn't commit offences?

The Judge ordered an adjournment—strangely, as the session had only just commenced. All were to be back in court in half an hour, when sentencing would take place. Christian was taken down and his mother, though shaken, remained calm. The next thirty minutes stretched out interminably. Clarissa went out into the corridor and rang Jim.

"Ready?" he asked.

"Not yet. He's guilty. But the Judge asked for a short adjournment before sentencing. Why do you think that is?"

"Sounds a bit odd. Perhaps he's got diarrhoea or something! No seriously, it sounds as if he's having a job making his mind up what to do."

"You mean it might be a lenient sentence?"

"Don't build your hopes up, Clarrie, and don't take it so much to heart. Whatever happens it's not your fault."

"Call for me in about forty minutes' time. I don't want to be hanging around here afterwards. See you soon."

Clarissa returned to the Courtroom just before the Judge re-entered. Addressing the defendant, he said "Christian McKenzie you have been found guilty of three serious crimes, for each of which a prison sentence is applicable. In the course of the driving offence you endangered the life of Mrs Clarissa Coniscliffe and caused her a severe degree of trauma. You also endangered the lives of other motorway users on a night of severe traffic conditions because of extremely heavy rain. The sentence for this is a fine and three months in prison (suspended) and relinquishing of your driving licence. There is a statutory prison sentence for possessing drugs which it is in my power to apply. For the offence of selling these same drugs I have it in my power to impose a prison sentence of three years. Bearing in mind, however, your youth and the unfavourable circumstances of your childhood I intend to impose one year's suspended sentence and a six months' sentence which you will serve. The social services of your area have been advised to arrange some residential rehabilitation care for you at a Drugs Centre during the period of your suspended sentence. It has emerged that you have some artistic ability and you would be well advised to build upon this foundation and make something of your life. Do not expect the same leniency if you come up before this court or any other again. Have you anything to say?" Clarissa thought she heard a muttered "thankyou" from Christian but nothing more.

As he was taken down to start his six months' prison sentence his mother did not lose her calm demeanour, but buttoned up her coat and walked out of the Courtroom. Clarissa wanted to run after her and say some words to her—to what effect she did not know. She really wanted to know where Christian would serve his prison sentence, but she wasn't sure how to set about getting such information. As it was, Jim would be waiting outside and she really did want to get away. She determined to find out this information as soon as she could but now was not the moment, she told herself. There was a sense of anti-climax, as for actors after the curtain has come down. She did spot Michael Baines and she smiled her goodbye. He came over to her and asked her what she thought of the verdict. She said that she thought it was fair, but was disturbed by the plight of the young lad and others like him, who didn't stand a chance in life. She thought she might enquire from him where Christian was likely to serve his sentence.

"Well, he'll probably go to somewhere not necessarily near his home to be assessed and then, my guess is to a Young Offenders' Institution. Why do you ask?"

"I'd like to visit him."

"Hm! I'd keep well out of it, if I were you. Anyway he's not likely to want to see you, is he?"

"Probably not. But I'd still like to know, but how do I find out?"

"I'll find out for you. If you give me your 'phone number or e-mail address I'll let you know. O.K?"

"That's very kind of you. Thank you."

They said goodbye and Clarissa ran out to find Jim, for by this time she was late.

"Has the bad man gone to prison, mum?"

"I'm afraid he has—for a short while—and then he's going to be helped to become better and possibly go to art college later on, as he's good at drawing."

"That's good—going to college I mean, mum, but I'm sorry he's going to prison. That will be horrible."

"Well, he'll probably go to a place where young people go and he'll do a lot of interesting things to help him when he comes out. He'll probably be able to do some drawing."

"So", said Jim, "the Judge was lenient with him just as you hoped. So come on, it's all over now so try to put it out of your mind."

Not so easy, thought Clarissa, but she didn't tell Jim just exactly *what* she had in mind. She wasn't altogether sure that her motives for prison-visiting were entirely altruistic.

* *

Clarissa, having anticipated a possible meeting with Sam, had packed something attractive for daytime and for evening. She dressed with care and with some success, for Jim, who thought she looked 'magnificent' in whatever she put on from tatty gardening togs to wedding finery, and really couldn't care less, whistled as she turned from the mirror. "Wow! Is that new?"

"This old thing. I've had it ages. Do I look OK?"

"You look magnificent. You'll certainly impress him. It is 'him', isn't it?"

"Hm. But it's my writing I need to impress them with. Sam's only one of them, remember."

"Sam, eh? I see."

"What do you mean 'I see'?"

"Oh nothing. Bit of a 'luvvy' name, that."

"Don't be silly, Jim. He's not a 'luvvy', as you put it. Anything but."

Jim merely grimaced and dropped the subject. There was an uneasiness between them which their daughter sensed. "Mum isn't leaving us, is she, daddy? Are you cross, like you were with Tom?"

Jim didn't say anything, so Clarissa jumped in with reassuring noises and said it was time they all went down to see if their visitor had arrived. They sat down in the foyer to wait.

"By the way, Jim, you never did tell my why you were cross with Tom—that time you rang me in Dorset. Was it about him and Amy?"

"In a way, yes. But now isn't the time to go into that. Could this be your visitor now?"

Sam was standing just inside the main entrance looking around. Clarissa stood up and waved to him. He came over to them and Clarissa felt almost faint with emotion but she managed to introduce her husband and daughter to her 'friend' with composure. Sam was all friendliness, without being gushing or out to charm. He put Jenny at ease immediately. Even Jim had to admit later that there was nothing of the 'luvvy' about him at all.

"Let me get us all a drink. We'll have them out here if Jenny isn't welcome in the bar."

When they were settled, Sam said that he was very grateful to Clarissa for being willing to help the group out and that he quite realised that it might entail some inconvenience for Jim and the whole family, but he hoped that would be minimal. "How do you feel about it, Jim?"

"Well, I've hardly had time to think about it as I've only just found out. I'm not absolutely sure what it is you do, but I know that Clarissa is wanting a change of some kind—so really it's up to her."

"Let's wait until we've had something to eat (you're probably starving, Sam) and when Jenny's in bed we'll discuss the thing," suggested Clarissa.

Of course Jenny objected to this and wasn't placated by being told that she would find it all very boring and daddy would tell her an extraordinarily good story when she was in bed.

The meal over, Jenny was taken off to bed in spite of her protests and Clarissa and Sam were left alone.

"It's good to see you, Clarissa. As stunning as ever."

"Don't, Sam. If I agree to do this it must be understood that we're are colleagues and nothing more."

"If that's what you want."

Clarissa was silent in a way that suggested to Sam that it was not at all what she wanted, but he produced some papers from the brief case he had under his chair and passed them over to Clarissa. "We would like you to make something out of this jumble of material."

"Where did you get all this?"

"I went to see the old man after you'd left. I took a tape recorder with me and this is what he told me. He gave me the name of a lady living in Dorchester and I called to see her. You won't believe this but she was Emma's daughter! She had some of her mother's things but she had deposited a handwritten diary in the Dorchester museum as being of value with its Hardy connection and being of general importance as local history. I went to check up on her story and sure enough I came across a tattered old note book written in pencil, mostly in note form but clearly not the work of an ill-educated person, as I think you'll see for yourself."

"They allowed you to borrow the book?"

"Yes, but only on the premises. As you can see these are photocopies of the material and I'm under obligation to destroy them as soon as we're finished with them. We would like you to put this into some kind of narrative form, so that we can make a script."

"Have you decided the angle you're going to treat 'The Return' from?"

"Not really. We might have to widen the topic to something like 'Models for Hardy's heroines' or something like that, though I know a lot has been done on that already. That's why we would like you to meet up with us and have a brainstorming session. You couldn't stay on for a few days next week?"

"It'll be difficult, but I'll see what I can do." Clarissa knew that she would have to be more amenable to the Group's demands or she'd have to back out.

"So you see I was quite busy all the time I wasn't in touch with you and not just with the project either."

At that moment Jim returned from seeing to Jenny, so there was no chance for Clarissa to go into Sam's personal problems.

"Could you possibly spare your wife for a couple or so days next week? If we can get a script roughed out we could each get on with our bits at home."

For a moment Jim was silent. "If you need Clarissa's writing skills and she stills needs to do whatever, then she'd better go ahead." Turning to Clarissa, he said, "You might as well stay on as you're down here. We'll manage. Stay as long as it takes but don't make it too long, for Jenny's sake, and don't forget Christmas is coming and your pageant and all."

"Thanks, Jim," said Sam, "that's good of you. We'll work her hard for the next couple of days and then send her back to do her homework."

"Well, have you two made progress with your whatever?"

"We've a hell of a lot of work to do," replied Sam.

"I'll have to be back by Wednesday for school."

"By the way, Sam, where are you staying?" Jim enquired.

"Nowhere as yet—I haven't booked in anywhere. This place looks rather nice. I'll see if there's a room."

Whatever Clarissa and Jim thought about this they kept to themselves, but Jim's face spoke worlds.

"I suppose this is the excitement you're looking for," said Jim, while Sam was away asking about a room.

"It's work, Jim—the sort I want. I can't pick and choose. Where else would I get a chance like this?"

Sam returned, having secured a room, and suggested a nightcap. Over their drinks Sam centred his attentions on Jim, asking about his job, hobbies, etc. Whatever his private thoughts, Jim was forthcoming and polite and the half hour or so to bedtime passed quite pleasantly, on the surface at least.

CHAPTER TEN

Jenny was not pleased to be leaving for home without Clarissa. Only the promise of a visit to the Canal Centre at Stoke Bruerne on the Grand Union Canal near Northampton cheered her up and Clarissa promised all sorts of delights when she returned.

When they'd waved off Jim and Jenny, Sam suggested a drive out to a well—known beauty spot for discussion over a coffee.

As they drove along they chatted desultorily. "Jim's a nice guy," said Sam. "Sensible and 'together'."

"Yes, he's good to us all and quite marvellous with Jenny."

"But?"

"Yes, 'but'. I suppose our relationship's getting a bit 'tired'. Marriage is an impossible situation—don't you think? How does a couple keep it alive, fresh and meaningful?"

"Well it's no good asking me. I'm no expert. One partner down and another about to go."

"Do you want to tell me about your 'other' problems?" Clarissa was not doing very well at keeping their conversation on a business level, but she just had to know how things stood between Sam and Esmé.

"I think she's found someone else. I can't say I blame her. She needs more than I can give her. She has a handicapped son and needs a much more supportive partner than I could ever be. For one thing my job is insecure, to say the least, and to keep Matthew (her son) comfortable needs financial certainty. I have money—quite a bit actually—but it's tied up in various projects at the moment and not easily accessible. Also I'm not good with Matthew. I get easily irritated and I suppose I selfishly resent the amount of Esmé's time he takes up. I care for them both—very much—but all the problems are putting a great deal of stress on our relationship as an 'item'."

"Do you mean things have got worse than they were when we were in Dorset?"

"Oh yes, much worse. In fact I moved out after a particularly acrimonious row. I don't think Esmé expected that. I still support them both—just—it's quite a struggle. I feel I've done the right thing. I keep in touch constantly. In fact it was when I called to see how Matthew had got on after a hospital appointment that I found her 'friend' in situ."

"So you weren't at Esmé's when I rang and left the message?"

"No, Esmé passed on the message and was suspicious—thought I was carrying on behind her back and she thinks she's reacting to my behaviour."

"And have you—been carrying on?"

"No, absolutely not, unless you count our innocent—er—interlude in Dorset as carrying on. Were we carrying on?"

"Not at all. We simply found that we had things in common, wouldn't you say?"

"I think that if we hadn't had commitments to others we would have—I don't like the expression carrying on—taken our relationship somewhere significant."

"We still have commitments."

"Well you have, but I feel my commitment is becoming more an obligation. There is a difference."

Sam pulled into the car park of the spectacular Clifton suspension bridge which spanned a deep gorge.

"Coffee," he said "and work."

"Yes indeed."

From the window seat in the coffee shop they had a splendid view of the bridge, gorge and river. Over coffee, Clarissa studied the documents more closely. The transcript of Will's story presented no difficulties apart from achieving the authenticity of his dialect, but Emma's note book was going to prove more of a problem with some of its pages tattered and the pencil faded in many places. What was clear, however, was the tone of the jottings. Emma had undoubtedly been a refined, intelligent, and educated woman and Clarissa felt, instinctively, the style she would adopt for Emma's narrative. What she needed to know now was what exactly was the group's objective.

When she first went down to Dorset 'The Return' was going to be her jumping off point and she could see points of contact between what she had in front of her and Eustacia Vye. The contrast between the two women was stark. The one an over-indulged, romantic dreamer who stage-managed her own tragedy and the other who had been dealt a raw deal, had struggled to overcome the consequences of her choices in life and made something of, not just herself, but her daughter. And where did she, Clarissa, fit in? Her mind wandered guiltily over her own life. Everything had fallen into her lap. She had suffered nothing but the death of her father, which—though sad because of its premature nature and her own youthfulness at the time—could not be counted among the overwhelming tragedies of life. And here she was on the threshold of . . . .

"A penny for them, Clarissa Coniscliffe!"

She jumped. "Sorry. I was day dreaming."

"Pleasant dreams, I hope?"

"Not really, but we won't go into that. We were talking about Hardy's models last night. From a brief glance this one looks almost a model for Tess. If I'd lived a hundred years ago, Hardy wouldn't have had to look far for a Eustacia."

"What do you mean? From a beauty point of view, yes. You really are an attractive woman, Clarissa, but I don't see any other resemblances."

"You don't know me."

"I'd like to."

"You wouldn't."

"Clarissa. First of all please stop running your self down and, second, let me discover you. If I discover the monster you make yourself out to be, I'll run a mile. But I don't think I'll need to."

"Oh Sam! What am I going to do?"

"You mean what are we going to do? I suggest we relax and enjoy each other—wherever that takes us—and it need not take us to outright infidelity, but I think it will."

He leaned across the table and kissed her firmly and lingeringly on the mouth. Clarissa responded for all she was worth.

Afterwards, in Clarissa's bedroom, post coital on the bed, sipping a glass of wine, Clarissa lazily remarked, "Now we really must get down to work."

"Yes, you're right." Was the reply, but neither moved.

* *

After about an hour, the 'phone rang. "Clarissa, it's Jim. We've just got back."

Though the call was expected, Clarissa felt a guilty jolt go through her. The effects of the wine, however, helped her to reply relaxedly. "Oh good. How's Jenny? Did she get her treat?"

"Yes, we called in at the Canal Centre and, believe it or not, even at this time of year, we managed a boat ride into the tunnel; we had half an hour in the adventure playground and a good children's Christmas special in the pub, so all's well. How about you? Done much work?"

"Yes" lied Clarissa, "lots. It's being very useful."

They chatted on for a few minutes longer, and with the promise that she'd see them the following evening, Clarissa returned to Sam's arms. She felt that whatever happened in the future she would never forget this afternoon with Sam. After a cold, fine spell, the weather had turned Christmassy. Outside, in the gathering gloom, light flakes of snow began to meander down past the window to settle gently and increasingly thickly on the festively-lit fir trees in the hotel garden. There was a misty glow over the city and in their room the lamps and the fire light offered all that Clarissa thought she wanted from life. They rang room service for tea and langorously fed each other snippets of buttery muffin, laughing and joking as easily as any two people in the first throes of romantic love.

CHAPTER ELEVEN

All the way north, Jim thought about what was happening in his life. He was on automatic pilot in his replies to Jenny's questions which, until after the canal visit, were lighthearted and excited, anticipating the treat ahead. When she began to get tired she started to fret about leaving Clarissa behind and was convinced that her mother had left them.

"I heard you say that mummy was going to leave us, when we were by the river."

"That was a joke, darling. The kind grown ups make."

"Well, why isn't she coming home with us?"

"Well, mum is helping Sam with some writing for a film. Don't you think that's quite exciting?"

"What sort of film? Like Harry Potter? Did she write a story first?"

"I don't think the film is like Harry Potter, but your mum is going to write a kind of story."

"What about?"

"Have you heard of Thomas Hardy?"

"Mum has some of his books on her shelf."

"Well, she's going to write something to do with him."

"Why can't she do it at home?"

"She will, but she has to discuss it first with Sam and some other people. Now why don't you try to get a bit of sleep and, before you know it, we'll be home."

"I'll put my earphones on and listen to my music."

"OK, that's a good idea."

Before long Jenny's eyes closed and her chin dropped onto her chest. He stopped at the next service station and gently eased her into a more comfortable position and took the 'phones off. Left to himself, Jim began to take stock of his life. He felt privileged to be alive at this period in history with all its exciting possibilities. As far as his personal life was concerned, he'd had nothing to complain of up to now. Attractive wife, lovely kids, job he enjoyed and plenty of interests. Now, however a new emotion was entering his personal emotional gamut—'jealousy'. He'd never been an envious person, being content with life, but the thought of Clarissa staying in that hotel with Sam was more than just niggling at him. He trusted his wife and up to now had just laughed at her crushes. Perhaps he ought to have seen them as warnings that all was not well. He 'fancied' some of the women he met in the course of his work and interests, but not in any serious way. It simply gave him a 'buzz' and added an interest to the day. He had no reason for thinking that there was anything other than 'the project' between Clarissa and Sam. He wasn't at all sure that it would be more than a flash in the pan, for he could not believe that anyone in their right mind would take on an unknown to work for anything as demanding as TV documentaries. And Clarissa would not stand the pace, she hadn't enough confidence. The moment things got stressful she'd panic. But this line of reasoning simply led him to the uncomfortable conclusion that Sam had engaged her services because he fancied her.

Perhaps he'd taken his wife too much for granted. Perhaps she did need more than he could give her. Was he, in fact, boring? She'd been excited enough by him at the beginning and enjoyed all the contacts he introduced to her through his work in London. She'd loved being a mother and done wonderfully by the kids but, there was no doubt about it, she'd been difficult to live with lately. Well one thing was for sure, he wasn't going to make a 'big deal' of it and act the heavy-handed husband. Perhaps if he gave her her head she would get it out of her system and they would move forward from there.

It was almost dark when they reached home and as he waited for the kettle to boil for a warm cup of tea, he rang Clarissa at the hotel. He couldn't say why but he felt that not much work had been done on their project. Clarissa sounded tipsy, which was odd so early in the evening and he sensed that she was not alone. He suspected, too, that the rest of the group were not around, though Sam had implied that the discussion would be group-based. "I'm getting paranoid," Jim thought to himself. They'll arrive tomorrow morning." He abandoned the tea and poured himself a fairly stiff whisky. He saw Jenny off to bed and settled down to an evening of mindless TV, accompanied by a few more whiskies.

He must have dropped off in front of the screen for the next thing he knew was the clashing of the front door followed by Tom striding into the sitting room.

"Oh dad, I didn't realise you'd be back tonight."

"Is that a problem?"

"No, no," and Tom slumped into an armchair and sat there in silence.

Jim said, "Hi dad, have you had a nice break?"

"Oh sorry, yes, did you have a nice break?"

"Yes it was OK. What's up with you? You don't look too good. Is anything wrong? Why are you here? Not that you're not welcome and all that, but it's not your patch now."

"I wanted somewhere quiet to think. My room's fine when the drinkers have left but a bit noisy until then."

"What's the problem? Can I help."

"Doubt it."

"Try me."

"Things aren't going too well between Amy and me. Or more precisely Amy's parents."

"In what way?"

"They don't think I'm a suitable boyfriend for her. They're committed Muslims and naturally they'd prefer someone of the same faith for her."

"You see her as a long term partner—whatever that means nowadays?"

"I suppose so. We just seem right together."

"How does Amy see things? Is she OK with you being what you are?"

"Oh, yes. She's all for inter-racial partnerships as long as there is mutual respect for the other's culture or whatever."

"Well that's all that counts, surely."

"Well, it's never as easy as that, is it? To be honest, mum didn't help matters with her remarks at the play."

"I realise that and so does she, but it's difficult to take your words back."

"Yes, but it goes deeper than that. Mum doesn't think Amy is good enough for me. That upsets me and shocks me, considering what we've been brought up to think. So there you are—enemies both sides."

"Are you wanting to move in together?"

"We'd like to but we've no money. I'm thinking of applying to University to read politics and I probably will have to go away from the area, so everything is up in the air."

"Not a time to make decisions long term, I agree. Are they forbidding her from seeing you?"

"Well, they can't—not at her age—but they're making things difficult and a bit unpleasant. I never go round there now. We meet at mine and of course they don't like that."

"Good job there aren't any burly brothers!"

"Eh? What did you say?"

"It was something your Mum said. I meant it as a joke. Unfortunately your mum didn't!"

"Come on. She's not being press-ganged into an arranged marriage or anything. As far as I know I'm not going to be knifed!"

"Well you can count on my support whatever happens, but I'm really tired after a long drive and several whiskies so I'll have to say goodnight."

"Not like you to over-imbibe. Where's Mum, by the way? Is she in bed?"

"She might be, but not here she isn't. She's staying down to discuss a writing project with Sam."

"Ah, sexy Sam, eh?"

"Do you know him, then?"

"No, but I've spoken to him on the phone. He rang a couple of weeks ago about some writing or something. Did you meet him down there? I thought it was the trial of that guy who harassed Mum. How did that turn out?"

"He was sent down, but only for six months. Lenient really, but it upset your mother. Incidentally he was black with a disadvantaged background and all that. Your mum wants to help him or his mother if she can."

"Hmm, that's *very* interesting. Very interesting indeed. However, as you say, time for bed. Do you mind if I doss here tonight?"

"You know I don't. Help yourself. Goodnight and try not to worry."

Jim tossed and turned in bed wondering what on earth Tom had meant by 'sexy Sam'. He had to admit that Sam hadn't struck him as a womaniser, though he had only seen him in the presence of one woman so far—his wife! He tried not to imagine what they might be up to, so turned his thoughts to Tom and his problems. Poor old Tom! His first girlfriend and trouble already. Tom wasn't a frivolous lad and whoever he gave his heart to meant something more than just a 'conquest'. If anything went wrong between him and Amy it would hurt him deeply. So there they were, father and son, both with woman problems. He told himself to grow up. This was a *job* Clarissa was trying to pursue, not a love affair and—for his own sanity—he had to believe that. He hoped to God she wouldn't prolong her stay in Bristol. He didn't want to have to arrange carers for Jenny, especially as she was anxious about her mum 'leaving home' as she feared. How on earth had life become so complicated all of a sudden? It was beyond him. He switched the light on and read for a bit until sleep eventually overcame him.

CHAPTER TWELVE

"How do you fancy a trip to London?"

Clarissa and Sam were lingering in bed over breakfast brought to them by room service.

"What, today?"

"Why not? It'll only take a couple of hours and you can meet the group."

"But what about Jim? He thinks the group is coming here and he's expecting me back tonight."

"Tell him there were problems with that and it's easier the other way round. You can get a train from London just as easily."

"But it snowed last night. Won't the roads be bad?"

"We'll take a chance on it. The motorway should be OK."

The main roads were fine and Sam was a skilful and fast driver so their journey took just over two hours. Sam contacted the others in the group and arranged a meeting in their usual place—a room in a pub in Chelsea.

Clarissa was introduced to the rest of the group (Leo, Martin and Guy) who were high-powered with degrees from prestigious places and experience as diverse and rarified as the Conzertgebow, the National Film Centre, Oxbridge and the Bristol Old Vic. All were dedicated to what they were doing as a group and seemed not too bothered by the, as yet puny, rewards of their efforts as arts promoters in a small way. They were all very friendly and welcoming to Clarissa, but she was even more convinced that Sam must have had a mental aberration to have engaged her. The beautiful Francesca, whom Clarissa had glimpsed in Dorchester, was not present.

After some refreshment they got down to work. Various ideas were put forward as to what the aim of their film would be and Clarissa surprised herself by being just as forthcoming as the others. She was flattered to have her idea of a contrast between Eustacia and Emma under the title "The Willing Tragedy Queen" accepted as a jumping off point. Having made only a cursory reading of the material she confidently outlined a possible script contrasting the lives of Emma Bailey—the woman of the tattered note book—and Eustacia Vye, the beautiful and sultry heroine of Hardy's novel. Eustacia is comfortably stationed in life and spends her time falling in and out of love according to the dictates of her over romantic and capricious temperament. There has to be a lover in her life and if he promises an exciting future in the social world so much the better. She spends her time dreaming of love, often in melancholy mood which she would never try to lighten by turning her hand to anything useful. She marries Clym Yoebright, attracted by his having worked successfully in Paris and to where she constantly pesters him to return with her on his arm. When he disappoints her by wishing to remain in his native area and study to become a teacher she estranges herself from both her husband and her mother-in-law. She returns to a former lover and fearing that he has abandoned her she throws herself into the waters of Shadwater Weir. By contrast, Emma is born poor and marries a local lad who treats her despotically. She tries to bring some brightness into her life by arranging the flowers at the local church at Stinsford each Saturday afternoon. She has a talent for drawing and sometimes sketched the flowers she picked and arranged. On one such afternoon she attracted the attention of two gentlemen, one elderly—a Mr Thomas Hardy—and the other an aspiring young architect—a Mr Justin Austin who takes not only an interest in Emma's drawing abilities but her pretty face and figure.

Unhappy in her marriage and flattered by the young man's attentions she quickly falls prey to his charms and gives birth to his child. Both are generously befriended by Mr Hardy. A mysterious package is pushed through Mr Hardy's letter box addressed to E.B. containing an exquisite diamond and sapphire brooch, which Emma surmises can only have come from her husband, Will, leaving open some channel of communication between them. When Emma realises her lover cannot marry her for social reasons, she returns to her husband begging him, for the sake of her child—Felicity—to take her back as a skivvy. He exploits her shamelessly in terms of the labour he inflicts upon her, all of which she endures without complaining. But when he tries to force sexual relations upon her, thus breaking the pact they had between them, she flees with her child and subsequently endures all manner of hardship and degradation to earn money in the hopes of making a decent life for her child. This she succeeds in doing, mainly by her own efforts but aided greatly in her child's education by financial gifts from Mr Hardy. Eustacia sinks without resistance beneath what she perceives as life's unfairnesses. Emma takes responsibility for her errors and struggles to raise herself and her child. Clarissa sees the film taking various incidents from their histories and pointing up the contrast between their respective ways of managing life.

Clarissa promised a sample scene or two within the week. She felt inspired as she had not done for a long time and, tired as she was with the trial and very little sleep, she felt totally in control of, not just the task in hand, but of her life and where she was going. She felt and looked radiant.

"What a beauty, Sam. Where did you find her?"

"She seems to know her stuff, Sam. A pleasure to look at too, if that's not a politically incorrect remark!"

The comments in the Gents would have made Clarissa's ears curl. "Yes, she's a find, isn't she?" Sam did not go into details, but said he'd met her on a course and had been impressed in all the ways his colleagues clearly were. "And yes, Leo, your remark was a tad wotsit. She's a talented colleague so cut out the sexism, please. No offence."

After having made such rapid progress, there was no need for a further session that day so they broke up with Sam promising to send details of their next meeting. Sam and Clarissa had a few hours before the train North. They both knew how they would have liked to spend the time left to them but decided against that inviting option and went to an exhibition at a small gallery in Chelsea and then went for an early meal near the station.

"You realise you blew them away this afternoon—the group I mean. You really were impressive."

"I hope I can keep it up. I've got masses to do at school and, with Christmas and all that, I was a bit optimistic promising what I did. But I felt really switched-on. What an interesting lot. I should have felt overwhelmed, and at first I did, but I just felt I knew what was what in the discussion. You're doing me good, my darling, in more ways than one."

"When do you think you'll dare get away again?"

"I don't know, but I do want to visit Christian's mother and Jim knows that. However it's not going to be easy. We're a bit of a problematical family at the moment. Might you get up my way at all?"

"I'd love to if I can get round *my* problems. I'll do my damnedest."

"Why are we doing this? We've all these problems to overcome. Wouldn't it be simpler if we said goodbye and went our separate ways?"

"Is that what you want? You've more to lose than I have."

"We'll lose whatever we do! I can't tell you how 'alive' you make me feel. I don't want to lose that."

They parted. Clarissa made Sam leave her at the station entrance as she couldn't bear a prolonged goodbye waiting for the train to pull out. She felt 'alive' all the way to her station where Jim was waiting for her.

CHAPTER THIRTEEN

Romance in her life made a noticeable change in Clarissa's mood, which was one of euphoria and renewed mental energy. The whole family commented on the change, particularly Jenny who thought mummy was lovely since the holiday which had made her better. Tom kept looking at her in a wry, quizzical way and was occasionally heard to mutter something which sounded like 'sexy Sam', but on the whole he was taken up with his own problems. Rob was only to spend a couple of days with them as studies were pressing. Jim's bedroom experience took a turn for the better, which in his mind gave the lie to his recent suspicions. Clarissa would dearly have loved to contact Sam, but they had agreed to 'cool things' during the holiday so she was delighted to receive a message inside his Christmas card stating how much he was missing her and how soon could they meet again? She replied in hers that, much as she was missing him, she didn't see how they could meet very soon because of all the problems she had at home. The thought of him being in her life was enough to console her for the lack of his physical presence.

Clarissa kept her promise to get a first draft of a couple of scenes sent off to her colleagues. The pageant at school was declared a great success. Christmas day with the family—including two grandmas—was declared the best yet, with lunch particularly delicious. Only Tom seemed less than full of Christmas cheer which was noted solely by Jim. The more energetic members of the family went for a walk after lunch with the dog and returned to a blazing fire and tea. Clarissa had lit candles around the house and spicey scents wafted from the pretty oil burners to mingle with the smell of the evergreens decorating the pictures and mirrors. She had managed a quick call to Sam when the grandmas went for a nap and though his answers were almost in code (he was with Esme and Matthew who had pleaded with Sam to spend Christmas with them as usual) he seemed glad to hear from her and managed to convey his longing for her. Though he was hundreds of miles away, Sam was her knight in shining armour and she was conscious of the charged emotions she had sought for so long. She loved everyone and nothing was too much trouble for her. She had treats geared to everyone's specific fancy—lavender 'falderals' for the grandmas, a gadget for Tom's bike, a sophisticated puzzle for Jim and the latest 'Harry Potter' for Jenny.

It was when they were in bed that Jim remarked on Tom's withdrawn-ness and told Clarissa of the trouble between him and Amy. It was clear that whilst Clarissa felt entitled to feel as she did about Amy as a suitable partner for Tom, she was put out that Amy's parents should feel the same way about her beloved Tom.

"I thought you'd be pleased," observed Jim. "It would suit your book, surely, if they broke up."

Clarissa was silent. After a while, she said, "I'm ashamed to say I didn't notice anything wrong with Tom. He never has been the life and soul of the party. I don't think Amy is right for Tom, but I hate the thought of him being unhappy over her."

Jim didn't quite know what to make of this somewhat ambiguous statement. As it was late and he didn't want to spoil what for most of the family had been a happy Christmas day—thanks to Clarissa's efforts—he muttered something non-committal and settled down for the night.

CHAPTER FOURTEEN

The rest of Christmas passed pleasantly enough and, as is the way with happy holidays, it was soon over and the depressing months of January and February loomed. Everybody except Clarissa faced the return to work with a sinking feeling in the pit of the stomach. She was all too conscious of how she'd felt a year ago at the prospect of the new year's toil, but this year she was filled with a zest for life unfelt for a very long time. The return to school didn't present a problem for she had determined that she would give notice of leaving at Easter and, ironically enough, she prepared her lessons with enthusiasm. But what engrossed her was working on the script for the film. When she'd pieced together all the oddments, the note book, letters and diary entries Sam had unearthed from the Museum, she was fascinated by what they revealed. She cast the material in the form of two short autobiographies—that of Will and a more detailed and extended version of those events by Emma. These were the basis of her script for the film.*

January and February were dull and miserable with rainfall above average but March was beautiful, at the beginning fine and cold and as the month progressed warm and sunny. When she was not teaching, Clarissa dropped Jenny off at school, took the dog for a long walk in meadows a few miles from their house and mused pleasantly on how good life was. She threw sticks for Bess, who never tired of the game and then sat down on a log overlooking a pond which appeared every winter and slowly disappeared as the year advanced. She supposed the Waders, water birds and winter migrants were aware of the temporary nature of their habitat,

---

* *These are to be found in full at the end of the novel. All references to Emma's relationship with the Hardys' household are fictional.*

but at this time of year the pond was alive with gliding geese, nesting moor hens and the odd brooding heron. Bess sometimes disturbed a pair of birds peacefully going about their business as she rushed into the water with a stick triumphantly retrieved. The air was then filled with warning, honking cries which excited Bess even more. Clarissa couldn't imagine how she'd ever thought the morning walks with Bess merely a tedious duty. They now afforded her ample reflection on her relationship with Sam and the exciting times ahead with her new colleagues. On returning home she would get down to work on the script and eagerly await Sam's daily call. It was easier for the calls to be that way round as Sam was itinerant and couldn't easily be located.

The time was fast approaching when she would need to meet with the rest of the group to discuss the mechanics of shaping up the script to the requirements of a TV format, about which Clarissa knew nothing at all. Sam suggested, during one of the calls, that he and Leo—the film man—could come up to her and stay in a local hotel where they could have their discussions. He hinted that Leo could be persuaded to leave him and Clarissa on their own from time to time to follow their pursuits and Clarissa wouldn't feel she was deserting the family. This was certainly a sensible idea but Clarissa wasn't keen on another dose of Sam and the Family. He was in a special category as far as she was concerned and the possibility of a threesome (foursome or any other some) which brought Sam and Jim together again, with her in an uncomfortable position in the middle, did not appeal.

She decided to approach Jim about going to meet Sam again on the grounds of needing to see the group in order to be able to get on with the next stage of her writing. She also wanted to see their son, Robert, who was at Birmingham studying law and on whom she could call on the way down to Dorset (where Sam and Leo agreed to meet Clarissa for local colour's sake). Robert had never caused Jim and herself a moment's worry. He'd worked sensibly at school and sailed into university certain of what he wanted to do. He would doubtless meet a suitable partner in time and settle down to a comfortable life. He wasn't smug about the smooth running of his life. He simply got on with it and was kindly disposed to those around him without making a song and dance. Consequently he had tended to get somewhat overlooked or rather taken for granted. Robert would be OK everyone thought and so, as yet, neither of his parents had been down to see him in his new surroundings as a first year undergraduate.

If she went before the Easter holiday she would be back to look after Jenny during the break. Maria came to the rescue again; she didn't offer to have Jenny to stay at her house but would see to her after school and babysit when required. The two grandmas voiced disapproval again and were joined by Jim, who reluctantly agreed to her further absence.

She spent a pleasant evening with Robert who shared a house with friends on the outskirts of the city in a rather dingy suburb of big Victorian houses turned into student accommodation. Rob was surprised by his mother's career change and impressed that she'd been taken up by TV people. She played it down as Sam had done to her, but she was secretly quite proud to be talking scripts and takes and other jargon with her son and one of his housemates, whose mother was on an ITV production team in Yorkshire.

Rob was also interested to hear of Tom's relationship and would have liked to know more, but Clarissa was very cagey about the details and was non-commital about her opinion of Amy. She informed him that Jenny was fine and didn't tell him about the sleep problems she'd had. She told him the details of the trial and said that she was hoping to visit Christian or his mother. Perhaps he might like to accompany her when she'd worked out some arrangements? Rob thought this would be a good experience for him and agreed. Altogether Clarissa enjoyed the company of her uncomplicated son and was sad to be leaving him so soon.

She had left the hotel accommodation to Sam and was delighted to learn that he had not booked rooms at The Greenwood Tree. She arrived at The Partridge by mid-afternoon and found that she had arrived first. She went to her room—a sunny, comfortable and spacious one with two single beds—unpacked, had a shower and was enjoying a cup of tea in the lounge when her two colleagues arrived. Sam greeted her with a kiss on the mouth and a warm hug and Leo with the fashionable continental embrace of London and the south of England. Clarissa couldn't help contrasting this encounter with that first meeting with Sam at the Greenwood Tree. Now she was all confidence and sparkle and knew she was entrancing both men by her looks and her conversation. After a decent interval of chat, Leo discreetly left the lovers whilst he sorted out his things and had a nap. Sam followed her to her room where napping was the last thing on both their minds. Their feverish embraces conveyed how much each had missed the other and when they at last got round to talking there was no further need to express their longing in words.

"So how have things been with you, truly?" asked Sam.

"Apart from being separated from you, marvellous. For me personally that is. Things have been problematic for others though," and she mentioned Tom's problem and her awareness of Jim's suspicions, though unspoken.

"As you know things between Esmé and me are pretty bad. I'm thinking of settling a sum of money on her to help with Matthew's future care, then I needn't go round. It won't stretch very far but it's all I can afford at present. Joe, the chap she's seeing now, seems better with Matthew than I could ever be, so we're virtually split up."

"Do you mind?"

"I mind that people who once cared deeply for each other can find themselves so estranged—and that's happened to me twice now, but there was no future with Esmé and me—and before you say it, it was on the rocks before I met you—so, no, you're not to blame."

"You said when I asked the question before—'what are we going to do?'—that we were to let things take their course or something like that. Do you see any more clearly where that course is leading?"

"Yes and I think you do too. I'm thrilled by that, but you have so much more to lose than me."

"And a lot to gain. For me, life with you would allow the essential *me* to grow, as a writer and a woman. Yes, you see how confident I am now. I believe in myself as a writer. I know I can make a success of this job and even if things went wrong between you and me I would still continue to write. Oh yes, of course I'm revelling in the first flush of new love. I can't think about anyone else but you. I'm so energised by you that nothing's a trouble. They had the best Christmas ever because I had too much love and happiness for just myself. The strange thing is I want to give this to Jim. Can't we have a ménage â trois, quatre, cinq, six or however many? But I know it isn't just a passing whim. You have found me and given me to myself."

"What can I say to that? I'm overwhelmed, delighted, scared of such responsibility and very much humbled. Also scared that you'll run away now that you've become so rightly confident."

"I won't ever *run* away, but I may be drawn away against my wishes. But let's not dwell on that now. We've work to do and incidentally I'm starving. Exercise does that to one I've discovered. Away with you and let me get changed. Shall we meet in the bar for a pre-dinner drink?"

Sam kissed her before he left and said, "I love this new confident woman just as much as the tentative one, perhaps a little more. Let's meet for that drink as soon as we can."

Just before she went down Clarissa called home and got no-one, so she left a message saying that all was well and asking after each of them. She was conscious of how stunning she looked in a cream cowl-necked sweater over slim fitting slacks and ran down the stairs in anticipation of a stimulating evening ahead.

* *

Dinner was a lively affair. The meal was good and imaginative, the wine—like the repartee—was sparkling and Clarissa learned a great deal about film techniques, though she was rather dismayed to realise that she would have to dispense with much of her written material in the interests of making a point quickly without using up too much of their precious and limited budget. Leo gave her guidelines to work to and suggested an example of how a scene could be organised to best effect.

"Do you really need a script writer? Couldn't you save money by dispensing with me and one of you doing it? Surely it's not beyond the wit of any of you to add words to the scenes you set up! No Sam, this isn't one of my usual self-denigrating tacks. To tell you the truth, judging from what you've outlined, I think I'm too good for this sort of thing!" Clarissa joked.

"I told you we were a Mickey Mouse set-up but when we spot talent we grab it as long as it doesn't cost too much. Isn't that right, Leo?"

"Too right. It's lucky you're a wealthy woman, Clarrie my girl."

"Where did you get that idea? It looks as though I'm going to be a kept woman from now on—well from Easter, anyway."

"Oh Christ, you haven't given up the day job have you?"

"'Fraid so. So this'd better work."

After a few drinks in the bar they planned the next day to search out some sites for the film and get a feel for the local colour and parted, Leo to his room and Clarissa and Sam to hers.

"I said to you earlier that you made me come alive as a woman, a writer, but I forgot to mention as a highly sexual being. I didn't realise it could be like this." They were lying for the moment sated and enjoying the drowsy murmurings of afterwards.

"What about with Jim?"

"Possibly, but if so I've forgotten. And you and Esmé?"

"I know I brought it up, but I don't like comparisons. Combinations of people are all different. All have different needs, different expectations and different levels of satisfaction. Sorry, that sounds pompous. All I care about is that we're good together."

"Does Leo have anyone?"

"He's between, at the moment. Was married and is on the lookout, I believe."

"Do you think he minds about us? Feels 'de trop' or anything?"

"Doubt it. He was keen to come. Probably fancies you."

"I'm sure he does. He's an attractive guy. Very fanciable."

"If I were a jealous man, I'd be jealous. As it is . . ." The rest remained unsaid as there were more important things to say and do!

CHAPTER FIFTEEN

The next morning Clarissa said that she would like to re-visit Will as part of their site locations search. They decided that it would be best if Clarissa went on her own as Will might feel overwhelmed if all three descended. The two men would take her to a spot somewhere near his home and drop her to walk the rest of the way. They would hover nearby. It was a greyish sort of morning, rather like Clarissa's very first day in Dorset wandering around aimlessly on her own, but there was nothing aimless about how she felt now. She was looking forward to seeing her 'time warp' again and to renewing her acquaintance with Will. She was determined, however, not to accept any proffered 'drop o' zummat' this time. Sam and Leo dropped her at the Quiet Woman site and she retraced the way she'd first trod with Will.

It took her a little over five minutes to get to his place but as she drew near to the place she sensed something was odd. There was a total lack of sound, no clucking of hens or, as she grew nearer, no warning bark of a dog. At first Clarissa thought she'd not yet reached the spot, for there was no shack to be seen. Then she realised that the rickety chunks of stone and brick rubble were all that remained of the foundations of Will's home. There were a few remnants of what looked like the rugs from Will's floor and a rusting old tin bowl which might once have held the old sheepdog's water. Clarissa was so shocked and taken aback that without uttering a sound she turned and ran back to the Quiet Woman.

"He's gone. He's gone", she cried out to Sam and Leo who were strolling about photographing the place. "They've knocked down his home."

"Will's, you mean?"

"Yes, yes. What on earth has happened to him?" and Clarissa tried to keep back the tears which had sprung to her eyes.

Sam made her sit down on the isolated stretch of wall and put an arm round her shoulders.

"Shush, calm down, darling. He was a very old man remember. Anything could have happened. Maybe he's in a home or living with some relative or something."

"But why destroy his home? It seems so brutal, so callous. And they've ripped up his lovely old rugs and thrown them on to a tip. Poor old Will." And now the tears flowed.

"Let's go back to the car, go somewhere for coffee and think about this," suggested Leo.

They went to the tearoom near Hardy's cottage where Clarissa pulled herself together and they discussed how they might find out what had happened to Will. "Why don't we contact his stepdaughter? That seems the obvious thing. She must know something about him even though they were estranged." Sam's suggestion was agreed upon and Sam 'phoned her there and then on his mobile and reminded her of his previous visit. Could he bring a couple of his colleagues to discuss the film they were working on. At least that might get them access, whereas the mention of Will might put her off.

Felicity lived in a modest terrace house near the centre of Dorchester. Nevertheless it was full of fine paintings and tasteful objets d'art as befitted one who had studied at the Slade and been an art teacher and since retirement was being successfully exhibited locally.

They learned from her that Will had died before Christmas and that she had arranged and been present at his funeral—in fact the only 'mourner', though that hardly was a reflection of her feelings towards Will. The owner of the land where Will's shack stood had long wanted to sell the fields and woods around and had lost no time in demolishing the flimsy structure. She'd gone over and recovered Will's belongings and had sorted out what was worth keeping from a financial and sentimental point of view. They had intended to mention their television project first, but Clarissa couldn't contain her feelings about what she considered the despoliation of Will's home and had burst out with what she felt. When they did get round to their project, Felicity had evidently given the matter some thought since she had spoken with Sam and in principle was in favour of the idea, provided they kept in touch with her and didn't abuse the information they had about her mother.

She plied them with tea and cake and the time passed pleasantly. Clarissa was fascinated by their hostess. Though the time scale dictated that she must be in her sixties she was a still beautiful woman with a presence and composure which were truly remarkable. She revealed that she had never married (no doubt she had been warned off men by her mother's experiences) but she did refer briefly to a partner without divulging the nature of the relationship. Her dress style was 'individual', as befits artists, but not in a poseur way. Clarissa noticed that she was wearing a sapphire and silver brooch.

CHAPTER SIXTEEN

Over dinner that evening Leo revealed that, if the age gap between himself and Felicity had been a little less, he would have found himself very interested in her. He soon convinced himself that the gap was not all that significant and in any case it didn't matter. Sam and Clarissa exchanged amused glances, believing the wine was talking and changed the subject. They had a strenuous day ahead of them to get round all the sites they wanted to photograph and record and Clarissa was to return home the day after that, so they retired early. In spite of passion's demands the two lovers were soon asleep, companionably curled around each other.

More in the interests of speed and convenience than 'three being a crowd' they decided to split up with Leo going off on his own. Sam and Clarissa went to Hardy's birthplace and afterwards strolled up to Rainbarrow. It was hard to imagine the 'Heath' of the novels, the area being now covered with mature pine trees obscuring the valley Eustacia might have looked down into when walking from her home at Mistover to Rainbarrow. They sat down near the barrow marked by a sprawling, low, holly tree and discussed the possibilities of the panorama rolling away down below accompanying the opening credits of their documentary and the desirability or otherwise of computer technology stripping away the modern accretions of afforestation back to the heathland of Hardy's imagination. They discussed possible soundtracks. Elgar? Folksong? Or the sounds of nature, pure and unadulterated?

They were hardly aware of how passion stole upon them stealthily and they made love up there on Eustacia's barrow. They ended up giggling at the 'corniness' of their situation and their mirth was part of the delight they had in each other. They pulled apart, brushed themselves down and got down to the business of recording the scene. After which hunger drew them down to the nearest inviting pub they could find for lunch. They longed to return to their hotel room to continue the business begun on Rainbarrow, but sheer willpower drove them on to the church at Stinsford and on to Dorchester and the ugly surrounds of Max Gate—a major road and a modern housing estate—which they could only see by standing on a brick wall and peering through the hedge.

"Next time I'll wear my professional hat and get proper access to the place by prior appointment." Sam's comment underlined Clarissa's realisation that much of their so-called business was simply a pretext for adultery and a shadow remained over the rest of the day, made more oppressive by the thought of returning home.

There was a message for them when they got back to the hotel. It seems Leo had decided there was an urgent need to return to London straightaway, so he'd packed and gone.

"He's a strange guy," remarked Sam.

"Perhaps he got fed up of playing gooseberry."

"Perhaps he's gone to visit Felicity."

"No, he wouldn't"

"Well, he seemed very struck with her."

"No, he'll have got what he came for and gone. He's a bit of a restless sod."

"And tomorrow, I go. Oh how I don't want to and goodness knows when I'll get down again."

"Aren't you wanting to see Christian? Only a suggestion but why don't you stay on now and go to see him. Have you an address?

"Yes. Charles Baines 'phoned me. I've got it here somewhere."

"Makes sense but I'm not pressurising you, much as I want you with me."

"It's an idea, though Jim will hate me for it. I really must get home the day after tomorrow as I have school the day after that."

"I'll leave you to 'phone and I'll go and get the bill so that we can have a quick getaway tomorrow morning."

Someone would be at home at this time. Clarissa's heart pounded as she dialled but she managed to simulate the casual (she was getting to be quite skilled at covering up her true feelings) as the answering service invited her to leave a message. That non-plussed her as she was certain Jim would be home at this time and her information was somewhat fumbled.

"Going to try to see er my er stalker—no I mean Christian—so be back a day later than I intended. Hope everything is fine or at least OK. Sorry. Clarissa."

Once again it crossed her mind that romance entailed a great deal of unwanted emotion and behaviour.

As Sam was a long time getting the bill she quickly freshened herself up and went downstairs to look for him. After searching reception she eventually tracked him down in a corner of the bar speaking to someone on his mobile. She stopped a little way from him so as not to appear to be snooping and heard him say goodbye to Francesca. The twinge of jealousy she'd felt in Dorchester went through her again.

"I was trying to raise Leo but no luck. Then I rang Francesca."

"Oh?" was all Clarissa could manage.

"As she missed the meeting I thought I should put her in the picture."

"Did you get our bill sorted out?"

"No, sorry, not yet. I got side tracked by the calls. Tell you what. Let me get you a drink and I'll join you before we go in for a meal."

Clarissa sat over her gin & tonic, almost stunned. She couldn't believe the intensity of her jealousy and hurt. She tried to rationalise the situation. Of course as part of the group Francesca had to be informed but why now, when their time together was so short?

Once again Clarissa's dissembling skills had to be brought into play as Sam plonked himself down beside her with a beer.

"Have you worked it with Jim?"

"Not very satisfactorily. There was no one in, so I could only leave a message. Perhaps I'd better go home as arranged."

"Well if that would cause you less trouble, do so by all means."

This was not what Clarissa wanted to hear but pride would not let her back track, so as they went into dinner it was assumed that she would stick to the original agreement in spite of the message she'd left, though Sam did confess he was sorry she felt she had to go. Clarissa felt down and on edge all the way through the meal and on occasion was almost sharp with Sam in replying to his most innocent remarks.

"You must be tired, Clarrie. I know I am. Let's opt for an early night after the meal." Clarissa had no quarrel with that.

When they got to their room the 'phone was ringing. It was reception, putting through a call for Clarissa. It was Jim.

"So you're not coming home tomorrow. I got your message. Sorry I wasn't in. I was delayed at work and Maria had Jenny. It's OK. I'm taking a couple of days off work so I can cope."

"Are you sure?"

"Yes. I'm getting to be quite a dab hand at running a home and working. Don't know what you women complain about. It's a doddle! Only joking!"

"You sound very cheerful. Clearly you thrive when I'm away."

"Can't grumble. Jenny and I get along famously. Anyway you go and see your precious Christian, but I think you're on a fool's errand."

When she put the 'phone down she turned to Sam and said "I'm staying. Is that OK with you?"

"What do you mean, 'is that OK with me?' What do you think?" and he drew her into his arms.

"There's nobody else you'd rather see?"

"Like who?"

"Like Francesca."

"Francesca? What on earth do you mean?"

"Well you 'phoned her earlier."

"Clarissa. Francesca is a colleague. I told you why I called her."

Clarissa was silent and Sam didn't say any more, but after they'd made love he studied her face and said gently "You are lovely, you know" and then firmly, "but you still underestimate yourself. Our path ahead is going to be difficult, especially as we're at opposite ends of it—so to speak. Geographically, I mean. We've got to trust one another or it's going to be hell. You're going back to a husband and family. I could be jealous. I've got a finished relationship."

"But Francesca is beautiful and you're free—well, apart from me."

"Exactly. I don't hare after anything in a skirt. And Francesca is married. Yes, at one time I did 'fancy' Francesca. Who wouldn't? But anything there was is long since over and she's very happy with her Anthony and I'm happy with you."

"I daren't say sorry or you'll whop me, but I *am* sorry. I was rather upset by not reaching Jim personally and I took it out on you. You see you're beginning to see what I'm really like. Please say you've got a less than perfect side."

"Come here and I'll show you. I'm a sex monster as far as you're concerned, my love and we've wasted enough time for one night. Suddenly I'm not sleepy anymore!"

CHAPTER SEVENTEEN

"Have you a visitor's pass, madam?"

"Visitor's pass? I don't know what you mean."

Clarissa's path was blocked by a burly prison officer. "Who've yer come ter see?"

"Christian McKenzie"

"Are yer a relation?"

"No, a friend. I've never been before."

"Just a mo'," and Jack Fellowes went to consult a list. Then he rang someone. All his body signals were negative with much shaking of the head. "Sorry madam, he's got his full quota of visitors for this month."

"What do I do to get a visitor's pass?"

"Well really it's up to the prisoner. He has to make the application. He's allowed three visitors a fortnight. I'll tell him you called, if you like."

"No, don't do that. Can I write to him?"

"Yeah, that's OK. Make arrangements with him."

Clarissa went back to the car where Sam was waiting outside stark red brick walls topped with barbed wire.

"No go?"

"Afraid not. It seems I need a visitor pass which can only be pre-booked. As Jim said 'a wild goose chase'."

"Do you know where his mother lives?"

"Yes, at least I have her address somewhere." Clarissa looked through her diary and found where she'd written down where Mrs McKenzie lived. She showed it to Sam who had vaguely heard of the area. It was the same side of town as the prison but about four miles further out. The suburbs were sprawling and seedy.

"That's a full blown prison we've been to, isn't it? I thought Christian would have been in a young offenders' institution. What a grim place for a youngster to be in."

"Yes, the University of Crime, I'm afraid."

They drove past a bleak looking Council Estate and pulled up to enquire the way to Landesdowne Close. A weary looking young woman pushing a baby buggy thought she'd heard of it, but declared the place to be like a rabbit warren with lots of streets, closes, crescents with virtually the same name. She advised them to go further into the estate and enquire again, which they did. Eventually they found Mrs McKenzie's house which stood out as a bijou residence in a street of unkempt broken-down dwellings, quite a number of which were boarded up. Sam stayed in the car and Clarissa walked up the path in the neat front garden and rang the door bell.

It was a few minutes before the door was opened, not by Christian's mother but by the friend who had accompanied her on one of the days in court. Clearly Clarissa was not easily recognised, for the woman looked at her quizzically and not too pleasantly.

"I don't suppose you remember me but I was one of the witnesses at Christian's trial. I spoke to his mother afterwards and said I would be in touch. I'm sorry I haven't made it earlier, but I live in the north of England and that makes it a bit difficult. I wonder if I could possibly speak to her, if it's not too inconvenient at this time."

"Well it is. She's not well. That's why I'm here to see her."

"Oh dear, I'm so sorry. I hope it's nothing too serious."

"It's depression. She's been like it ever since Christian was put away."

"Do you think she would see me, just for a very short while?"

"Just hang on, I'll ask her. What did you say your name was?"

Clarissa told her to which she responded "Oh yeah, I remember now. Didn't he stalk you or something? Just wait there a tick."

It seemed Mrs McKenzie would see her so Clarissa followed the woman into the house which was just as neat and tidy as the garden. Mrs McKenzie was lying on a settee looking pale and strained but without the composure she'd shown at the trial. She seemed both on edge and apathetic, an unusual combination since one usually cancels out the other.

Mrs McKenzie barely looked up as Clarissa entered the room. She went over to the settee and put her hand on her shoulder "How are you?"

"Alright," she murmured.

"I've come to talk to you about Christian. How is he?"

"Well, I don't see him that often since . . . . well you know . . . ." Her voice trailed off.

"I know. I wonder if I might visit him with you or write to him. I know he must hate me but I would very much like to talk to him."

"He'll hardly talk to me. He says he doesn't like visitors. He hates that awful place he's in. He should be in the Young Offenders but I don't think he's been very co-operative and that's put him back."

Mrs McKenzie seemed to go limp after her spurt of talking. Her friend said that she thought she'd had enough and needed to be left in peace. "Come out into the kitchen and I'll put you in the picture. I'm Angie, by the way."

Out in the kitchen she continued. "He's been causing trouble—even in there—so they've put back his transfer till they've reassessed him."

"What's the trouble he's caused? Drugs again?"

"Yeah. One of his mates smuggled some in—don't ask me what—I'm not up in that stuff—and of course Christian being Christian couldn't be discreet about it and got caught. The trouble is the lad's bored stiff. He's put down for all sorts of courses but nothing seems to happen. You know he's *really* good at Art. I'll show you some of his stuff if you like. Give you something to talk about if you do contact him."

Clarissa peeped into the sitting room while Angie was going to fetch Christian's work and saw that Mrs McKenzie had dropped off to sleep. Her face in respose resembled that of her son and once again Clarissa couldn't help reflecting on the contrast between the circumstances here and the comfortable, middle class surroundings of her family and she felt the familiar pang of guilt that she was set on a course which could destroy all the advantages, material and emotional, of what they all enjoyed. Even more she was determined to help these people across whose path she'd strayed and when she looked at Christian's folder of art work she thought she saw a way. There was raw talent here, not yet fully refined, though some of the cartoons were quite sophisticated.

"Do you mind if I ask my friend to see these? I think they're very good and I'd like a second opinion, in addition to yours I mean."

"Yeah, go ahead."

She went to the car and told Sam she wanted to show him something. Sam followed her into the house looking somewhat bemused. On seeing the work he voiced the same opinion as Clarissa.

"I'd like to have a word in private with my friend. We'll talk in the car. Do you mind?"

"Suit yourself. I'll make you a cuppa if you like."

"That would be lovely, thanks."

In the car, Sam was all curiosity. "What are you up to? What's the mystery?"

"Have you got anyone to do the graphics for the film?"

"Well that's not really my pigeon. Leo usually sees to that."

"That boy's work is good. Think of the ideals of our group and give this lad a chance. It could be the making of him."

"First you and now him. "I *am* taking risks," joked Sam. However my instincts have proved sound with number one risk so perhaps I could be persuaded to take a second. But I can't stress enough that it's not really up to me."

"We'll have to speak to the powers that be, and to Leo to see if we can meet Christian and arrange something. One step at a time. Let's go back and talk to Angie and see if we can apply for a visitor pass."

Over a cup of tea they outlined to Angie what they had in mind.

"Sounds great to me. I think he needs pushing in the right direction. Here's his address. You'll need to contact him first. His mum isn't in a fit state to make a decision about anything, but I don't think she'd object to what you want to do for her son."

****

Clarissa was bubbling over with excitement at the prospect of doing something concrete to help Christian and his family and could talk about nothing else on the journey back to the hotel. Sam was silently amused and somewhat puzzled by Clarissa's 'need' to do something for this lad. This was a side of her he was only dimly aware of and whilst it didn't detract from her attractions for him he did wonder if she was given to enthusiasms which might prove temporary. After all, hadn't she already taken on a tremendous new challenge which, together with her family responsibilities and all the rest, would take up all her energies? Only time would tell.

The weather had taken a turn for the worse and after a light lunch at the hotel, they decided to spend their last afternoon and evening together in a not unexpected way.

As they lay sated with enjoyment of each other, Sam whispered "So you're addicted to 'good works', my beautiful philanthropist?"

"Not really. Why do you ask?"

"Well, Christian, for example!"

"Hardly good works. Not even conscience! I can't explain it but I feel genuinely concerned for that boy . . . . and his mum."

"Would that more people felt that way towards perpetrators—or at least some of them. You clearly feel that Christian would benefit from a real interest being shown in him?"

"Of course. His poor mother *is* interested in her son's welfare, but has been too busy trying to put food into his mouth to do much else for him. Though her job was to make some extra to help him get some kind of a qualification."

"It says something about our society in the twenty first-century that the poor creature had to come to this. Unfortunately I think we've got an uphill struggle trying to get Leo to take on an unknown, to say nothing of opposition we might get from others, not least Christian himself. So please don't raise your spirits too high."

"Well, I can but try."

"*We* can but try. I'm with you in this. All I'm saying is don't be too hopeful." Sam turned towards her and brought the conversation to an end in the time honoured way with lovers.

CHAPTER EIGHTEEN

Clarissa made her way north in a state of elation. Life seemed very full and satisfying. This time the radio had done with Requiems and Tragedies and by the time she was on the homeward stretch a jolly jazz programme was being broadcast. She turned off the motorway on to a country road through a rather upmarket village whose store catered for those with a discerning palate. She decided to pick up some goodies for an evening meal (to atone perhaps?). A bottle of good wine would be nice too.

She arrived home in a thoroughly happy mood, bearing gifts and expecting to be welcomed if not with open arms exactly, with a slight degree of enthusiasm, from Jenny at least. She was disconcerted, therefore, to find the house in darkness and empty. Assuming that someone would be home soon, if only to put Jenny to bed, she set the table with care adding a candle for effect. As the evening wore on hunger got the better of her, as she hadn't eaten since early lunchtime, and she toyed with the supper bought in excited anticipation.

At nine thirty, Jim came in with Jenny.

"Where on earth have you been till this time?" Clarissa burst out.

Jim raised his eyebrows and gave his wife a meaningful look. Jenny answered. "We've been to the cinema. It was great."

"That's right. We've been to see . . . ." And he mentioned a current film which all the kids were going wild over.

"Didn't you think about school? Couldn't you have waited until the weekend?"

"We could have but I didn't see the harm for once. Anyway I can't always be asking Maria to have her and we're running out of things to do, aren't we sweetheart?"

"No dad, you're great. Fab, in fact."

"Well, off to bed now, young lady." This from Clarissa.

"Oh shit. Sorry, sugar. Do I have to? I'm starving!"

"Jenny. Never let me hear you say that word again." This again from a shocked Clarissa.

Jim took his daughter out into the kitchen, gave her something to eat and then shepherded her upstairs to bed. Clarissa followed, intending to settle her daughter down.

"I want dad. Fab dad."

"Well, she's got a bit used to me and we're in the middle of a serial I'm making up for her."

Clarissa bit back any further comments and retreated downstairs. Later Jim stood in the dining room doorway and surveyed the table.

"Were we expecting someone? If so I'm afraid it's slipped my mind."

"I was expecting you. I stopped off and bought something special for us to eat."

"Ah well, you should have said. How was I to know?"

"Naturally I thought you'd be home to see to Jenny or at least you could have left a note."

"Now don't let either of us adopt the 'martyr' role. I'm peckish so let's dive in now. Mm, nice wine." Jim studied the bottle.

"I've eaten. I couldn't wait all night."

"Well, let's have a glass of wine then," and he began to uncork the bottle."

No. Don't let's waste it. It was quite expensive and deserves an occasion."

"If it was an occasion *then*, why not *now*?"

"Well things have all gone a bit pear-shaped, wouldn't you say?"

"I don't quite know what shape you expect 'things' to be when you breeze in and out of this house like a lodger."

"Look we've been over all this before. It's my work, remember?"

"Yes, and I've got my work too, don't forget. It's not easy fixing things here when you always stay longer than we bargained for. You simply can't expect people to take over your responsibilities whenever you feel like it."

"Which people in particular?"

"Maria, for one. And me for another."

"I think you're being unreasonable, Jim. When I left the message you seemed perfectly alright. Has something gone wrong since?"

"Not especially. In fact, though she wasn't very tactful about it, Jenny was right. We've got along well."

"She sounds out of control to me. Staying out of bed till all hours and where did she pick up that horrible expression she used earlier?"

"From Maria's kids, probably. Pat's just at that age. I'm doing my best, Clarissa."

"The martyr mode again."

"Look, let's stop bickering. We're both tired and it's getting us nowhere. Bed?"

Clarissa shivered inwardly. A few months ago she could deal with 'both beds', but she'd reached the stage with Sam where sharing her body was becoming unbearable.

"As you say we're both tired so let's sleep alone tonight. I'll take the spare room." And without allowing any chance for Jim to demur, Clarissa went upstairs to the spare room.

CHAPTER NINETEEN

Jim and Clarissa were sitting over breakfast on the Saturday after her return. Jenny was playing some rather loud, raucous music in her bedroom and Clarissa was biting back comments on yet more evidence of the way her daughter was changing for the worse and deciding that the subject was best avoided. She enquired about Tom instead, whose name hadn't come up yet since she'd got back.

"I really don't know how he is. I don't know *where* he is either."

"What do you mean, you don't know where he is?"

"He's off on the rounds of university Open Days. I expect he'll contact us when he's anything to report."

"Any news of the girl friend?"

"Nope."

"Oh. Which universities?"

"LSE, Sussex and Birmingham, I think."

"Will Rob know his whereabouts?"

"Could do, I suppose. He'll probably stay with Rob for the Birmingham day."

"I can't understand you! How can you be so casual about where he is and what he's doing?"

"As I recall, getting involved didn't do very much good, not so long ago! He's a big boy now, Clarrie."

"I wish you wouldn't call me that." As with her body, she didn't mind *Sam's* use of the diminutive but Jim's use of it now grated on her as indicative of an intimacy between them which no longer existed.

"Sorry. You're in films now. Script writer par excellence. Shall I ask the kids to call you 'mother' or maybe 'ma'am'?"

"Don't be stupid. Anyway to get back to Tom, I think I'll give Rob a call." Jim shrugged his shoulders and went out of the room.

Clarissa went upstairs and called in to Jenny's room to ask her to turn her music down. The child had her back to the door with earphones glued to her ears. She was gyrating and mouthing to the music with a look of rapture on her face. Clarissa had to touch her on the shoulder to announce her presence.

Once more Jenny came out with "Oh sh . . . . ugar", but had the grace to redden. She removed the earphones and stared rebelliously at her mother.

"You scared me."

"That's no reason to use that language, my girl. I want to use the telephone so kindly keep that row down."

Jenny deliberately turned the 'row' up for a blast or two and Clarissa found she'd slapped her across the face before realising what she'd done. They both gazed in horror at each other before the child threw the control gadget and earphones to the floor and rushed downstairs howling. She collided with Jim in the hall and flung her arms around him, screaming "I hate her. Tell her to go back to that man, dad". Clarissa went pale and sank on to the stairs. Jenny's sobbing went on for about twenty minutes, hysterical and desperate.

"Let me get past you please, Clarissa. She needs to lie down. Go and make some coffee."

Clarissa trailed into the kitchen and mechanically made a pot of coffee. She couldn't believe what she'd heard from her daughter's lips. Surely Jim hadn't said anything to the child about what he feared between his wife and Sam. Clarissa wasn't sure that Jim really believed that anything *was* going on, though he'd have to be naïve not to suspect.

Jim came down soon afterwards. "She's asleep." He sat down at the kitchen table and beckoned Clarissa to sit down too.

"I haven't said anything to her. Believe me. As if I would."

"Then where did she get the idea from?"

"I can only guess. You remember that conversation down by the river at Bristol and the joke about you leaving me?—well I thought it was a joke! She's spoken about that once or twice. And don't forget she met Sam and she's obviously put two and two together."

"And what score do *you* make?"

"What score should I make?"

"We're colleagues. Yes, he stimulates me because we have things in common, but that's all."

Clarissa lied more glibly than she cared to admit. But the time wasn't yet ripe for decisive family rifts so she glossed over a complicated situation as craftily as she could. Nevertheless the ugly incident upset her. She'd never laid a finger in anger on Jenny (or any of the children) until today and she hated herself for handling the situation so badly.

When Jim went out to post a letter Clarissa went upstairs to Jenny's room. She was sleeping though still emitting the occasional sob, as is the way with children after a prolonged, frantic bout of weeping. Clarissa stood looking down at her from a moment or two and then went downstairs to ring Rob from there.

Rob answered the phone and when Clarissa announced herself he said "Are you OK, mum? You sound odd."

"I've got a bit of a cold, that's all. I'm a bit worried about Tom. Your father says he's off on University Open Days but we've no idea where he is. Thought you might know as Birmingham is one his choices and we thought he may have arranged to stay with you."

"He hasn't been in touch with me as yet. I could let you know if he turns up—that is if he wants me to."

"Why shouldn't he want you to?"

"Well, he's his own man and if he wants you to know his whereabouts he's perfectly capable of letting you know himself."

"I suppose you know about Amy?"

"Yes."

The tone of his reply implied that he didn't want to pursue that any further. Nevertheless Clarissa continued "I'm a bit concerned about it all."

"I'm not going to discuss Tom's affairs. I haven't met the girl and anyway it's not got nothing to do with what we think, so let's drop the subject. How's Jen?"

"Getting a bit out of hand. Into loud music and bad language."

"So, normal then!"

"She's only seven, Rob"

"Kids grow up fast these days, mum. But I must say, it doesn't sound like my sweet little sister."

Clarissa knew she would break down if they went on any longer about Jenny, so she rang off saying she was in a hurry and would he remind Tom that he *did* have family who cared about him.

* *

Although Clarissa was very troubled about her relations with Jenny, she tried to put it to the back of her mind by concentrating on the script she was to prepare according to the instructions she received from Leo. What she was expected to do was quite different from anything in the creative line she'd ever done before. She knew that most of what she wrote would be discarded. Script writers have to be succinct almost to the point of brevity and have to give the most detailed directions in all areas—dialogue, movement, background, lighting, camera angles and so on. She had yet to select significant episodes from 'Return' to complement what she decided to use of the Will and Emma stories, so it wasn't so much a case of trying to put the Jenny problem on the back burner, it was a matter of *having* to if she were not to be a drag on the others in the group.

Jim, of course, thought she was not taking the Jenny thing seriously enough. According to him she was neglecting the emotional needs of the child, shutting herself away in her study instead of spending the extra time he felt was needed to repair the situation. To combat this, Clarissa devoted her evenings to Jenny (to not very good effect) and started her own work after her daughter had gone to bed, working until the early hours. She got up much earlier in the mornings and did more than an hour's work before anyone was about. Consequently she was worn out, tetchy and totally unresponsive in the bedroom. This did nothing to repair relations with anyone and she felt she was almost in the situation she was in before she met Sam. The difference was that the work totally absorbed her and in spite of all the difficulties she knew this was what she wanted to do above all else.

Late one night she was working on one scene she *had* to include in the film—probably the opening one after the credits. This was from 'Return', very near the beginning when Eustacia stands high on Rainbarrow like some Queen of the Night, seemingly growing out of the very summit on which she stood, gliding away and leaving the place to the peasant folk and their bonfire, returning later to keep tryst with her lover. She wanted to capture the flickering and flaring effect of the fire as it concealed and then highlighted the faces of the Heath folk. It was all there in Hardy's text, almost as though he had written it with a film in mind. She need only refer to the novel itself where the directions were written down far more effectively than she could give them.

But she knew she would need to meet Leo at least to discuss what they both could achieve. The meetings loomed on the horizon. How could she contrive to keep on getting away? "But this is my work", she thought. "Why should I have to keep on apologising for its demands?" She would hire a nanny part-time, when she needed to go away. She would be firm with Jim and not *ask* to go away but announce it. She e-mailed through the work she'd just finished to Sam and on a separate one she told him that she was available to see him and other group members whenever was convenient to him. What else she wrote can be left to the imagination.

She deliberately disturbed Jim getting into bed, as she felt in the mood to tell him what she'd decided to do about Jenny and her necessary absences from home.

"I've worked out a solution to my having to go away so often with my work and leaving you to cope with Jenny." Jim mumbled something but clearly hadn't taken on board what she'd said. At risk of irritating him she persisted. "Did you hear what I said, Jim?"

"It's very late. Can't it wait?"

"It's important, so please wake up and listen." Jim opened one eye and, seeing her serious expression, roused himself. "Go on, then."

She repeated what she'd already said and continued. "I'll engage someone part-time to see to Jenny when I have to go away. I can afford it. I don't expect you to pay."

Jim, being completely awake by now, looked at her long and hard. "I think you're missing the point, Clarrie—sorry, Clarissa. Jenny needs *you* here at home."

"Look Jim, I know I've found my Métier." Jim smirked but Clarissa continued. "I'm not easily letting it slip through my fingers. I've simply got to meet up with the others from time to time—not all *that* often, but as often as it takes."

"And what about Jenny, your daughter? Don't you give a fig about what happens to her?"

"Of course I do, Jim, don't be stupid. You know I adore her. But she's your daughter too and you and she seem to getting on very well together, in spite of my reservations about her behaviour recently. I've done most of the caring up to now. I could give up this writing job and become resentful and miserable as I was before and that wouldn't be in her best interests or yours for that matter."

"Oh, blackmail now! You know, Clarrie, you sound like a spoilt child, a blackmailing, threatening one, at that."

"I'm trying to be reasonable. At last I've found what I want to do as ME, not just as wife, mother and halfhearted teacher and I'm coming up against the classic opposition—husband!" She had raised her voice and Jim's heated reply pushed them into a full scale row which quickly lost the disciplining bounds of logical rationality. Too late they realised the folly of their behaviour as Jenny burst into their bedroom, scared and tearful. She ran straight to Jim. "I didn't mean it, daddy. Don't tell mummy to go away." Once again Jim had to calm her down assuring her that all was well, in spite of evidence to the contrary and once again Clarissa took herself off to the spare room where she fretted the night away. Of course she felt guilty about Jenny but she was determined to stick to her guns as far as her new role in life was concerned and Jim's opposition strengthened her decision to seek out and employ a carer for her daughter. She would set about it the very next day.

CHAPTER TWENTY

Before settling down to work on the script, Clarissa rang Maria to sound out just how she felt about being called on to look after Jenny rather more often than had been the case up to now. Jim was certainly making a big deal of it.

"Oh, I don't mind looking after Jenny, though she's not always the easiest to deal with these days. She seems to prefer Pat's company to Sally's. Some sort of childish crush on him, I think."

"Mm. She seems to have increased her vocabulary, too." Clarissa told her friend about the outburst of a couple of weeks previously.

Maria sounded rather 'miffed' at the clear implication that her son was a bad influence, but whether it was that or a genuine situation that caused her to say that changed circumstances would make it very difficult to have Jenny in future, Clarissa was not very clear about. She put the 'phone down in a mood of peke and upset. She turned to the yellow pages and started thumbing through the child minders and carers section. "No, this will not do," she told herself. She wouldn't simply stick a pin in to select someone to look after her cherished child. She would ask around at school and see if any of her upwardly-mobile colleagues with well-paid husbands—there were some even in the staffroom of an 'ordinary' comprehensive—could offer her any advice.

There was an e-mail from Sam acknowledging the work which she'd sent the previous evening and stating categorically that a meeting between her and Leo was essential. He added a cryptic comment which he said he would be expanding on in an immediately following e-mail. They didn't want any electronic overlapping of business and the personal and they'd decided the personal messages were to be destroyed. The second message hinted at some mysterious liaison between Leo and a lady. He would bet his bottom dollar that a bit of sniffing around would reveal Felicity as that lady! He also offered Clarissa accommodation in his London flat on her next trip south, from where they could more easily visit Leo's flat which also doubled as his studio.

This suggestion both thrilled and frightened Clarissa. So far their relationship had been conducted on neutral ground which had kept it in the realm of romantic uncertainty and excitement. She had the feeling that Sam wanted to move it on and sharing his flat would give that movement some impetus. She was dying to see Sam in his everyday 'context' so to speak but wasn't at all sure what that would bring in its wake. She would have to stall for a bit, however, at least until she had appointed a nanny and a decent spell of time had elapsed between the last visit and the next. However besotted she was with Sam, she wanted to keep her feet on the ground to deal with problems presented by her children.

In addition, she had not yet done anything about securing a visitor pass to the prison. She decided to do something about that immediately. She wrote a letter to Christian saying that she realised that she was most likely the very last person he wanted to see, but that she had a proposition to put to him which she thought would interest him as a talented cartoonist. She put it in the hall to post later. With coffee at her elbow, she settled down to work on the script. She selected an episode from Emma's story which she thought would best complement the 'Bonfire' scene from 'Return'. That scene seemed to Clarissa to be the essence of Eustacia—romance, theatre and intrigue—and it took her some time to find an image which encapsulated the essential qualities of Emma she wanted brought out in the film.

She was so absorbed in her work that she was unaware that the front door had opened and shut and that someone had come upstairs to her study and was standing looking over her shoulder. It was only when she had saved her material on the word processor that she stretched, stood up and turned round to face her mother-in-law. She jumped.

"God! How long have you been"—Clarissa nearly said spying on me but said instead—"standing there?"

"About a minute." Then after a significant pause, "So this is how you fill in your time."

Clarissa flushed with irritation near anger. "I don't have to *look* for things to do. This is my work."

"So I'm led to understand."

Ignoring the loaded statement, Clarissa went on diplomatically, "It's always good to see you, Moll, but you've taken me by surprise this time. You scared me."

"Sorry. I thought you were expecting me. Jim rang this morning and said you might welcome a visit. It seems you're getting in a tangle, going off and leaving Jim to cope with Jenny."

"I don't think that's quite the right reading of the situation. My friend Maria has been on hand to look after Jenny on the *two* occasions I've needed to be away. And I don't think Jim minds looking after his own daughter once in a while. Remember I've looked after three children *and* worked."

"Jim tells me you're thinking of hiring a nanny part-time. Do you think that's wise, the way Jenny is at present?"

"I suppose it depends on who I get and I intend being very selective in the matter of who I take on for my daughter."

"Will I do?"

"You'd do admirably, Moll. However I'd like to be independent of everybody. If someone is paid to do the job then I'm not beholden to her (or him for that matter)."

This last throw-away comment seemed to incense Moll. "You mean you'd let a man look after her?"

Clarissa, who knew very well that it was highly unlikely that she'd employ a man, but a rebellious streak at what she considered this uncalled-for interference had taken over and made her want to shock, replied,"Of course, if the right man applied."

Moll, who prided herself on not interfering, pressed her lips together and said nothing further, but her look spoke worlds.

"Well, you know where I am if I'm wanted. My only concern is the welfare of my granddaughter. I suppose Jim can cope. Goodbye." She turned and walked towards the door.

"Please don't go Moll. Stay and have some lunch."

"I'd rather not if you don't mind. I've got to get back to see to a friend. Give Jim my love." And with that she almost ran down the stairs and was gone.

Clarissa was left shaking. She had always got on reasonably well with her mother-in-law in spite of finding her rather cold with her stiff upper lip attitude to everything. And it was true that she had not tried to interfere in her son's marriage, so Jim must have painted a pretty complicated picture of their family affairs for her to take the step she had. This angered Clarissa and made her less fearful of Jim's reaction to his mother's hasty departure than she would otherwise have been. She got no more serious work done that day. She longed to speak to Sam but she didn't want to introduce a whingeing element into their relationship so she smothered the urge to ring him.

* *

As expected, Jim was upset that his mother hadn't spent the day with Clarissa and stayed on to see him and perhaps talk some sense into Clarissa over an evening meal and a bottle of wine. They wrangled on half the evening 'sotto voce' so that Jenny wouldn't hear, but being the child she was she sensed the atmosphere was all wrong. She picked up on granny's short visit. She wasn't overly fond of her somewhat buttoned-up grandma but knew that Moll was very fond of her and always produced some little gift to please her.

"I expect grandma doesn't like mummy now, dad. Is that why she didn't stay to see me?"

Clarissa almost exploded. "I've just about had enough of this."

Again Jim stepped in to pour oil on very troubled waters. "She just dropped in for a short while and then had to hurry back to visit a sick friend. You'll be seeing quite a lot of her very soon. She's coming to look after you when mum goes away."

This caused an outcry from both Jenny and Clarissa. "When's mum going? Is she going to that nasty man?"

From Clarissa, "Over my dead body!"

"Let's sit down all three of us and sort this out." Jim ushered both of them into the sitting room.

"Mum has a new job, Jenny, which means she has to go away from time to time to talk about what she's doing, with Sam and other people. I can't always be here to look after you in the evenings so I've asked Granny if she'd come and help out. Would you like that?"

"Or," Clarissa jumped in, "I could arrange for a nice person to come and stay—somebody who'd play with you, someone young and full of fun." Clarissa glared at Jim, daring him to contradict her.

"Why can't Pat come? I really like him."

Whilst persuading her that, nice though Pat was he wasn't quite old enough to be a nanny, Jim shooed her towards bed as playfully and unthreateningly as he could and told her they'd chat some more and she could think about it in bed.

When Jim came down Clarissa had already ensconced herself in her study so as to avoid any further 'eruptions' that evening. Jim took the hint and left her in peace.

Surprisingly, for she was in turmoil, she made good progress on selecting the companion scene from Emma's story to the 'Queen of the Night' scene from 'Return'. Whilst Eustacia was all darkness, mystery, 'drama' and self-seeking, Emma was open, generous and willing to face up to the realities of life. She worked on the episode where Emma and her little daughter were walking along in the afternoon sun before sheltering in Miss Winston's outhouse. She concentrated on the warmth of the afternoon, the games and laughter, the devotion she showed towards her small daughter and her determination to do all in her power to protect her from the indignities of being at the mercy of men simply because she was poor and uneducated. As always Clarissa was not unaware of the resonances of what she was writing with her own present situation. She realised that her devotion to her own child was not exactly dedicated at present and intrigue rather than openness characterised her current behaviour. And now she was in a mother-in-law situation not totally unlike that between Eustacia and Mrs Yoebright.

Common sense, her own instincts of fairness and duty all told her to disentangle herself from the romantic side of the course she'd embarked on, but she knew she couldn't give up the career opportunity which had opened up for her. Sam was a major part of that and she couldn't go on seeing him as a colleague without wanting all of him. Indeed she feared that without the energy and inspiration of his love everything she had newly discovered about herself would evaporate.

* *

The ensuing weeks followed an almost relentless pattern for Clarissa. The days free from school were spent in intense and satisfying work on the script. Sam wanted an outline of the film and at least two sample scenes to submit to his agent as soon as possible. She dreaded the evenings.

Jenny was silent with her to the point of rudeness and Jim was politely uncommunicative. When he was available she left him to see to Jenny. When he was not, Jenny was so 'off' her mother that she quickly became independent and organised her own evenings, mostly in her bedroom, her activities accompanied by the loud music Clarissa so much detested. She went to bed without a goodnight and firmly shut her door discouraging her mother's company. Clarissa fumed and despaired by turns. The truth was she didn't know what to do. In normal circumstances she would not have tolerated such behaviour from a seven year old and would have sought to find out the causes behind it but, knowing that what was needed was a complete reversal of her own present behaviour, she realised the futility of a heart-to-heart with her daughter.

CHAPTER TWENTY ONE

Clarissa did indeed find the person she was looking for to look after Jenny. Gillian Fairclough had impeccable qualifications. "Trained at *the* college for nannies and had worked for Lady Whatever", according to the staffroom snob. Occasional work suited her fine and she and Clarissa came to a mutually acceptable arrangement by 'phone. An end of term do was held for Easter leavers and Clarissa left with more cards, presents, expressions of regret at her leaving and warm good wishes for her new venture than she would have expected. Her classes expressed disappointment that they would not be having 'Miss' for English any more and said she was a super teacher. It was true that her work had possessed renewed verve since Sam and the writing and the thought that she could return to teaching with such glowing recommendations was not unacceptable to her, though she sincerely hoped she would not have to.

She arranged with Sam that she would go down to London after the holiday and meanwhile she, Jim and Jenny spent a few days in North Northumberland. Clarissa had wanted go to Rob's in the hope of tracking down Tom from whom they still had no word, except from Rob who assured them that Tom was OK but would say nothing further. Jim was adamantly against going so they booked up at a small former coach house now guest house they'd been to before in happier days, almost into Scotland. Clarissa took her lap top with her as she could not afford to relax from the script completely. Jim had plenty of reading material with him and as long as they kept Jenny amused during the day they had the evenings to do as they pleased. There were very few guests at this early season and they were often alone in the sitting room after dinner and immersed themselves in their separate activities, with very little in the way of conversation.

They were very close to Lindisfarne, a place they all loved for varying reasons and they spent part of each day there, according to the times of the tides. They preferred to be there at high tide when most people had left and they had the island almost themselves. Jenny loved playing around the upturned fishermen's boats and down by the harbour throwing pebbles into the water. Jim wandered around the ruined abbey and took photographs of the ever changing sea and sky scapes and Clarissa revisited, as she always did, the castle with its Lutyens' interior and the garden designed by Gertrude Jekell to withstand the harsh North Sea winds. There was indeed much to enjoy, but the tensions remained as at home with Jenny clinging to her father and both of them sharing private jokes and asides together, or so it seemed to Clarissa.

It was on the afternoon of their last full day that a 'phone call came from Christian. Jim and Jenny had gone off to play on the large stretch of grass behind the castle and Clarissa was dozing after a very filling picnic on a lounger outside the car, lap top on her knee.

"This is Christian here. You remember? You wrote to me about some cartoons or something'."

Clarissa was very enthusiastic in her response. "Oh Christian, hello. Lovely to hear from you. Where are you ringing from?"

"From me mum's. They're letting me out one day a month, especially as mum's not well."

"I am sorry. Please give her my best wishes. I expect she's all the better for seeing you."

"Dunno about that. Anyway, I've kinda mentioned it to one of the teachers and he says you need to speak to the prison authorities about it."

"You're keen to have a go then?"

"Yeah, might as well. It's better in this place. You sent the letter to the old place but they've moved me. They sent it on. I get to do a few courses in 'ere and they like you to choose your own project."

"That's marvellous. I'll get in touch with the powers that be as soon as I can and get down to see you too."

"I'll 'ave to go now, Mrs C. Cheers."

His manner was different from that displayed in the dock. More genuinely confident and still with the touch of cockiness, but also clearly pleased to have his talent recognised in spite of the 'couldn't care less' mode of speech. She hoped against hope that the group would give him a chance. She should have warned him that nothing was cut and dried yet. It wouldn't do to let him down. With this in mind she rang Sam.

"Hello my darling. This is a pleasant surprise. Is all well?" Avoiding his question she plunged straight into telling him of Christian's response to their suggestion and how it was essential not to let the lad's hopes down.

"Better not to build them up, my love. Don't say anything until it's all sewn up. You haven't told him it's certain, I hope."

"We—ll, not exactly."

"Clarissa! You know it's not up to me."

"You've got the most clout! Have you told Leo yet?"

"Not yet, I'm afraid."

"Sam, you promised."

"I know, I know, but I've been somewhat busy to say the least. When you come down you're going to see your scenes with actors. Well, one to be precise. How about that?"

"Surely not. Don't we have a say in the choice of actors?"

"Oh, it's only Francesca standing in to see how it looks." Clarissa felt pole-axed! Here she was in the far flung North enduring all manner of angst, juggling with pressure on all sides to keep the writing going with all that it entailed, alienated from her family because of Sam's strong attraction for her—and there was he cavorting around with Francesca in the role of Eustacia!

"Oh fine, fine!" she burst out. "Don't you think you might have waited until I came down before you started mucking about with my script?" Just at that moment Jim and Jenny came back from their 'play' and she hastily said good bye and switched off.

"Oh, dear, dear. Trouble at t'mill?" mocked Jim. "Temperaments to the fore, eh?"

"Oh, that was one of the technicians playing about with the script."

"You said 'mucking', mum, didn't she dad? Mucking about. Mucking about."

"That's enough, Jenny." This from Jim. He could see that Clarissa was uptight and he sensed that it was no technician who had upset her.

"It's a bit thick! I thought we were supposed to be relaxing up her away from it all!"

"I'm afraid we've got deadlines to meet. We've got to keep in touch."

Jim said nothing further, but indicated that they'd better pack up and catch low tide to get off the island.

* * * * * * * * * * * * * * * * * * * *

That night there was another couple in the sitting room after dinner, which avoided the strained atmosphere which otherwise would inevitably have prevailed. The conversation was desultory but pleasant enough to carry them through to a respectably acceptable hour for retiring. They learned of a garden in the area which had just been made over and reopened to the public and which would afford something of interest to both themselves and Jenny. They left the guest house straight after breakfast and took in this place on their way home to Normington. Their short holiday had not put anything right, but at least it had afforded the adults rest from everyday chores and Jenny interesting things to do.

Jim went back to work on the Monday, which meant that Clarissa and Jenny were thrown into each other's company rather more than either of them would have wished. Clarissa was not able to do much to the script during the day, not because Jenny demanded her time—as usual she kept to her bedroom or visited a friend—but because her powers of concentration were impaired by 'having to cope' with the child present or absent. But more than that she was tormented by the thought of Sam focusing his attention on Francesca—'film star'. She had not been in touch with Sam since the truncated 'phone conversation on Holy Island and the unpleasant feeling remained with her. As usual with her, she did not want to be the first one to break the silence. When Jenny was in bed and she could have got down to some work, the temptation to contact Sam was there and she constantly scanned her e-mails to see if there was any word from him. On the Saturday night before she was due to go down to London, she plucked up the courage to ring Sam. Jim was downstairs watching TV when she made the call.

Sam's response was cheerful and welcoming and to Clarissa's enquiry as to whether she was still expected on Monday, his reply was an astonished "Of course," as though her question was incomprehensible to him. Neither made reference to their last communication and Sam launched into how much he was missing her and longing for her visit. Clarissa could not help but reciprocate and, after finally arranging that Sam would pick her up at the station, she bad him a prolonged and passionate goodbye.

She turned round to find Jenny staring at her accusingly. "I thought you loved daddy."

"Of course I do, but you can love other people as well."

"You don't talk to us like that."

Clarissa went over to her daughter and put her arms around her. "When people live together day after day, all the time, they sometimes forget to say nice things to each other. They sort of think their family know without words. But, oh! Jenny darling, I love you very much."

The child drew away. "But you're always leaving us!"

"Just because I *have* to. I need to have meetings with the others about what we're all doing together. That's why I've arranged for a very nice lady to look after you when I'm away. I'm sure you'll like her. Her name is Gillian."

"Will she look after dad too?"

This was a new one on Clarissa. She'd spoken to Gillian Fairclough by 'phone but had not yet met her. Her voice suggested 'sensible' rather than 'sensuous' and it hadn't occurred to her that Jim might like some TLC other than her own, which was given very sparingly these days. The thought was slightly disturbing!

"Daddy is very good at looking after himself and he'll be here to help Gillian to look after you. So you really needn't worry."

"I'll look after daddy. He'll be alright."

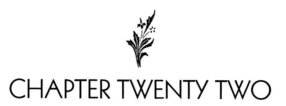

CHAPTER TWENTY TWO

So it was with mixed feeling that Clarissa boarded the train that morning. Jim dropped her off at their local station. She kissed him goodbye with more concerned warmth than had recently been her wont. "Take care of Jenny", she said. "And of yourself, too."

Once on the train, Clarissa forced herself to put all thoughts of Jim, Jenny, Sam and Francesca out of her mind and got down to some concentrated hard work. This proved therapeutic and the journey flew by so that, by the time Sam picked her up at Kings Cross, she felt restored to something like her confident new self. A taxi whisked them to Sam's flat where the table was laid for a late lunch à deux. The flat was just off Kensington High Street in an elegant building in a quiet cul de sac and therefore free from traffic and noise. It wasn't large, though his sitting room was well-proportioned, occupying the whole front of the apartment. One end served as a dining area and the rest as sitting room cum library/study. One of the long walls was home to books from top to bottom and a small upright piano and music centre occupied the wall opposite the dining area. It was the room of an individual comfortable with all aspects of the Arts. There were some excellent prints and original paintings on his walls and a number of interesting objects stood on the surfaces of his good and restrained furniture. Clarissa was impressed by the accuracy with which Sam's surroundings reflected the man she was beginning to know in some depth.

"Very nice Sam. I imagined you in a place like this."

"Kind of you to say so, my darling. It's even nicer having you here to share it with me for a while."

The lunch was light, yet satisfying, served with a good white wine. "This afternoon is for ourselves—relaxation and enjoyment. Tonight we work" and Sam poured her out a second 'Forty E-cup' as he called the capacious glasses in which he served his wine.

In bed, Sam knew instinctively how to please her and bring her to climaxes written about in sex manuals, but hardly ever experienced in reality—not with Jim anyway. In lovemaking they seemed ideally suited and mutual affection and respect made their coupling almost spiritual—or so it seemed to Clarissa. It was as they were relaxing afterwards that Sam asked the question that both thrilled and filled Clarissa with dread.

"When are we going to make this permanent? We both want each other and I don't know if I can bear this situation much longer."

"Please Sam, don't. I can't leave my family stranded just now. Jenny and Tom both have problems and, though neither of them would admit it, they need me. Jim couldn't cope with them on his own. I want you desperately but if you can't accept the situation as it is for the moment, then I shall have to let you go. It's not fair to hang on to you when these circumstances make you unhappy."

Clarissa couldn't believe she was saying this. Only a couple of days ago she was out of her mind with jealousy over what she imagined Sam was getting up to with Francesca. Today his ardent pursuit of her emboldened her to state terms.

"You don't have to desert your *children*, but Jim—I think you underestimate his powers of coping. You will have to make a choice between him and me."

"Sam dearest, 'How do I love thee? Let me count the ways' to quote somebody or other, but I cannot for the life of me understand what *you* see in *me*. I concede that I'm not bad looking but what do I possess that so spell-binds you? I'm lacking in confidence, unsophisticated and pretty much a 'wannabe' as far as writing is concerned."

"I love you for just those traits. You are stunning and I'm fascinated why you haven't the confidence commensurate with such looks. Perhaps I'm kidding myself, but I feel I've encouraged you in a talent which had made you feel better about yourself. I don't want to be your Svengali but I want to help you to take your writing as far as you can. We could make a great team with or even without the others."

"Can't we go on as we are—just for a while longer?"

"How *much* longer? Jenny is only seven. Do we have to wait until she goes to university or whatever?"

"It's usually the other way round—our situation I mean. It's usually you guys who are asking for more time and who are content the way things are, etc, etc not we women who are supposed to be the 'clingers'."

"Now you're generalising, my love. In my opinion every case is different and I want you for all the spoken reasons and many unspoken ones as well. I'm jealous of your life with Jim and your family—however problematic. You're always rushing back to the 'bosom of' and where do I go?"

"To this lovely apartment, freedom and . . . . Francesca?"

"The freedom to be lonely in this lovely apartment. I'll ignore the last remark. Please don't bring her up in that context again."

They remained silent for a long while, both sunk in their own troubled thoughts.

Eventually Sam leaned over Clarissa, kissed her and said "I'll wait."

CHAPTER TWENTY THREE

Leo's flat/studio was, on the surface, the complete opposite of Sam's. The paraphernalia of living was cheek by jowl with that of work or rather mixed up with it in a higgledy-piggledy tangle. Wires criss-crossed each other over the furniture and dangled from the ceiling in an alarming way. Speakers and cameras were everywhere and video monitors vied with each other for dominance. Coffee mugs in various stages of 'drunkedness' littered the already overloaded surfaces. One wall only had any semblance of order simply because a huge screen covered practically all of it. But it was clear as the evening progressed that Leo knew where everything was and how it worked.

Leo was sitting at a computer screen viewing images of some sort when they entered in response to his yelled "Come. Look at this," he said, without turning round.

Sam and Clarissa obeyed his summons. A swirl of flickering flames and human forms gave way to the clarity of a sunny afternoon, blue sky, autumnal trees and the figures of a woman and child dancing and skipping in a meadow. A plaintive folksong accompanied the images and a mumbo jumbo of text scrolled down the screen.

"What do you think of that, eh?"

"It looks most effective if it is what I think it is," said Clarissa quietly.

Leo jumped up and made a vain effort to tidy his unkempt hair. "I'm so sorry, Clarissa. Sam did say you were coming but I forgot just when. Do excuse the mess. I'd have tidied up a bit if . . ."

"Don't apologise please. Remember I've got three kids so mess isn't an unusual spectacle to me. How are you Leo?" And she kissed him on both cheeks.

"All the better for seeing you, my dear. Can I get you a coffee or something?"

Clarissa thought it would be kinder to say 'no'. She wondered if there were any unused pots in the place and no doubt a great deal of rinsing under taps would be necessary. They agreed to have one later after they'd done a bit of work.

Clarissa turned her attention to the computer screen again. She scrutinised the female forms. She could see that despite the very different contexts and costumes the 'actress' was the same. Especially as Eustacia, Francesca looked beautiful. Again the stab of jealousy.

"Who is the child?"

"Francesca's daughter."

"Quite a family affair."

"Well," said Leo, "we were anxious to see what the final result might look like with people so we asked Francesca and little Susannah to stand in. We didn't think you'd mind."

"Of course," said Clarissa without conviction. Will we have any say in the matter of actors if and when it comes to the real thing?"

"Possibly, if we can suggest anybody with a bit of box office draw who's cheap! Rather difficult!"

"Has Sam mentioned our friend Christian for graphics?"

"Sorry, Clarrie." Sam jumped in. "I did promise, but I've had so much on my mind."

Clarissa looked daggers. Leo sensed the tension between the other two.

"Is there something I don't know?"

Sam hastened to explain the Christian thing. At first Leo looked doubtful, but after all the arguments for it had been aired he decide he thought it might be possible. "I'll have to see his work first, though."

Clarissa produced some examples immediately—the samples she'd taken away from Mrs McKenzie's house.

"These are good. Unpolished but promising. Can I get to see this character?"

"As soon as we can get a visitor pass. I'll see what I can fix up."

They spent a couple of hours discussing the technicalities of the next stage of the film, based on Clarissa's work. The opening shots established the essence of the two women. Now the salient points of their contrasting narratives had to be set up in a more or less chronological way which presented a few difficulties, but both Sam and Leo—experienced in what would appeal to some arty director not to mention the viewers—were anxious to point up a modern application. Clarissa—who had found the methods she'd adopted early on in her teaching career combined with a good sense of humour had served her well right up to the end—had not gone in much for modern applications of texts. She tended to regard such glosses as often strained and contrived unless in the hands of someone with vision, which she was sure she was not.

They discussed 'applications' and 'resonances' without agreeing firmly on anything, until a coffee break and the great wash-up beckoned. Leo disappeared into another room, presumably the kitchen, and was away for quite twenty minutes without any sounds of gushing taps and clanking of crockery. When he returned he bore a tray on which exquisite china coffee cups and saucers were set out, together with scrumptious-looking homemade shortbread biscuits. As if from nowhere, three solid oak occasional tables appeared and were set down in front of them. Allowing for the jumble around them, gracious living was the order of the day!

"Didn't expect this, did you?" grinned Leo.

"Bit tame for you though, isn't it? Coffee and cakes, even if they were made by your own fair hand."

"Oh don't you worry, my lad. I know how to entertain a lady. And anyway the night is young."

It seemed that, in addition to all his other talents, Leo was a bit of a genius in the kitchen and a wine connoisseur. When Clarissa helped to clear away afterwards she saw that if his studio was all chaos, his small kitchen was all order and to judge by the lingering smells, cooking of some distinction went on there.

"You're going to be a catch for someone," began Clarissa and then, realising she might have made a faux pas, she continued, "Sorry I'm assuming, aren't I? Perhaps you *are* a good catch for someone already."

"I'm working on it," joked Leo, "but I'm saying no more at a present! Anyway, I'm a good catch for myself. I look after you alright, don't I mate?" And he slapped himself on the shoulder.

"When do we get a glass of one of your magnificent wines?"

"Don't be in such a hurry, Sam. Let's do a chunk more work on Clarissa's excellent script and, if you're a good lad, you'll get a glass of the warm South or something. If not, I'm sure Clarrie and I can demolish a bottle or two between us."

Even without wine the two men engaged in a bout of mock fighting and clowning around. It was clear they were very fond of each other and for a second Clarissa felt she was an intruder into a close and longstanding relationship. She didn't indulge in self pity but she was becoming familiar with the feeling of being an outsider—at home and now here. She was glad when they started to work again.

By the end of the evening she was getting au fait with terms she'd hardly ever heard of before—slug lines, rushes, camera movements, dissolves and cuts. It seemed she had to be yet more economical with her dialogue, leaving the actors to 'flesh it out' with vocal intonation and body language. Sam had 'tweaked' the sections she'd sent him so far, without telling her, which upset her a bit though she conceded that this showed his protectiveness of her. "It takes some time to get used to script writing, especially if you love using words as you obviously do," observed Leo.

"And remember," added Sam. "you need a good narrative to work on. All the best films come from good novels—not strictly true, but you know what I mean. What you've done with the bits and pieces we gave you at the beginning is marvellous."

"Now for that wine." Leo disappeared once more into his kitchen and returned with a bottle and some glasses.

Clarissa and Sam snuggled up together on Leo's sofa (after the removal of several yards of cable) and Leo sat at their feet. In the course of demolishing two bottles of wine and an assortment of nibbles it was revealed that Leo was head over heels in love with Felicity and had visited her several times in Dorchester. She was, apparently, fascinated by Leo but kept him at arm's length. "Can't believe I'm serious. Worried by the Age Gap and all that. I'll persuade her though!"

Clarissa, mellowed and relaxed by the wine, waxed eloquent on how privileged she felt to be connected to Thomas Hardy by however tenuous a link. Leo, her colleague and, now, she believed friend, in love with the daughter of a woman who had lived in the same house as the great man! Leo bent over and deposited a big sloppy kiss on Clarissa's mouth. "You're gorgeous, Clarrie. You're a lucky sod, Sam."

"I hope to be, but she's not mine yet. I can't prise her away from that husband of hers."

"Sh. Let's not spoil a happy evening by indulging in reality."

"This is reality. You, me, Leo, Eustacia, Emma. Surely you must see that, Clarrie!"

As often happens with drinking parties, the mood suddenly changed from the lighthearted to something darker. The emotions, given free rein, spill out and cause the owner of them some embarrassment when sobriety returns. And to stop this Leo intervened by offering coffee and a bed for the night, since the other two were in no fit state to drive home to Sam's. The interval of preparing for bed calmed everyone down and Sam recovered from his outburst. Everyone, tired out with work and wine, slept well.

CHAPTER TWENTY FOUR

The next morning Clarissa suggested she ring the Young Offenders' Institution at Bristol and find out if by any chance they might get in to see Christian that day. After some bureaucracy, as a great concession because they were classed as 'educationists', they were given the go-ahead to visit Christian.

They met him, after being frisked and relieved of their possessions which were locked away, in a large common room with low tables and chairs liberally scattered about. At weekends these would be filled with visitors but today there were only themselves and another group of people at the other end of the room. A couple of warders patrolled the perimeter or perched on the tea counter with bored expressions. Clarissa made the introductions and asked Christian if he'd mind showing his work to Leo.

"Yeah, sure I've got 'em 'ere," and he handed an art folder to Leo. Leo had an easy manner with the lad and was encouraging in his remarks.

"Where did you learn to do stuff like this, Christian?"

"Just at school. Art was the only subject I liked. The teacher was a good bloke."

"Do you do any art work in here?"

"Yeah, lots. There's a woman that comes in. I've told her about your film an' that and she says she'll help me with whatever you want me to do."

"You do realise that nothing's definite yet?"

Christian looked a bit crestfallen and Clarissa jumped in with "Now be fair Christian, I did say nothing was settled."

"What's your English like, Chris—it's alright if I call you that?"

"Fine. My English? Well I was pretty bad at school but I'm doin' a class now and takin' an exam next year some time. Why?"

"Do you do any reading?"

"A bit. 'Ave to for this exam."

"Well look, sunshine, read this." Leo produced a copy of 'Return'. "And this." He handed over Clarissa's scripts of the 'Emma' and 'Will' stories. I'll give you three weeks. Any questions and you ring me on this number. Here's my address. Make notes on what you think of Eustacia and Emma."

"Bloody 'ell, that's a lot."

"Do it and then we'll get down to the art."

A bell rang, signalling that they must leave. They said goodbye to Christian, collected their belongings and left.

"That was a bit much," said Clarissa when they were back in the car. "I doubt if he's read anything more demanding than a comic."

"It'll test him. I won't hold him to it but I thought I'd see how serious he was. Oh hell! We should have had a word with the powers that be. Shall we go back?"

Sam wasn't keen. He wanted more time with Clarissa and she suspected as much, so she offered to make contact with the prison officials concerned as soon as they got back to London. Leo was muttering about being so close to Felicity that it would be a shame to pass up the opportunity to see her but as they were in Sam's car he was over-ruled and in a couple of hours they were back in London. They dropped Leo off and returned to Sam's, where they were soon in bed.

"Who does have the final say in who does the graphics?"

"We're a democratic outfit so we need to have a group meeting but actually Leo holds a lot of sway. The rest will do as he says and I'm pretty certain he's sold on your Christian."

"When will there be a meeting?"

"We'll try to arrange one before you go back. Now enough of work, my darling." He folded her to him and caressed and kissed her until all thoughts of Christian, graphics and the rest were put completely out of her head.

* *

They woke late. After the last two days of work and dashing to Bristol and back, they were feeling somewhat battered so the extra sleep was welcome. It was actually Leo who woke them by 'phoning to tell them that he'd been very impressed by Christian and, if everybody agreed, he'd like to take him on. Sam said he'd contact everyone and arrange a meeting for as soon as possible, which turned out to be that afternoon. Clarissa put in a token presence to support Christian's corner and then left for a shopping spree in Oxford Street, arranging to meet Sam for a meal in the evening. She wandered in and out of fashion shops and bought herself a couple of summer outfits. She trawled the bookshops, where she bought books for herself and one for Jim—a book of aerial views of London with an accompanying CD-rom to 'get mapping' on his computer. She bought a novelty tote bag for Jenny to carry her 'gear' to school and some expensive aftershave for Sam. She would have liked something more out of the ordinary than this, but that would take more thinking about than she'd time for on this expedition. She feared the comments which he predictably offered when they sat down in a pub for a drink before their meal.

"So you think I need this to disguise the smell?" and "Is this to turn you on?" etc, etc, but it was clear that he was pleased. They hadn't as yet bought each other gifts, their time being taken up with other things.

"Tomorrow we buy you something special."

"Well it doesn't have to be a tit for tat arrangement, you know. I just wanted to say 'thankyou' for changing my life."

"There are *more* changes I want to make but I know you're not ready for those yet, so enough of that. You've made a pretty monumental change in my life too, darling." He kissed her.

"I'm starving." Clarissa said then they broke away.

"Ok, let's go and eat. I know just the place. Here, let me take your parcels."

He flagged down a taxi which set them down not too far away from Sam's, outside a discreet looking restaurant with a little striped awning over the front. Sam seemed to be known there and Clarissa couldn't help thinking that, for someone 'working for a song', he had a pretty good life style.

As the evening wore on there were one or two faces which seemed familiar to her (as seen on TV, she gleaned from her partner) belonging to people with whom Sam had at least a nodding acquaintance.

"Now I'm living." She thought. "How on earth am I going to settle down in dreary old Normington, after this?" She hoped he wouldn't raise the question of her leaving Jim again that night or she feared she would commit herself to a drastic course of action.

Fortunately or unfortunately, depending on one's point of view, one of the 'nodding acquaintances' came over to their table, slightly the worse for drink.

"Don't I know you?" He addressed himself to Sam by putting his hand on his shoulder, but looking or rather leering at Clarissa.

"I'm sure not." Sam brushed him off.

"What about you, gorgeous? I'm sure I've had the pleasure," he sniggered.

Clarissa didn't reply, but produced the basilisk's stare she reserved for precocious teenagers in the classroom.

"If you'll excuse us, my colleague and I are trying to conduct a business discussion."

The man gave a dirty laugh but backed off and tottered back to his table where he was ignored by his companions, none of whom seemed to notice his presence or absence.

"I *do* know him as it happens. He's a minor producer with TV. The sort we have to submit our work to. He looked at something of ours and met us but he won't remember. He was drunk then too!"

"What if you have to meet him again and he remembers your snub?"

"He's on his way out. Don't worry, he's not a threat."

Having finished their meal they both decided they would rather get out. It was still fairly early in the evening and Sam suggested a late film. A foreign film was showing at the small Arts cinema ten minutes walk away. As it happened it wasn't so far removed from the sort of project they were involved with themselves and it afforded them plenty of discussion material for the rest of the night. Thankfully the difficult topic was avoided again.

CHAPTER TWENTY FIVE

The next day Sam was to meet with the group's agent and the business was likely to last until late afternoon. He was worried about leaving Clarissa all day, on her own, but she assured him she would be fine. She would get down to more work on the script and catch up with her correspondence. She had no intention of snooping but she welcomed the opportunity to get the 'feel' of Sam's flat in more detail. After he'd gone she sat down at his desk and looked around and imagined him working here. When he raised his head from his work he would look straight at a water colour of a pastoral scene, in the right foreground of which just appeared the porticoed frontage of an imposing Georgian mansion. Clarissa got up to take a closer look and saw that not only was it signed by the artist but dedicated to Sam. Whether this was 'her' Sam or an older relative was impossible to decide. The house suggested a family of some wealth and could explain Sam's relatively 'well-heeled' lifestyle.

She crossed to the living end of the room and picked up a photograph of a family group on the steps of what was probably the house in the painting, and could recognise Sam as a youth of about eighteen surrounded by three girls and a boy, of assorted ages. If they were his siblings he appeared to be the oldest. There was a middle aged woman, quite possibly his mother, but no one who could be his father. There was, however, a face she did recognise, that of Francesca! That woman again! Though she was devastated she was determined not to let the discovery disturb her fragile equilibrium. She turned the photograph to the wall and herself to the bottle! Between swigs of a rather nice wine whose quality was lost on her but whose initial stimulating faculties enabled her to get on with some script editing, she made quite good progress. It was not until her mobile rang that the wine's effects kicked in. She swayed across the room to where the 'phone was hidden away in her bag, and fumbled to get it out and answer it. "He-ll-o." She expected the caller to be Sam and breathed sexily down the instrument.

"Clarissa? You sound peculiar! It's Jim here."

By this time the wine was seriously taking its toll.

"Ah, darling Jim! How are you? Don't I know you? Ah yes, my husband! Checking up on me, darling?"

"You're drunk Clarrie. A bit early for that sort of thing, isn't it?"

"Oh Jim, love, I'm not drunk. Only a bit merry."

"Are you getting much work done? I rather doubt it! Is Sam with you?"

"No darling. Naughty Sam's gone to a meeting with his girlfriend and I'm making myself at home here. Isn't that nice and cosy?"

"Where's 'here'?"

Clarissa had not told Jim that she was staying at Sam's flat and he'd assumed that she was staying in a hotel. The only number he had was Sam's as Clarissa had no hotel number to leave him! Discretion had gone completely to the winds by his time and Clarissa admitted she was at Sam's. Jim made no comment and merely said "I did have something to discuss with you but it's pointless with you in this state. If I were you, I'd go to bed and sleep it off. I'll ring again later." He was gone.

Clarissa stumbled back to the desk and finished the rest of a second bottle of wine, knocking one bottle and a sheaf of papers to the floor as she did so. She attempted to carry on with the script until she was seeing double on the screen and her hand written notes became illegible. Before she blacked out she managed to stagger to a settee and fell on to it in an ungainly sprawling attitude and knew no more.

****

Which was how Sam found her on his return in the evening. At first he thought she had been taken ill until he investigated further. The dishevelled state of his desk, together with the empty wine bottles told him the astonishing truth that Clarissa was in a drunken stupor. He roused her with difficulty, then, being convinced that she'd taken nothing more dangerous than alcohol and, being unable to get any sense out of her, he carried her to the bedroom and put her into bed where she promptly fell asleep again.

He was mystified as to why she was in such a condition. She was a moderate drinker, occasionally had a bit too much as they all had the other night at Leo's, so what on earth had induced her to get into such a state on her own. Then he spotted the photo facing the wall. On turning it round he gathered the cause of Clarissa's drinking spree. He had in fact seen Francesca at the meeting. They'd had lunch together as they often did on such occasions, but he realised he must not let that fact slip. He had known Francesca since childhood and there was a time when their two families had hoped that they would make an item, as had Sam himself. They had been romantically related in their late teens, but had drifted apart when they'd gone to different universities.

It was when Sam and the others set up the group and needed secretarial and administrative skills that he thought of Francesca. At that time he still carried a torch for her and would gladly have resumed the romance, but again things didn't work out between them and she married her Anthony and he met and married his wife. He cared for her deeply but as a very close friend, not a lover. How was he to convince Clarissa of that fact? Here was renewed evidence of Clarissa's lack of confidence, that she could become so jealous as to end up in her present state. He thought he'd bolstered her self confidence, but apparently not.

As he'd promised, Jim rang later that evening. Sam answered Clarissa's phone.

"So she's staying with you—in your flat I mean?"

"Yes, for convenience and cheapness. Didn't she tell you?"

"No. It must have slipped her mind. How is she? I rang this morning and she sounded very drunk?"

"I'm afraid she is, yes. I've been out all day and when I came back she was sound asleep on my settee. She still is. "He didn't think 'in my bed' would go down too well."

"It doesn't sound like Clarissa to drink herself silly, especially on her own."

"She's getting a bit stressed out about the film. We've been given a deadline and we're all feeling stretched. I expect that's all it is."

"Ask her to ring me when she's in a fit state, will you?"

"Sure. Is everything OK with you?"

"Hectic, but I suppose we all are. Better go. Things to do."

Sam went into the bedroom and got in beside Clarissa who, though still asleep, responded to him putting his arm around her. Gradually she came to with a splitting headache and the room spinning round. For the first half hour or so she gabbled on about how sorry she was; how could anybody think she was any good at anything and how she didn't deserve anyone's love and similar self-denigrating remarks. Sam held her and gently laughed at her until he made her laugh at herself, though it was difficult as she felt very sick and indeed made on or two sorties to the loo to get rid of not very much since she had eaten very little all day. Eventually she was able to take a cup of tea and sat beside Sam on the settee with her head resting on his shoulder.

"This is all to do with Francesca, isn't it?"

"She bugs me Sam. And now I've found out you've known her for years."

"I'll tell you the story of Francesca once and for all and then we'll lay it to rest," and Sam told her of his two attempts at relationships with her and of their failure. "We're firm friends and love each other as brother and sister, but that's all. She's happily married and I've got you."

"And if she suddenly weren't married, what then?"

"I don't believe in 'third time lucky'."

Clarissa couldn't say with hand on heart that she was convinced, but she knew it wasn't wise to pursue the matter any further even were she recovered enough to do so.

"Jim rang this evening. Apparently he rang this morning when you were well on the way to being blotto. He wants you to ring when you're sober. Leave it until the morning."

"I think I will. I couldn't cope with family stuff at present."

"We're going down to Dorset in the morning. Something to cheer you up I hope. It's a secret."

CHAPTER TWENTY SIX

Clarissa felt a great deal better than she deserved to do when they woke the next morning, early. Before seven they were on their way and within two hours were driving along the twisting roads into and beyond Dorchester and into the Piddle valley. About ten miles beyond Dorchester they turned off onto a steep and tortuous minor road which wound its way between steep sided hills and woodland where cows were lazily meandering and chewing the grass. Clarissa was dying of curiosity to know where their destination was to be. The end of the world it seemed, for they went deeper and deeper into isolation. At last Sam pulled up outside a pub in a small village.

"You should recognise this," he said, "if you're a Hardy enthusiast. I'll just park the car here and drop in and let them know we've arrived and then we're going for a walk."

Sam bounded in and out of the tiny pub, took her by the hand and led her up a winding lane away from the front of the pub. About one hundred yards on the left hand side a white cottage thrust its gable end, topped by a chimney, out into the road, completely cutting off any view round it.

"Does this ring any bells?"

"It sort of does, but I can't really say what."

"Study it a bit longer. Who rested her back against such a place to get warm?"

"Of course, Tess! Is this Flintcombe Ash then? It doesn't look like a 'starveacre' place, as Hardy puts it."

"That is where we've just been. Imagine those steep fields in the middle of winter."

"Yes or in 'horizontal' rain. This is fascinating. What a lovely surprise!"

"That's not all." He pulled her round the angle of the cottage, further up the lane which was rising steeply. He stopped outside a church gate on which was fixed a hand bill advertising a recital by a well known eminent pianist and his son, that very evening.

"Oh God, I've been a fan of his for years. You don't mean we're going to that?"

"We most certainly are. And here is the concert hall." Sam opened the gate and they went into a very well kept churchyard surrounding a large Victorian church.

"That's his house over there." Sunk a little into a hollow was a large but unpretentious 'manor house'.

There were stables, and horses grazing in the fields around. "His wife is in charge of all those. He bought that church when it became redundant and he and his wife run a music festival here every summer."

"There's some money here, then. So this is where he hides himself away when he's not performing."

"Yes. He's just one of the villagers, according to the locals. No side. He lets the village kids use his swimming pool and tennis court."

"Do you know him?"

"A bit. I know his son better. We've worked together. That's how I got the tickets. The concert's a sellout, largely because Heinrich's playing. Anybody who's anybody in the musical world will be there tonight."

"Why on earth didn't you tell me? I've brought nothing remotely suitable to wear."

"We'll go and buy something, then. This will be my treat to you. No, I insist. But I could kill for a coffee. Let's go back to the pub and see what they can rustle up for us."

On their way back to Dorchester they turned off to revisit Hardy's birthplace whose garden was ablaze with colour at this time of they year. Once again they found they were running out of time but they promised themselves a ceremonial visit on a future special occasion.

They had lunch at L'eau à bouche and once again were warmly welcomed by Françine and Emile. They went easy on the alcohol this time as they had the difficult task of 'getting something suitable' ahead of them.

That 'something suitable' took Sam's breath away when Clarissa put it on for the concert that evening. She'd chosen a simple cream sheath with the skimpiest of shoulder straps which showed her figure off to perfection. Her dark hair glistened and her skin glowed with health (though how she managed it after her drinking bout of the day before was nothing short of miraculous). Sam, who'd been to these do's before, took the precaution of presenting her with a fine wool stole of a forget-me-not blue to put round her shoulder as they took their places for pre-concert drinks on the grassed area before the entrance porch.

This was quite the most 'upmarket' gathering Clarissa had ever attended. The well-bred faces, the cut-glass accents, the expensive clothes were set fair to overwhelm her when Guy their music man breezed up.

He greeted Clarissa with a "You look divine, darling" plum-in-mouth accent and proceeded to slap Sam on the back with a "Hi up, me old mate." Clarissa cringed. "Why was Guy behaving in this clownish way, so uncharacteristic of him? The two men laughed, rather raucously Clarissa thought, and then moved over to a group of particularly upper-crust looking individuals who to her amazement greeted them with open arms. For a moment or two Clarissa was left on her own and was beginning to panic—what on earth was she doing in company such as this—when Sam took her arm and brought her into the circle where it was clear her stunning appearance made an immediate impression. She limited herself to one glass of wine only as she didn't want to repeat the events of the day before, but it was enough to dispel her timidity and make her realise that these people were only human after all—some of them quite ridiculous with their braying laughter and over-projected voices. They filed into the church and Clarissa, Sam and Guy took their seats somewhere near the middle where visibility and sound were excellent.

Heinrich Heller almost shuffled on to the platform in an evening suit which had clearly seen better days, ill fitting and dingy. His bow was perfunctory, not out of hauteur but more out of a sense that the audience's applause for him was unnecessary and that the music to come was of far more significance. His son, Adam, was casually dressed in black and was somewhat more flamboyant than his father. As soon as Heinrich touched the keys in the piano introduction to the first sonata of the evening, his unique quality was apparent. Father and son played as one, their parts intermingling and complementing each other in a truly musicianly way. There was no attempt on either part 'to steal the show' but they interpreted the composer's intentions as scholarship and commitment guided them. The result was thrilling and brought rapturous applause but, just as at the beginning, Mr Heller modestly acknowledged the applause and walked clumsily from the platform patting his son on the shoulder as he did so.

A few minutes into the interval, outside the church Clarissa spied Heinrich galumphing back to the house, head down, hands folded behind his back, his page turner (whom Clarissa recognised as an eminent conductor who didn't think it beneath him to perform this lowly task for the world famous pianist) beside him. Adam followed, surrounded by a group of young people, earnestly congratulating him on his performance.

"I'm not paying another bloody five quid for a glass of wine." Guy again. "I've got some in the car. Follow me."

Clarissa would rather have mingled with the crowd in front of the porch, queuing for refreshment. She had spotted a number of celebrities from the worlds of music, theatre and other fields, but she was unceremoniously dragged off by the two men to where Guy's car was parked in a small cul de sac in front of a disused stable. Just as they were waving around their garish plastic breakers, which were all Guy supplied by way of wineglasses, a very elegant well-preserved blonde walked past, stopped and spoke to them in a tone which implied she thought they were interlopers. "Can I help you?"

"Don't think so luv." Guy once more in his brash-northern-lad mode. "Unless yer going 'to give uz ur money back for this trash!"

Clarissa froze and looked at Guy in utter disbelief. To her amazement the elegant blonde's face lit up with a radiant smile. She rushed up to Guy and Sam and hugged and kissed them soundly—on both cheeks 'luvvie' style.

"Guy, Sam, how wonderful to see you both! But why are you lurking around down here?"

"Can't afford your Dorset wine prices, Bella my love. Oh you know me darling. Can't stand all that down-from-London claptrap. 'Oh Gawd, 'fraid the country odours are kicking in, don't yer know' type stuff."

"Well you must join us afterwards at the house. Promise!"

"Before you rush off, Bella, let me introduce you to a new colleague of ours. Clarissa Coniscliffe, meet Isabella Heller or Bella to her friends."

"Oh don't try to hide your smile, Clarissa. Bella Heller—a bit of a joke name. That's why I stick to my professional name mostly, except when I'm doing the wifely thing. Bella Lambton. I'll look forward to catching up with you later. Must dash."

The second half of the programme was even more exhilarating than the first and ended with a great flourish of scales and repeated chords from both instruments and thunderous applause from an adoring audience. As they emerged into a rather cool Summer evening Clarissa threw the blue wrap around her shoulders and was escorted by Sam and Guy both taking an arm down the pathway, lit up with flares set into the soil and grass, to the house, brilliant with light and welcoming. They caught up with Adam who was delighted to see Sam again.

Through a softly-lit flagged hall they entered the drawing room of fairly grand proportions, comfortably and not pretentiously furnished. Food and wine were ready waiting around the room. They joined the group around Heinrich who had thrown off his jacket, collar and bow tie and was urging people to partake of the eats rather than gather round the 'maestro', dishing out gushing compliments. A large, black Labrador mingled with the guests and was a favourite with everyone. Adam joined them in jeans and a casual top.

"It's wonderful to see you Sam. What are you up to these days?" After Sam had introduced Clarissa to Adam and their circle generally, Sam gave an account of the project and Clarissa's part in it.

"When's your deadline?"

"End of July, so we're working flat out."

"I'm looking for a researcher/writer." Adam looked directly at Clarissa.

"You're not having her," said Guy. "She's booked—in more ways than one." The innuendo was not lost on the others.

"She may have time after July, though," observed Adam.

"No. She's got masses on. Really," jumped in Sam

"Does she take sugar?"

"Pardon?"

"Does she take sugar? You know that radio programme for the handicapped, where it's implied that the public perceive anyone disabled to be an idiot who can't speak for himself. Well you're doing that to me. Might I be allowed to speak for myself?"

"Well what do you say?" said Adam.

"I'd have to know exactly what the job entails and then I'd be able to give you a considered answer."

Sam looked grim. Guy grinned at Sam's discomfiture. Everyone else had their eyes glued on Clarissa.

"I'll certainly be in touch." Adam squeezed her hand. "And now what about some light entertainment while we wine and dine?" He pointed to several in the room and then to the grand piano at the window end of the room. Almost immediately a jazz ensemble was performing. Three other

Hellers were on bass, cello, clarinet and a friend on saxophone. Adam went off to get some refreshment but was soon taking his brother's place on bass. Heinrich occupied a comfortably-worn leather armchair and stretched out with his eyes closed whilst his wife stood behind his chair and massaged his shoulders and neck. Soon a few couples took to the floor and moved to the music.

Sam took Clarissa in his arms and they slowly did one or two turns around the room, but he was constantly being interrupted by greetings from people he knew. He was clearly a well-known and popular character amongst a fair number of the guests who showed a great interest in his charming companion. Bella, having seen that Heinrich was comfortable and relaxed, made a beeline for her and questioned her in some depth as to her role in the group, how long she'd known Sam, clearly fishing for information on the exact nature of their relationship about which Clarissa remained very cagey.

Bella was evidently fond of Sam whom she'd got to know quite well through his collaboration with her son. At that time Sam had been in a relationship with Esmé and Bella discreetly asked about her. Clarissa made some noncommittal reply and changed the subject to Heinrich and his forthcoming plans. Bella took the hint and gave an outline of Heinrich's concert engagements stretching well into the future, but it was clear that she would be drawing information out of Sam when the opportunity arose. She then introduced Clarissa to the page turner whom Clarissa had rightly recognised as the one-time conductor of a well known orchestra, Richard Joopsen. He was a thoroughly nice man and drew her out in a very considerate manner. She'd seen Richard at a dress rehearsal at Covent Garden when she and Jim lived in London. It had been a prestigious production and Richard remembered it well as having been fraught with problems right up to the opening curtain. Clarissa knew the bass lead (from whom the invitation had come) very well.

Richard knew Guy, their music man, from their time together at music college and they chattered on easily about various aspects of Opera and other miscellaneous topics. As she chatted to the celebrities gathered there she was conscious in the back of her mind of the difference between her present stimulating lifestyle, thanks to Sam, and the one back in Normington—dull, predictable and ordinary. These extraordinary people made her feel special too. She was proud of being Sam's 'partner' and whilst she basked in his reflected glory she felt more sure than ever that she could hold her own as an interesting, attractive and talented woman.

The 'ad hoc' music ensemble were now strumming out some folk songs and she quietly sang along to the ones she knew. Before long Adam beckoned to her to join them round the piano and Guy made sure she did so by putting his arm around her and gently but firmly propelling her towards the performers. Everyone fell silent as she sang effortlessly a simple and haunting north country ballad, accompanied by the clarinet. This was an aspect of herself she had said nothing about to Sam or anyone in the group and as she held the last note steadily and sweetly she was aware of Sam gazing at her fixedly. There was a pause before an outburst of enthusiastic applause. She had created a mood no-one wished to dissipate.

"Is there no end to this girl's talents?" Guy held her at arm's length and looked her up and down—and then let go of one hand and presented her to her audience who cheered and clapped with renewed enthusiasm.

"That was delightful my dear." Heinrich had come up to the piano. "What lieder do you know?" and he played the Schubert 'Heiden Roslein'. This charming lied was just about singable by someone as out of practice as she currently was and she was satisfied that she had done it justice even without the calls for 'encore'.

"You have a very beautiful voice, but I know singers like other musicians need to warm up first and be in practice. You, I think, are not in practice at present. You should be. Come up to the house in the morning and we will have a session together—that is if you are able to?"

Clarissa was speechless. This couldn't be happening to her. Her idol, *Heinrich* Heller, asking if *she*, Clarissa Coniscliffe, were able to have a music session with him. She looked at Sam who nodded and she in turn nodded to Heinrich. "That's settled then. Would eleven suit you? You should have got rid of the 'frogs' by then."

"That's very kind of you, Mr. Heller. Thank you so much."

"See you in the morning."

As they walked back to the pub Sam was very quiet.

"Are you alright, Sam?"

"Why shouldn't I be?"

"It's not like you to be so quiet."

"Bit tired, that's all. *You* enjoyed yourself."

"I've had a wonderful evening. I can't thank you enough. What a marvellous surprise!"

"Speaking of surprises, you've kept that lovely voice well hidden."

"Good Lord, I'm totally out of practice. But I used to do a lot of singing before Jenny came along. I trained at the Guildhall as a part-time student just after Jim and I were married and I've had singing lessons on and off since then. But life became too hectic when I went back to teaching so I gave up."

"Well, old Heinrich was certainly impressed. He's a very busy man. He doesn't give up his time for just any one. Looks like we'll have rivals for your services after July!"

"Don't be silly. I don't anticipate a career in singing. Heinrich is just being kind. It'll be a one-off thing."

"I think he's come under your spell like everyone else. Adam is taken with you too." The rueful tone in Sam's voice caused Clarissa to squeeze his hand.

"You're not jealous are you, Sam?"

"You don't have a monopoly on that emotion, my love!"

"Oh alright. Point taken." She avoided the implied query in the remark about Adam by reiterating her delight in the evening they'd just spent with such stimulating people.

"They're quite a pain, some of them. OK in small doses."

"Something's put your nose out of joint. What's on your mind?"

"I'm not going to dampen your evening by telling you now. I will tomorrow." Clarissa had to be satisfied with that.

They made love that night, but it wasn't the consummation either of them had looked forward to earlier in the day. Both slept fitfully and woke anything but refreshed the next morning.

CHAPTER TWENTY SEVEN

It was with shame that Clarissa realised that she had not rung Jim or given him any idea of her whereabouts so that he could contact her. Her mobile wasn't functioning so she used the pub's pay phone to ring home. To her amazement her mother-in-law answered.

"Oh it's you, Clarissa," Mrs Coniscliffe said coldly.

"I could say the same to you, Moll. What's the matter? Why are you at our house? I don't mean to be rude or anything, but I wasn't expecting to get you when I rang."

"Everything's the matter. That Gillian girl's gone."

"Why?"

"I told her to."

"*You* told her to!"

"I told her to. If you don't give a fig for your daughter, I do. She's gone and that's that."

"That most certainly isn't that. How dare you throw your weight about in my house!"

"I'm not going to argue on the 'phone, but I suggest you get back here as quick as you can. And by the way, it's Jim's house too." And with that the 'phone was put down.

"What was that all about?"

"Yet another drama at home." Clarissa looked shattered. "Mother-in-law has dismissed the nanny and God knows what else besides. Bang goes my hobnobbing with the lovely people. I shall have to go home today."

"You could have your session with Heinrich and still get back today particularly if I drove you home."

"I don't feel up to an intensive singing lesson now. I'd be rubbish."

"I think you should. It could be therapeutic for you. Then we'll collect our things and go straight from here."

"But you've got masses of things to do. I couldn't let you waste time sorting me out."

"I won't be wasting time, not in my opinion, as you well know. Do what you have to do in preparation for your lesson and I'll walk up to the house with you and spend some time with Adam, if he's available. Go on!"

By the time she was ushered into Heinrich's music studio, Clarissa was feeling reasonably calm. The short walk to the house, on a beautiful early summer morning, through burgeoning trees and shrubs with the birds singing away (without any tuition!) had raised her spirits somewhat.

"I think we may all be feeling the worse for wear after last night's jollification, so take a few sips of water and we'll go through some relaxation exercises and see how we both get on."

There was no sense of the great maestro handing down advice from on high. He assumed they were equals and she could teach him as much as he could her. He questioned her about the techniques she used and together they discussed how such-and-such an effect could be achieved. After some graded vocal exercises he produced the lieder book of the previous evening and they worked for a while on 'Heiden Roslein' as a way into some more advanced singing. Halfway through the session he went to the door and summoned his clarinettist son and the three of them together worked on Schubert's 'Shepherd on the rock', which explored all facets of the vocal gamut from sheer 'bel canto' to 'colaratura'. The piece was taxing for the instrumentalists too and there was much camaraderie, laughing and joking as they fluffed bits here and there, got frustrated by their occasional ineptnesses and set to with renewed determination to sort out the difficult passages.

"When did you last sing that?" enquired Heinrich.

"Oh years ago. I sang it at a music society do and I'm afraid I fluffed that top B, just as I have this morning."

"Do you enjoy singing?"

"I love it, but I just haven't the time to do any serious work."

"We have a small group of excellent singers who perform each year at our festival. Your voice would fit in very well with them. I would be more than willing to recommend you, if you'd like me to."

"I'm flattered Heinrich, but I live in the North of England."

"We rehearse for three weeks only before the festival. You could make that perhaps?"

"May I ask for time to think about all that's entailed? I would love to, but I do have a family to consider."

"Have you? I wondered about that."

Heinrich didn't elaborate, but Clarissa detected a tone in his voice which disturbed her. "He's wondering about my relationship with Sam," she thought to herself, as she recalled how it must have seemed to him the evening before as the two of them danced intimately together.

"Think hard before you break up the family. Believe me, I know what I'm talking about. Now, I would like to offer you more sessions but I'm afraid my future commitments are taking me out of the country for some months. However, I suggest you keep up the practice along the lines we've discussed and on my return you might have come to some decision with regard to our festival. You can contact me here."

Heinrich took Clarissa's hand and kissed her on both cheeks. "It's been a real delight, my dear. Thank you."

Clarissa was overcome with confusion and stuttered out her profound thanks.

"You were right Sam, that's done me the world of good. What a great guy he is. Not an ounce of 'side'. He made me feel as though I was the expert. He suspects, however, that something's going on between you and me and I'm not sure he approves."

"Well, it's not for him to approve or disapprove."

"Has he been divorced? He sort of suggested he knew all about family breakdown."

"He's not divorced, but I think his marriage is tottering."

"It certain didn't look like it last night, the way she was soothing him after the concert."

"That's Bella all over. She loves to be associated with his fame. 'I'm the wife of the great Heinrich', but that's not the whole picture. As a matter of fact, her 'significant other' was there last night, keeping a low profile."

"That's sad. They looked an ideally suited couple. Though, having said that, they do look a bit like 'Beauty and the Beast'. She's so 'glam' and Heinrich—well!"

The ensuing silence suggested that they both realised that they really had no right to talk about anybody else's infidelities.

"Now to face reality. Don't look at me like that, Sam. Yesterday, at least, I was living a fantasy. And this morning."

"Will you join his choir?"

"I doubt it. I've enough trouble getting away as it is!"

"Things may well have changed, by then."

"Who knows!"

They sped north without collecting the things that Clarissa had left at Sam's flat. Fortunately she had everything to do with the script with her as she'd taken the view that she could work on it wherever she was when she got the chance. "If I have some of your belongings it'll guarantee your coming back," Sam said, half joke / whole earnest. They called at a hotel some ten miles away from Clarissa's and Sam booked himself in for a few nights. "As long as that? Can you afford to be away so long?"

"I want to see how things go with you before I depart. I'm going to get in touch with Leo and see if we get in to see Christian and get cracking on the graphics. If possible I'll call at the Young Offenders on the way back home. So don't worry, darling, I won't be wasting my time."

Sam dropped Clarissa near her house and, after a regrettably but necessarily short goodbye, he sped off and Clarissa walked the short distance home. She inhaled deeply as she opened the front door and walked in. The first sound she heard was that of Jenny's music, loud and brash.

"Nothing new there, then", she thought and walked into the kitchen, where Moll was making a cup of coffee. Clarissa greeted her coldly.

"Still here, I see."

"Obviously. Who else is there to see to things here?"

"I seem to think that I went to great lengths and some expense to make sure that *things* were *seen to* here, if by *things* you mean Jenny."

"That's about the size of it. It seems that to you Jenny *is* a thing. I dismissed that woman because she had no right to be here. You hadn't even met her. You engaged her over the telephone! You would have done more for the dog!"

"You said I needed to come back quickly for some emergency or something. You interrupted my work, I hope for some good reason apart from lecturing me on how to bring up my daughter. So what was it?"

"Isn't that enough? The child is out of control. She needs a child psychologist if you ask me."

"I recall that I went to a great deal of trouble and expense to bring in an expert in child behaviour. The one you took it upon yourself to dismiss." Clarissa knew she was stretching a point to call Gillian Fairclough 'an expert' or that she was brought in as anything other than a convenience to herself. How easy the art of glib lying was becoming!

"A child of that age needs her mother."

"I go away infrequently for my work and I make provision for those occasions. Jim used to be away for weeks at a time leaving me with two small children and I don't remember you, or Pa for that matter, offering any help. It seems Grandfathers are as bad as their sons in that respect!"

"What was the matter with the job you had? It fitted in with everybody's needs."

"Except my own, but I wouldn't expect you to understand that, Moll. I'd like you to leave in the morning. I resent your interference, however kindly meant." Kindness was not an adjective that readily sprang to mind in connection with Moll, but its diplomatic use on this occasion was appropriate, Clarissa felt.

"Jim asked me to come and I'm not leaving unless he tells me to."

Moll stalked out of the kitchen and up the stairs to her room, banging on Jenny's door as she did so and ordering her to turn down that infernal row.

Clarissa agreed with her about the infernal row but she wasn't going to stand for her child's being chastised in front of her own face. Infuriated, she ran up the stairs to her mother-in-law's room and ordered her out of the house there and then. "I'll 'phone for a taxi and you can book in at that B&B you've used before."

"Unless you intend manhandling me down the stairs I'm staying here until my son tells me otherwise."

Suddenly Clarissa felt unutterably weary. The fight went out of her. She dragged herself to the other spare bedroom and collapsed on to the bed. The throbbing of Jenny's music went on and on but ceased to bother her as she sank into a deep sleep.

CHAPTER TWENTY EIGHT

She awoke sometime in the early morning after a troubled few hours plagued by tormenting dreams in which she was the 'outsider' in all situations. The next few hours she spent tossing and turning, trying to figure out the rights and wrongs of the situations she'd brought herself and the rest of her family into—particularly Jenny and Jim. Perhaps it was mistaken to think in terms of right and wrong. It very much depended on where you stood as to your view point. Moll, of course was right, according to her traditional way of looking at things, that a mother's place was with her children and there was no gainsaying that Jenny's welfare was paramount. What was happening between herself and Jim probably would have happened anyway at some time, as things were far from satisfactory even before the advent of Sam. She could see nothing wrong at all with her own desire to find fulfilment both in her career and her emotional life. Perhaps making other people the sacrificial victims, again particularly her daughter, came into a morally dubious area, but one couldn't always choose the right moment for opportunities to come along and if you missed them they rarely came again.

It was pointless going over and over the problems in the dark, in her own head with nothing and no-one to shed any light on them, so she got up and quietly went to Jenny's room and tiptoed in. The room was in disarray and the child was lying on top of the bedclothes with her legs dangling from the side of the bed. Clarissa gently lifted her back into bed and arranged the duvet over her. She felt a sharp stab of guilt as she was struck almost for the first time how very much the 'little girl' her daughter still was, in spite of the teenage paraphernalia strewn around. She must try to repair their relationship, somehow and soon.

She didn't know whether Jim was in or out. He usually left his car in the drive instead of the garage and she lifted the curtain to see if it was there. It was. Should she go to their bedroom and slip in beside him? She didn't really want to, but if she didn't there would be no chance to speak to him before he left for work and there were things she needed to know.

"Oh! You're back," was his unenthusiastic greeting. He clearly had been lying awake for she had no need to rouse him.

"What's going on? Why did you call your mother in?"

"I didn't, she rang. I mentioned you were away on business and the next thing I knew she'd come."

"Who told her to sack Gillian Fairclough?"

"Again not my doing."

"You didn't stop her?"

"She did it when I was at work. But I must say I wasn't keen on having a stranger to look after Jen, so I didn't object too much."

"Well I've told her to go—your mother. Interfering old so and so."

"She thinks she's helping. Don't be hard on her."

"Did you know that she dragged me back under some pretence of an emergency or something?"

"I didn't know that. What emergency?"

"You tell me."

"None that I know of. None new, anyway. Jenny's been very difficult with her—she's fine with me."

"You must give us your secret!"

"Now can we stop the third degree please? I've a job to go to."

"Promise me you'll get rid of your mother tomorrow. She can't help any of us."

"I'll see what I can do. Goodnight."

Clarissa woke Jenny for school the next morning. The child seemed quite pleased to see her. "Hello mum, I'm glad you're back."

It appeared that she'd liked Gillian and hated Gran for sending her away. Jenny's tolerance of her grandmother had totally evaporated on being left in her charge. "She's an old fuddy-duddy and very strict. When's she going?"

"Probably today. But don't hate her, Jenny. She loves you and though she doesn't always understand young people she really does want to be good friends with you."

Moll didn't come downstairs until long after Jim had gone and Jenny had left for school with a friend's parent whose turn it was to do the school run. She came into the kitchen ready to leave. She put their house key she habitually kept with her back on the key rack. "I shan't be needing that again. I'm going because Jim has asked me to."

"Please try to understand Moll that there are certain things we just have to sort out for ourselves. I apologise for being so angry last night. Can we part as friends?"

"When I see you doing right by that child, I'll feel more inclined to be friends. Goodbye."

Clarissa tried to persuade her to have a coffee at least, but her mother-in-law refused and the last Clarissa saw was the back of her small red car disappearing in the distance.

She rang Sam at his hotel and they arranged to meet as soon as Clarissa could get there. Over coffee she told him how things stood at home. "Not as bad as the old dragon made out. However, I do need to devote more time to Jenny and I must meet Gillian Fairclough. It was stupid of me not to in the first place. Jenny seems to have liked her, though.

"If things are OK then I'll set off for Hartlocke this afternoon. I've been in touch with both Leo and the 'Young Offenders' and we can get in to see Christian. I waved the magic key of good publicity for them when this film goes out. Now let's not waste our precious minutes together. Come."

Saddened by everything that was happening around her in her family and by her lover's imminent departure, Clarissa couldn't respond to Sam's overtures.

"Sorry Sam, do you mind if we don't?"

"Of course I mind, my love, but if you feel you can't for whatever reason, that's OK. Do you want to talk?"

"Possibly, but not here. Let's drive out somewhere peaceful. I know just the place."

Clarissa drove them to a little lane not far off the main road and parked in the entrance to a field, with a rusting iron gate. "No one ever uses this gateway."

They climbed over a style and walked up a path which lay between ripening corn on one side and an overgrown hedge on the other. At the top of the field the path widened out and curved round into a wood and in about quarter of a mile led over another stile into a wide open meadow. In the distance was a small lake set against a background of low trees. They sat down on one of the many fallen logs which skirted the near side of the lake.

"I love this spot. I come here often when I need to sort things out. The prospect is ever changing with the clouds constantly forming and reforming and all mirrored in the lake. I play games to settle things in my mind. If a certain cloud has or hasn't reached a certain point, then such and such will or won't happen—superstitious thing that I am!"

"And what are you trying to settle this morning?"

"I daren't try it this morning. The outcome mighty terrify me."

"As bad as that?" Sam put his arm round her shoulders. "Would it help if we 'cooled' it for a bit?"

Clarissa's heart sank at the prospect, but she knew that the commonsense course was what he suggested.

"But aren't I needed? What about the work?"

"It's at a stage where you can send the stuff from home. You know how we work now and whilst it would be ideal if you could be in closer touch with what's going on, it's not absolutely essential. Nearer deadline time you will have to be on the spot, especially if you want a say in the actors and so forth."

"I'm a liability, aren't I? I did say so at the beginning."

"Nonsense. You're bloody good and for quality we're prepared to put up with some difficulties."

"Life is going to be almost intolerable without you to buoy me up!"

"There *is* a way. *I* know it. *You've* got to find it, it seems."

"I know what could be the right way for me, but it might lead to destruction for my family."

There was a long pause. Then Clarissa looked beseechingly at Sam.

"Will you come up to see me?"

"As often as I can. You know the constraints."

"Say goodbye now and when I'm 'down' I'll come here to find the flavour of you."

What they had failed to accomplish earlier was accomplished in earnest now. What hadn't disappeared was their sense of humour. "We're making a habit of this 'al fresco' lark. Where will the next time be? Hyde Park?" They held hands and ran back to the car.

CHAPTER TWENTY NINE

Life went on tolerably for Clarissa but she did not have the feeling that sustained her over Christmas. She attended to the tasks of family life almost mechanically. Fortunately the preparation of the script still kept her enthralled and Sam was in weekly touch with her. It seemed that Christian was producing excellent graphics. He'd read 'Return' and Clarissa's initial 'Emma' and 'Will' narratives and understood what was needed. There had already been a mention of what Christian was up to in the local press and TV and in various prison service bulletins. It seemed that all was on schedule for a submission of a draft of the film by some time in July.

Clarissa was determined to get her relationship with Jenny back on track. She invited Gillian Fairclough for tea one afternoon and she saw how well she and Jenny got on. Gillian was an attractive woman with a lively personality. Clarissa recalled her daughter's words "will she look after daddy?" and saw that Jim, if he were that type might not be averse to some looking after at her hands. She apologised for the abrupt dismissal by her mother-in-law, but Gillian had not been upset by it. "We nannies do cause a bit of friction in families—especially with grandmothers!" She was quite willing to look after Jenny on the terms stipulated before, though Clarissa had to tell her that the next time she would be away was likely to be about two months hence. Clarissa made herself available to Jenny more readily and frequently than of late and the child was more amenable to her mother's attentions than she had been. That is not to say that everything went smoothly. She was still insolent to her mother and continued to make references to 'that man'. She often made a show of ganging up with her father against Clarissa and there were still scenes with bad language from Jenny.

It was one evening after just such a scene, when Jim was out, that a phone call came from Rob.

"Mum, can I speak to Dad?"

On being told that Jim was out, he went on. "Will you get him to ring me as soon as he gets in?"

"Can't you tell me?"

"'Fraid not, Ma. It's about Tom. He's OK—sort of—but I can't say any more than that."

"Is it anything to do with Amy?"

"Sorry, I won't discuss his affairs. Just get Dad to ring a.s.a.p. How's Jen?"

"Bloody awful, if you must know. But she's not as a bad as she was."

"Doesn't sound like our sweet little Jenny!"

"She's taking it out on me because I have to go away from time to time with this new job. I don't think your Dad's that keen either."

"You and he are OK though, aren't you?"

"Not as good as we should be, I suppose. But don't you worry. It's nothing we can't sort out."

"I know you're taken up with this writing lark, Mum, but is it worth all this hassle?"

"Writing *lark*, eh? It's MY WORK! Can't men understand that women need much more than wiping bottoms and cooking meals? I thought you youngsters were supposed to be enlightened these days!"

"Calm down Mum. Keep your hair on. It's your problem. You'll have to sort it out with Dad. I'll have to go now. Don't forget to tell Dad."

Were it not that she was anxious to learn what Rob had to say about Tom, she would have left Jim a note and gone off to bed feigning sleep. She also had work to finish and e-mail, so she was up when Jim came in and passed on the message, in a somewhat ungracious manner. "I'm simply the messenger it seems."

Jim used the upstairs cordless 'phone and took it into his study and shut the door.

Clarissa went into the kitchen to make a drink and busied herself with odd jobs required before retiring for that night.

"I'm going to have to go down to Rob's to see Tom," said Jim when he eventually came down after a long 'phone call.

"Why? What on earth's the matter? Is Tom alright? Is he at Rob's?"

"He's at Rob's. At least he was, but he's got his own place now apparently. He's OK but in a bit of a fix, I'm afraid. Amy's pregnant."

"Oh my God." Clarissa slumped over the table and hung her head in desperation. "Poor lad. I knew no good would come of that girl."

"I don't suppose she feels over the moon about it either. It takes two to tango, you know."

"He's naïve. First girl friend. I bet she's been around a bit."

"From a background like hers? Don't be stupid, Clarissa. The poor girl will be terrified to tell her family, I'll be bound."

"Don't they know?"

"I'm not sure, but I rather gather not."

"I must go down to him."

"It's *me* he wants to see."

"Well, you can't. You've got your work."

"I'll take some time off, like I do to accommodate *your* work if you remember."

The firmness in Jim's voice and the innuendo convinced Clarissa she was beaten this time. She reflected guiltily that there was a golden opportunity gone to see Sam."

"When do you intend to go?"

"Tomorrow sometime. I'll ring the office in the morning."

Apart from pointless, endless speculation, there was nothing else to say. Clarissa went off to the spare room as was becoming the norm these days with Jim hardly ever questioning it. She slept not a wink but turned over in her mind various schemes of how *she* would deal with the situation, none of which would meet with Jim's approval.

CHAPTER THIRTY

Jim left for Birmingham late morning saying he didn't know when he'd be back, but he would ring and keep Clarissa informed. As soon as he was out of sight his wife tidied her appearance, locked the house, got into her car and went round to the Khatiri's house. Mrs Khatiri was in the house alone and was astonished to see Clarissa when she opened the door. She was, however, impeccably polite and offered Clarissa coffee which was not quite so politely declined.

"I haven't come on a social call, Mrs Khatiri. What I have to say will shock you, I'm afraid, unless of course you know already."

"Please tell me Mrs Consicliffe, then I will tell you if I already know your news."

"Your daughter is pregnant."

"You must be wrong Mrs Coniscliffe. Amy would not become pregnant."

"I hope you're right. My son rang us last night with the news. Of course that does not necessarily mean that he is the father!"

"What are you saying? That my daughter is a bad girl? Your son is her first boyfriend."

"She must get rid of the baby. You must see that. They both have their studies to think of."

"Please leave my house, Mrs Coniscliffe. I hardly believe what you say. If it is true we must think very hard before anyone acts rashly."

"I spent all night thinking. You must persuade Amy to have an abortion, *please*."

Mrs Khatiri politely but firmly showed Clarissa to the door. "Goodbye. We will see each other again, but please let us think. Don't harass us, particularly my daughter."

Clarissa was shaken by her visit to the Khatiris. Mrs Khatiri had treated her with admirable courtesy under the circumstances. Why was she behaving in this hostile way to these people? Her prejudice towards Amy, set in the context of what she thought were firmly held convictions, was irrational. It could only be explained by an overwhelming protectiveness towards her first born who, in spite of appearances to the contrary with his rebellious, rather tough, exterior, had always seemed to her vulnerable. She felt he'd been ensnared by the first romance he'd ever had and would be trapped in a situation he would soon tire of if he married simply to stand by the girl he'd made pregnant, however laudable that course of action might be. She couldn't help thinking of a friend's son who'd struck up a relationship with a Moslem girl. Her brothers, on the instruction of the parents, had made the boy's life hell, not to mention the girl herself who had been forced into an arranged marriage. She couldn't bear that for Tom. The whole thing cast a shadow over his prospects for university and a future career. Indeed she told herself it had nothing to do with Amy's different culture and background, she would have felt the same about any girl who had allowed herself to become pregnant by her son. She must make Jim see sense and use his influence on Tom.

On settling down to try to work Clarissa checked through her e-mails and found a message from Sam who had tried to ring her when she was out at the Khatiris'. He wanted to come up with a copy of the film so far, complete with Christian's graphics. He had a contact at the university local to Normington who would let him use the film studio in the Media Studies Department. He would stay at the hotel he used the last time. Clarissa e-mailed back immediately stating that now would be very convenient as Jim was away, though she couldn't say for how long. Just before Jenny got in from school, Sam rang to say he would arrive very late that same night and could he possibly see her.

"Go to your hotel first and I'll ring you there. It might be possible to come here after Jenny's well settled down. Oh! It will be wonderful to see you. Drive carefully."

Of course Jenny chose that evening to be difficult about settling down. She had not had a sleepwalking episode for quite some time or a nightmare, which relieved Clarissa as suggesting the child was back on an even keel, emotionally speaking. Her recent school report had been excellent too. It was just Sod's Law that it was after ten o'clock when she finally fell asleep.

Clarissa tidied up and then rang Sam. Jim had rung earlier in the evening to say that he was staying at Rob's for another couple of nights at least. He hadn't yet seen or spoken with Tom who was away for a few days and he intended staying until he *did* speak with him. He could give no news of Amy. Clarissa didn't divulge that she'd been round to the Khatiris' that morning, but she pleaded with Jim to 'make Tom see sense' and persuade Amy to think about an abortion as the most sensible, indeed the only course open to them.

"I'll do no such thing. That is entirely up to them. My object in seeing Tom is to assure him of my—our, I hope—support."

"It'll ruin Tom"

"I doubt it will ruin either of them, but of the two Amy is in the more vulnerable position."

Clarissa could see there was nothing to be gained from trying to change Jim's mind, so she rang off with "Keep me posted, love to Rob."

The conversation with Jim had renewed all the anxiety she'd pushed to the back of her mind by working on the script, but there was a credit side to Jim's call. She now knew that Jim was not likely to burst in on her and Sam unexpectedly. They were safe for the foreseeable future.

Within twenty minutes of Clarissa's call, Sam arrived. Though overjoyed to see him her first words were "Sh! Keep your voice down! Don't for God's sake wake Jenny!" Clarissa produced a bottle of wine and they drank it on the rug before the fireplace which, for the summer, was decorated with an assortment of potted plants. Their mutual response was ardent, as befits lovers forced to be so far apart . . . .

Clarissa was determined to keep her family troubles to herself and guided their conversation to the arrangements for showing her the rushes Sam had with him. She showed him her latest efforts which met with his approval.

"You're a quick learner, Clarrie."

"I'd have been quicker if you hadn't been so gentle with my efforts in the beginning."

"How could I not be gentle with you?"

"Because I want to be judged on my real merits and the sooner I learn the hard realities of the job I've undertaken, the better."

"I'll always be there to lend a hand."

"That's not what I want from you. I prefer it when you tell me where I'm deficient and let me learn the hard way. No, I mean it Sam. Don't cushion me."

Sam looked surprised at the vehemence of her statement but made no comment. After a while he said "I'm not to share the delights of *your* bed tonight, then?"

"I'd love you to, but I'm reluctant with Jenny in the house. Do you mind?"

"You asked me that question on a previous occasion and my answer is still the same. I mind very much but I'm not in the business of forcing you. We'll find a time and place (if that isn't too corny) before I leave. Now, much as I'd love another glass of that delicious wine, I must desist and drag myself away, before I'm unable to in more ways than one." They made arrangements for the next morning and he left.

* *

Their local university was not of the first rank but, as with so many modern 'seats of learning' it had a very good and well-patronised Department of Media Studies. The buildings were of the red and cream 'lego' variety and stood out rather starkly amongst the grimy remains of what had once been a thriving shipbuilding area. There were still some battered looking large sheds standing empty, uncertain of their future but fearful that the aptly-named demolition firm 'Tremble and Sons' would soon end that uncertainty.

Inside the university building Clarissa and Sam made their way up the escalator (there were no down ones in the interests of economy!) to a state-of-the-art media studies 'suite'. If before she had been impressed with Leo's set-up, Clarissa was overwhelmed by the technology now confronting her. Professor Marlowe too was intimidating in a 'nerdish' sort of way—consumed by his subject and determined to make all comers who were not so committed feel massively lacking in some way. He took it upon himself to address this inadequacy and held forth at every possible opportunity. It looked as though Sam just about passed muster as he discussed the ins and outs of this or that piece of technology and the vagaries of the media studies course with consummate ease.

Eventually Professor Marlowe left them to their own devices (or at least Sam's—if he *had* noticed Clarissa's presence, he gave no sign), with specific instructions on how the 'gear' was to be handled. They were to spread their wings and experiment, provided everything was left as they found it!

"You sounded pretty impressive. I didn't realise you were so clued up on this stuff."

"I'm not! But I wasn't gong to let old Charlie know. Actually I used to be—clued up—but since I met Leo I've left all the technical stuff to him so I'm a bit rusty."

Their only task was to put in the video disc and wait. By means of some technology unknown to Clarissa their work came up on a large screen, though it was intended for the small screen—whatever size that was in these days of multi-choice!

Clarissa was bowled over by what she saw. Leo had worked yet more on the opening scene and it was spectacular, especially with Christian's graphics. His style captured exactly the essence of the two women, the dreamer and the realist, the tragedy queen and the woman triumphing in spite of overwhelming odds. The plaintive folk song accompanying the whole was perfect in its simplicity and suggestions of pathos. Clarissa felt herself close to tears and she reached for Sam's hand. "Did we do this? It's bloody good!"

The rest of the film was sketchy and unpolished but showed signs of real quality. Francesca was still standing in reminding Clarissa that Sam must have been seeing quite a lot of her, but she made no comment and tried to stifle the jealousy that still plagued her in spite of Sam's assurances. They discussed ways in which the film might be improved and then left the studio, switching off the equipment they'd used but leaving everything else as they found it. They called in at Professor Marlowe's office to thank him for 'the use of'. He showed not the slightest interest in what they'd been up to but gave them yet another lecture on the wonders of modern technology and swept off to continue his proselytising elsewhere.

"Where on earth did you find him?"

"On one or other of my courses. He extended invitations to all and sundry. I never thought I'd take him up on it, but there you are. You came along, living in one of these far flung outposts of the British Empire and the rest, as they say, is history."

"You know that request you made last night? Something to do with a bed?"

"*Y—e—s?*"

"Well it might just be possible to try it out. If we hurry!" And they did just that.

* *

Jim rang to say that he'd spoken with Tom and was coming home later that day. This was the cue for Sam to leave. He and Clarissa had enjoyed two happy days together apart from the time Clarissa devoted to Jenny when Sam made himself scarce.

"You'll certainly be needed in about a month's time to finalise everything before we submit the film. Will that be OK?"

"Absolutely. Jenny will be fine with Gillian, though . . ." She broke off. She had almost let slip the trouble they were having with Tom, but remembered just in time that she'd vowed to keep that from Sam.

"Though what?"

"Nothing. I was getting a bit muddled with some dates Jim had mentioned," she lied. "But that's not till way after the film's submitted. Silly me!"

Sam looked less than convinced. "You'd tell me if there was anything wrong, wouldn't you?"

"Of course. Now off you go. We've both got work to do." She felt tearful as she always did when she parted from Sam these days, so she kissed him briefly and pushed him out of the door. He tried to take her in his arms but she shut the door firmly on him. He shrugged his shoulders, got into his car and was gone.

Jim looked all in when he walked into the kitchen on his return. He wearily poured himself a drink and, more or less ignoring Clarissa's enquiring body language, took it into the sitting room, slumped on to the settee and switched on the TV.

"Well?"

"Not now, Clarissa, I'm far too shattered. Later."

Realising that, as this juncture, discretion was the better part of valour, Clarissa didn't persist but returned to the kitchen to bring in the tray she'd prepared for his return.

"I'm not hungry, but thanks all the same. Everything alright here?"

"Fine." Then after a longish pause, "If you've nothing to tell me then, if you don't mind, I'll be off to bed."

"I've plenty to tell you but it will only lead to argument and I'm not up for that tonight."

"Goodnight then." Clarissa left the untouched tray and went up to the spare room she now considered her sleeping quarters. Once there, she burst into tears. She was dying to know how things stood with Tom and 'that girl' and didn't know how she could wait until Jim deigned to tell her.

She was not, however, going to beg for information. She felt aggrieved that Jim was all too reluctant to share what he knew with her, even allowing for his tiredness. Surely she should be the first to know whatever there was to know about her own son and she suspected that Jim was simply being awkward to spite her.

She heard Jim come up the stairs and go into their bedroom and close the door. She was relieved in one way that he hadn't come into her room, but she was kept awake all night by anxious curiosity and anger.

The next morning, well before their usual getting-up time, she went to where Jim was sleeping and roused him.

"Jim, sorry but I can't wait till tonight to hear about Tom. You've got to tell me now. I've a right to know. So come on, tell me." Clarissa sat down on the bedroom chair and dared him to remain silent at his peril.

"You won't like it, but here goes."

Jim's considered opinion was that Tom was determined to stick by Amy whatever she decided to do about the baby. He hadn't said as much in so many words but he was clearly crazy about the girl and, baby or no baby, he wasn't going to give her up without a fight.

"That's just about the right word—crazy. What does he know of life, of women and their wiles? She probably isn't pregnant at all, but just pretending so that she can trap him!"

"That's just biased speculation which gets us nowhere. OK, they've been foolish, but no more than lots of other kids of their ages and our role now is to support not condemn."

"Where's Tom living? With her I suppose!"

"Yes, but he wouldn't tell me where."

"Why not?"

"In case I told you and he doesn't want you barging in there, as I gather you did with her parents."

"Oh! So that news travelled fast!"

"Can't say I'm impressed with your diplomatic skills. Carry on as you are and you'll alienate not only Tom and Amy, but Rob as well. He can't see what you're making all the fuss about!"

"Just when I thought he'd pulled himself together after all that loafing about and now this. He's ruined!"

"Don't be so melodramatic, Clarissa. It's just delayed things for a bit, that's all."

"How's he going to support a wife—or whatever she'll be—and child?"

"They'll get benefits. Tom will have to get some kind of a job. And we can always lend a hand."

"If we do it for one we'll have to do it for all. I don't suppose her family can or would support them. It's a disaster and until he deigns to speak to me I feel disposed to wash my hands of him."

"Stop there Clarrie. Don't say things you can't retract."

CHAPTER THIRTY ONE

Clarissa had no intention of washing her hands of her son and his affairs, but there was little to be done if she was ignorant of his whereabouts and couldn't speak to him. Furthermore the pressures of the film were increasingly onerous as the deadline approached. Both her 'phone and her computer were red hot. She called Gillian in more frequently to look after Jenny, in the evenings and some weekends when she just *had* to get on.

After one such evening session she came downstairs to find Jim and the nanny in the kitchen chatting very companionably over coffee. It seemed Jim had got over his aversion to her 'kind' and after she'd gone was full of how much he found that he and Gillian had in common. It seemed she was hooked on non-fiction rather than fiction, as was he, and she shared a number of his interests. "She could be quite good for Jenny," he suddenly decided. This was just as well, as a number of the group's meetings were imminent and Gillian would be called on more than ever.

There were two such meetings before the final one on the eve of submission day. Clarissa stayed in Sam's flat on each occasion, but there was little time for anything other than work and sleep. If they had a long working evening they crashed out on each other's sofa or floor, mainly at Leo's since his flat housed all the necessary technical equipment.

It was at Leo's when Clarissa finally came to meet Francesca. There was no doubt about it. She was very beautiful in the voluptuous style of Eustacia Vye but, unlike Eustacia, she was practical and business-like—in a non-threatening way. She was a favourite with the group who relied on her common sense to extricate them from many a difficulty. They discussed the actors they would submit as their preferred choice, but there was no getting away from it, Francesca could have filled the role admirably if the opening scene with her as stand-in was anything to go by.

"No offence Francesca, but we're not likely to get a big name to fit the bill. So stand by! You'd come far cheaper . . . . And better of course!"

Francesca laughed. "You haven't seen my acting! I can stand around like a stooge but if I had to move or open my mouth, I'd be finished."

"I hardly think you're in the 'stooge' category, you gorgeous creature."

"Flattery will get you everywhere, Leo, except in my bed."

"He's not relying on you for that sort of thing, darling. Haven't you heard of his Dorset conquest?"

"Haven't we got work to do? Plenty of time for Leo's conquests some other time!" Sam cracked the whip.

The folksong as accompaniment had only been intended for 'rehearsal purposes' but they all agreed that it was exactly right.

"I hear you have a lovely voice, Clarissa", Francesca smiled. "It would be wonderful if *you* could sing it."

"I think it is perfect as it is, but thank you anyway."

Clarissa watched the interaction of Sam and Francesca closely. Over coffee the two of them discussed some financial matter. It was evident that they were very easy in each other's company and often touched each other in a familiar but non-sexual way, throughout their conversation. They certainly made a handsome couple though Francesca was slightly taller than Sam. There was nothing to suggest that they were anything other than good friends but that did not lessen Clarissa's suspicion that, given the choice, he would choose Francesca over herself.

They ended that evening with a send-off party for the film. They were pretty certain that it would be accepted, but whether or not it would see the light of day this year, next year, sometime or never was dependant on the whim of some TV producer. Sam was to deliver the film himself the next morning and they expected to hear the verdict in a month or two's time.

In bed, in the early hours of the next morning, too excited to sleep and sated with lovemaking, Clarissa and Sam discussed all that had passed between them in less than a year.

"Do you think we could stand each other, day in, day out, with all the sorts of pressure we've been through in the past few, hectic weeks? It's certainly been a bit of a test, wouldn't you say?"

"It makes a difference when you're both involved in the same pressure-making circumstances—and with no kids to make the situation worse."

"I think we make an excellent team. It's been great to have someone here in the flat with me to share things—good or bad."

"Someone?" queried Clarissa.

"You, you silly bugger!"

"Yes, we've managed pretty well together. But tomorrow I must go. I want to call and see Christian and I need to see my son Rob about something."

"Why don't I come with you?"

"For the simple reason that you've got a very important mission tomorrow. Don't tell me you've forgotten!"

"Hell! What's the matter with me! *You* could stay until the day after and then I could come with you."

"That would be wonderful, but it's a family thing with Rob and I really need to be on my own."

"There's something you're not telling me, isn't there?"

"We're having a bit of bother with the kids but I really don't want to discuss it with you just yet."

"Just as you wish, but if I can be of any help you need only ask me."

"Thanks. Now we really must get some sleep."

CHAPTER THIRTY TWO

Clarissa made good progress on the journey to Bristol to see Christian. He was now living with his mother and Angie had left, believing Mrs McKenzie to be much better since Christian's fortunes had taken an upward turn—thanks to Clarissa and the Group. They welcomed Clarissa very warmly with coffee and cakes. Christian couldn't wait to show her the latest thing he was working on, whilst replying to all her compliments with "Aw Miss, it's not all that good!"

"For goodness' sake, stop calling me 'Miss'. My name is Clarissa."

"Bit of a mouthful that, Miss."

"OK, Clarrie, then."

Christian was working in a supermarket, packing shelves during the day and some evenings and weekends, but he had enrolled for some evening art classes. He had to report to a probation officer every month for the next year and was steering clear of his old associates and drugs. He attended a Drugs Rehabilitation Centre one weekend a month on a residential basis and was making excellent progress.

"Ah wasn't really into that stuff, Clarrie. Ah sold a bit now and again an' a'm not sayin' ah didn't 'ave the odd joint but ah was never 'ooked, as yer might say."

"What would you like to do with your Art, Christian?"

"Chris, Miss, sorry—Clarrie. Well ah like what ah've done for you lot—graphics an' that. Be great working in advertisin' or the telly."

"Are you working towards a qualification at your Art classes?

"Yeah. 'A' level or summink and then ah might go to college. Mum wants me to do that."

Mrs Mckenzie beamed her approval and pride in her reformed son. "We can never thank you enough, Clarissa, for everything you've done for Christian. He's a changed boy altogether."

Clarissa left, assuring them of her continued interest and willingness to help in his future career in any way she could. She was just about to drive off when Christian shouted to her to wait. He ran into the house and rushed out flourishing a newspaper.

"See this Miss—sorry—Clarrie?" There was his photograph and a long article on his selection to do the art work for a proposed TV film.

"Yes, I heard you'd got yourself into the papers. Fame at last, eh?"

"For the right reasons, this time, Clarrie!"

"I'll let you know the result as soon as I know myself. Until then 'Go well'."

Clarissa did not anticipate that her next visit would be as pleasant as the last. Although time was getting on and it was unlikely that she would reach Rob's much before late evening, she delayed the 'evil' moment still more by stopping to have a light snack at a service station on the motorway. Inevitably her mind went back to the last time she'd used one and then to Christian. It seemed incredible that her stalker should have been in and out of jail and was now a colleague of hers in less than a year. She could not but feel proud at the part she'd played in the lad's rehabilitation. She must continue to keep an eye on him and support him as much as she could.

It was indeed late when she drew up outside her son's door. There were no lights on in the house, so it was with some trepidation that she rang the doorbell. After several ringings and what seemed like an age, Rob opened the door and peered out. On recognising his mother his jaw dropped. "Mum, what on earth are you doing here? What's happened?"

"I must say you don't look too pleased to see me. Sorry, I should have rung but I've been so busy that I simply haven't had the time. Can I come in?"

"Yes, yes of course," and Rob stepped back so she could pass him.

"I must have got you out of bed. Sorry again."

"Let me get you a coffee or something."

"I wouldn't say 'no' to that."

When they were settled down with their drinks, Clarissa said, "I suppose you know why I'm here!"

"I can guess, but if it's about Tom and Amy I can't tell you any more than Dad will have told you."

"And that's precious little. Where are they living? I have a right to know."

"Dad didn't tell you?"

"Said he didn't know."

"I thought he *did*."

"If he does he's not telling me. It seems I'm not to be trusted."

"Well you have made your feelings pretty clear on the subject and you did give Mrs Khatiri a bit of a bollocking, I gather."

"Can't you persuade him to see sense? Surely you can see the chances he's throwing away."

"I think he's a plonker, but it's none of my business. He's got his own life to lead."

"Have you met this girl?"

"Amy? Yes. She's lovely."

"But she'll spell nothing but trouble for him. He's wasted enough time as it is dithering about in that pub and now this. Do you seriously think she's pregnant or is it simply a ruse to get him?"

"Don't be daft, mother. She's an ace girl. She doesn't need to inveigle a fellah to take up with her. Tom's no great catch anyway!"

"For her he is!"

"What do you mean by that exactly?"

"Oh! Never mind. I can see everyone's on her side so it's no use discussing it any further. Is he alright, you know, health-wise and so on?"

"He's fine. Elated I'd say, at the prospect of fatherhood."

"New fangled, rather. Wait until reality kicks in. He won't be so elated then. Well I wash my hands of them both. There's nothing more I can do as he's cut himself off from me. Can you lend me a settee for tonight?"

"Take my bed. I'll russle up some clean sheets." Rob was adamant on that point, so without having made any progress as far as Tom was concerned, Clarissa went to bed and fell into a sound sleep.

CHAPTER THIRTY THREE

A few days after her return home Clarissa had two quite unpleasant surprises. She was doing a bit of general tidying up, having neglected household chores from months, and was in Jim's study trying to dust his desk which their cleaning lady refused to touch, in case she disturbed something important. On impulse, she went into his computer and brought up his e-mails. As she scrolled down the messages which were almost all to do with his work or his committees, she came across two from a Hazel Eastwood: Subject: 'Pink scarf and Guardian' and a third from 'Miranda': subject: 'Thanks for a pleasant meeting'. It would be easy to open them but conscience stopped her. She felt guilty as it was intruding into his privacy. Surely it could not be what these three e-mails suggested! Jim of all people!

At first she felt amused and then, irrationally as she realised, angry and jealous. She knew she had no business feeling so in the light of her own behaviour. Jim must certainly more than suspect what was going on between her and Sam. It was impossible to say anything about the e-mails without revealing both her prying and her adultery.

The second disturbing surprise was a letter, addressed to both herself and Jim, lying open on his desk, from Sahid Khariti:

Dear Mr & Mrs Coniscliffe,

The news of our daughter's pregnancy as a result of her relationship with your son clearly upset you, as Mrs Coniscliffe made clear when she visited my wife some weeks ago. May we say that we sympathise with you in this as we are devastated too by the news.

We had high hopes for our daughter's future career—the first in our large family to go to University. We also had hopes for her in marriage and had arranged for her to meet and hopefully marry her cousin—a doctor in the famous Leeds Hospital.

However that cannot be now, so we feel the only course open to us is to support the two young people in their difficulty and urge them to marry as soon as possible so as to avoid any scandal to our family.

May we request a meeting with you as soon as possible?

Yours faithfully,
Khalida and Sahid Khariti

The implication in the letter that her son was not good enough for the Khatiri's daughter sent Clarissa into paroxysms of anger. Jim came back to a furious wife who presented him with the letter as soon as he entered the front door.

"You really choose your times Clarissa. Always when I'm tired out. Anyway, that letter was in my study. What were you doing in there?"

"Your room does have to be cleaned sometimes, darling. And don't you think you should have shown it to me or left it out for me to read?"

"OK. OK. But let me get a drink first. Where's Jenny? We don't want her listening in to all this!"

"She's at a friend's."

Jim loosened his tie, poured out a couple of drinks and walked with them into the sitting room.

"I told you there would be trouble with that girl. It's a wonder we haven't had a relation of some sort banging on the door for revenge!"

"We've been over all this before, Clarissa. You can see from their letter that they are perfectly reasonable folks—which is more than can be said for you, I may say."

"They'll never stop thinking that Tom is second best after that precious doctor. There'll be trouble, not to say tragedy ahead. You'll see."

Clarissa's frame of mind was reinforced by current reports of a grisly murder in a Moslem family, plastered over every newspaper and in the TV and radio news programmes. A young bride of twenty one had been brutally stabbed to death by a cousin for daring to choose an 'unsuitable' partner."

"They've suggested a meeting and I think we should take them up on it."

"I can't face them. They know how I feel about it, but you do what you like."

"I know things aren't right between us, Clarissa, but we really should try to pull together on this one, don't you think?"

"You mean I've got to give in and go with the flow."

"Showing your degree of hostility won't help at all. It'll further entrench them. And anyway you know very well that, when youngsters are as committed as these two are, there's precious little anyone can say that will move them."

"Committed! They've been damned stupid and they've 'landed' themselves—putting a kindly interpretation on it! Of course Tom won't want to walk away, he's a decent lad. But should we encourage him to ruin his future when a small operation could sort it out?"

"You know damn well you're talking balls. No-one has the right to urge that on any woman and you know it. I'm going to arrange a meeting with the Khatiris and you can come or stay as you wish." Jenny came in and the subject had to be shelved.

CHAPTER THIRTY FOUR

"You can't possibly be going off again. Surely there's nothing to do until you hear the result and that's a month away at least."

"There's masses to do. We've the whole film to finish. If this lot reject it we'll do the rounds."

"I don't know how you can put your mind to it with all this hanging over us."

"The same way as you manage to do your job! You still don't think of my writing as *work,* do you? Just because I enjoy it, I suppose."

Clarissa and Jim had taken Jenny out for an afternoon one weekend to a nearby wild-life park. She was happily engaged feeding some wild birds on the lake with specially prepared food bags handed out at the entrance. They were 'relaxing' on the grass nearby, keeping an eye on her, and Clarissa had broached the subject of an imminent trip away.

"I suppose you'll be hauling that Gillian character in again."

"I thought you liked her. I rather gathered you thought she was better for Jenny than I am! What's changed your mind?"

"Oh she's very nice and all that, but she's not her mother. A child needs her mother."

"Look Jim, we've been through all this before. You'll have to get used to the idea that going away from time to time is in the nature of my work."

"It's more than just the work, though, isn't it?"

"What exactly do you mean by that?"

"I mean that you and Sam are having a bit of a 'ding-dong'. I'm right, aren't I?"

Hearing her relationship with Sam reduced to this coarse cliché shocked Clarissa to her very core.

She managed to reply without betraying her feelings too much. "I've told you—yes, we enjoy each other's company and OK, I find him very attractive, but I have no intention of leaving you and splitting up the family."

"Let me make two points. First, it seems to me that you've already split up the family. You've alienated both Tom and Jenny. Second, have you ever considered that *I* might leave *you*?"

Clarissa stared at him in disbelief. Jim, easy-going Jim, leave *her*? To judge from the e-mails she'd discovered on his computer, he was taking active steps to do just that. For revenge or an even more significant reason?

"You've certainly left us to our own devices for the best part of a year now, to gallivant about with your 'oh so important' job! Do you imagine that I sit here night after night, twiddling my thumbs? I find Gillian pretty useful too, you know, to get out now and again to socialise."

She didn't admit to knowing *how* he set about socialising and she deliberately put a rein on her own responses, for fear of letting slip too much information about her goings on with Sam before she was ready.

"Until the film's future is secure I've got to carry on, trips away and all, as well you know."

What she didn't tell Jim at this point was the exact nature of her next jaunt. It was nothing to do with the film and everything to do with her determination to find where Tom was living, visit him and put an end to the foolhardy course he was embarked on. She rang Sam and asked him if he fancied a few days with her in Birmingham.

"Birmingham?" Sam was dumbfounded.

"I haven't quite gone off my head. You did say that if I needed help with my family problems, I could call on you. Well I do." She outlined to him what must have sounded an outlandishly ridiculous plan to track down Tom. She didn't tell him all the details, but enough to raise his sympathy for her as a distraught mother.

Clarissa booked two rooms in a small hotel not far from Rob's place. She didn't intend that Rob should know anything of her whereabouts but, if by any chance he did found out, she didn't want him discovering the true nature of her relationship with Sam. Being in a run-down area, the hotel was dingy and unappealing but clean and adequate. She wanted to 'survey' Rob's entrance from morning to night so it was essential to be very close to his house. She told Sam that she *and* Jim had become estranged from Tom over his relationship with a girl, but not that the girl in question was Asian nor that she, Clarissa, disapproved. She knew with almost complete certainty that Tom would visit Rob at some point and she would note his departure and somehow follow him home. Sam agreed to act as 'relief shift' and generally kept her company in her vigil. Sam actually thought the whole thing preposterous, but his devotion to Clarissa and his promise to help made him acquiesce. It was good to be with his love even in these bizarre circumstances and, curiously enough, their passion was not diminished by the drabness of their surroundings or the necessity for creeping about in the dark from room to room!

They were at their post—a convenient side road opposite Rob's house from where they had a first class view of all the comings and goings at Rob's door—at seven o'clock in the morning. Clarissa had thought to provide flasks for coffee which the proprietor obligingly filled. He must have wondered what these two eminently middle class guests were doing patronising his lowly establishment, but he showed no curiosity and kept his own counsel. A little general store provided them with lunchtime snacks and they took turns to be the shopper. They spied Rob twice during the first day and Clarissa could scarcely refrain from calling out to him, which would have wrecked everything.

It was interesting, if depressing, to observe the activities of the seedy area, most of whose residents were Black or Asian. The houses, which were nearly all turned into flats and bedsits, must once have had a degree of elegance about them. The peeling, porticoed entrances denoted a more affluent past which made the attempts of a series of occupiers to paint them up, in now tattered shades of cream and bright red, even more pathetic. An assortment of bright plastic toys were scattered about in one or two of the longish front gardens and boxes and plastic bags adorned the steep flights of steps up to the front doors. The residents seemed bent on either coming or going, the traffic preventing much in the way of street socialising, though here and there young women with prams and young children laughed and chattered as they went along and the odd dog sniffed its way determinedly from one gate post to the next. It was a main road so the traffic was heavy especially at peak times and it was at these times that Clarissa and Sam had to be particularly vigilant, straining their necks to get the best view possible through the inevitable convoys of double deckers in both directions.

It was on the afternoon of the third day, when both were becoming more and more aware of the absurdity and futility of their task, that their long wait was rewarded by the appearance of Tom at Rob's front door. He evidently had a key to the place as he went straight inside. They had seen Rob go out earlier, so it would be an easy task to confront Tom in Rob's rooms. Clarissa knew, however, that this would bring her no further forward in finding out where Tom lived. He wouldn't tell her and she could hardly 'trail' him in such circumstances. He must not know she was anywhere in the vicinity until she arrived on his door step.

He left about thirty minutes later and walked back the way he'd come. Clarissa urged Sam to edge out of the side road and follow her son. This was easier said than done for obvious reasons and almost immediately they were upon him. If he'd turned his head he would have seen them and, even though he wouldn't necessarily have recognised them, he would soon have become conscious that he was being curb crawled. Clarissa was forced to get out of the car and follow on foot. Sam parked the car as soon as he was able and caught up with Clarissa. They kept about a hundred yards behind Tom, dogging him steadily until he reached a small parade of shops where he stopped and seemed to study with interest the contents of one of the windows ('Togs for Tots' as Clarissa grimly noted later). He hesitated outside the door, hovering on the point of going in, but apparently changing his mind and walking on at a quicker pace.

He gave them a fright by turning round to check on the arrival of a bus, which caused him to put a spurt on to catch it at the next stop ahead. Though this was a probability they had foreseen and feared, it came as a blow. They couldn't jump on the same bus as they would most certainly be discovered. They noted the number and route of the bus from the information board at the stop and made a quick decision that they should get in the car. Clarissa followed the bus as far as she could, a course which was made easy by the slowness of the traffic which was by now building up towards rush-hour. She kept just behind the bus as far as a busy inter section where the vehicle performed a complicated manoeuvre in order to turn right along a major traffic thoroughfare.

Fortunately Sam and car caught up with her at that point and, though causing much exasperated hooting, managed to pull up for her to get on board. With difficulty in crossing from the inside to the outside lane, they managed to turn right and get a couple of cars behind the bus. It took three-quarters of an hour and five to six miles of tortuous city roads before they saw Tom alight from the bus and enter a house in a slightly leafier and pleasanter area than Rob's.

"Now what do we do?" enquired Sam.

"You do nothing, but I'm going in."

Sam, aware of Clarissa's determination, said nothing further and Clarissa got out of the car.

"I'll be waiting for you. Take as long as you like." He went off to park the car.

Clarissa walked firmly up to the front door and pressed the door bell. Had she acted timidly she would have lost her resolution and run after Sam. Tom opened the door and stared in disbelief at his mother. "Who told you? Dad? Rob?"

"No-one told me. Let me come in and I'll explain."

"You're not coming in here. You've caused enough trouble already."

"Come out here then. Please Tom. We'll find a pub, a café anywhere, but we must talk."

"What have we to say to each other? I'm going to marry Amy and you're here to try to stop me. Impasse!"

"I know I can't stop you, but please Tom talk to me. I'm going out of my mind with worry about you . . . both," she added as an afterthought.

"Fifteen minutes then. I've got a job to do."

He went back into the house, shutting the door behind him. The two minutes it took before he reappeared were among the loneliest and bleakest of Clarissa's life. To be 'shut out' by the son she adored brought a pain to her heart. That closed door was a symbol of his rejection of her. She pondered on her predicament. Estranged from everyone she most cared about—even Sam who, though not knowing precisely the object of her machinations, yet seemed to disapprove.

Tom led her to a mobile kiosk selling drinks and snacks. He bought a coffee for his mother and a Coke and a hotdog for himself. Clarissa winced at this graphic evidence of his unhealthy life style which, of course, she attributed to his present predicament. He indicated a battered, decrepit-looking public seat, where they sat down next to a waste bin spewing forth its unsavoury contents, surrounded by cigarette butts and other detritus of an even more disgusting nature. The traffic had thinned a little but the air was heavy with petrol fumes.

"Sorry about the gracious living, mother, but I really haven't much time." Clarissa noted the formality of his address. "The plain facts of the matter as I see it are these. I love Amy. She loves me. We are having a child and we want to be together. Life will be difficult for a while, but we're prepared for that and we're looking forward to our baby. I doubt whether you have any adequate replies to these statements, so why waste your breath?"

"First of all let me make one thing clear. Neither your Dad (he didn't know your address anyway—Rob wouldn't tell him because of me!) nor Rob told me of your 'hideaway'. A friend helped me to trace you. It would be very easy for me to walk away from you and say 'it's your life'. Goodness knows I've got problems enough of my own! I could rid myself of any responsibility and worry on your behalf. But, as your mother who cares for you, I have at least to make you stop and think about the pitfalls—the ones you've already considered and the ones you haven't."

"It won't make any difference, mother, but if it will make you feel better as having done your duty, then fire away."

"You say you love each other. Fine now, but your feelings may well change. If you have no more than passion as a foundation, where will you be when that fades—as it will—coming from such different backgrounds with very little in common? You hardly know this girl! Are you aware that her family, though appearing supportive, would much prefer their daughter to be marrying a doctor from a muslim family than a penniless—whatever you're doing at the moment to keep body and soul together. Have you thought of the trouble you're storing up for your selves in the future—family feuds and the problems of mixed race children? I very much doubt it."

"What shared interests? Yeah sure, you and Dad come from the same background, but has that cemented your relationship? You're a snob, Mum, for all your fine egalitarian talk. If she'd had a white face and the wrong accent you'd have been the same. You're accusing us of something no more heinous than you're doing yourself. We're not betraying anybody. Are you? I fancy you have some problems of your own to work through before you start on ours."

"Please, *please,* Tom, think before you do anything rash. Don't break my heart."

Tom stood up and with a softer tone in his voice said with finality, "I don't want to break your heart, Mum, but you, in your turn, mustn't break ours." He started to walk away and then turned and said, "Where are you staying? Do you want to stay with us tonight or whatever?"

"No, I've got somewhere to stay, thanks. Please think hard about what I've said."

"I must say, I expected more understanding from you, Mum." Tom's face registered the disappointment and sadness he felt at his mother's attitude and he walked away without looking back.

Clarissa remained sitting on the battered seat, her eyes filling with tears. She experienced loneliness so deep that she was unaware that Sam had walked up and was standing behind her for quite some minutes before sitting down beside her and putting his arm round her shoulders. He comforted her without speaking and after a while he took her arm, raised her from the seat and led her back to the car which was parked a short distance away. They didn't speak until they were seated in the lounge bar of an indifferent looking pub drinking a stiff whisky each.

"Mission accomplished?"

"In the sense that I've discovered Tom's whereabouts, yes. In every other sense, no."

"Are you going to ring Jim?"

"Jim? Heavens no, he knows nothing about it!"

"But you told me he did!"

"He knows about Tom and his problems, but not that I've come down to search him out. He'd be wild he if he knew."

"Why? Wouldn't he be glad you'd made contact with his estranged son?"

"Jim and Tom aren't estranged. It's just me that Tom and Amy aren't happy with."

"Who is Amy?"

"Tom's girl, partner what you will. He's got her pregnant and she's Asian."

"And you have a problem with that?"

"I'm afraid I do. Please don't ask me why! Intellectually, with one or two rather important reservations, I don't, but emotionally I do. I can't explain it satisfactorily to myself, so I can't expect anyone else to understand."

"And you've trailed your son, found out where he lives, to do what exactly?"

"Try to get him to see the problems that lie ahead and think hard before he commits himself to a course that will rob him of his chances of a university education and a good career and bring huge problems in its wake."

"You're entitled to tell me to mind my own business, but don't you think you're attempting the impossible? Since when has 'thinking' altered the course set upon by the emotions? Take us as a prime example. Do you expect Tom to do what we, experienced and middle-aged, are unable to do? Come on Clarissa!"

"I'm tired Sam. I can't rationalise any more. Let's just leave it for now."

"OK." Then after a pause, "I've got an idea. Let's make this last night a good one. I'm tired of that dingy dump we've been in for what seems like forever. We've nothing to go back for. We need a posh place good food and a large comfortable bed. What do you say?"

"That would be marvellous. What are we waiting for?"

They drove out towards the leafier suburbs of the city and pulled up outside an imposing building, once a stately home but now taken over by a large expensive chain and run as a de-luxe hotel—impersonal, but giving the comfort and anonymity they wanted. A 'phone call squared things with their previous hotel and soon they had showered and changed and were enjoying pre-dinner drinks in the opulent bar.

"Do you want the good news or the bad news?" Sam startled Clarissa out of a lingering mood of depression.

"I couldn't take any bad news. Let's have the good news, please."

"Our film has been accepted. I had a call when you were talking to Tom."

Clarissa stared open-mouthed at Sam and then leaned over and hugged him.

"Oh that is marvellous. Wonderful! Congratulations, Sam!"

"To all of us, not just me, for heaven's sake! The others don't know of course, so don't go spreading the glad tidings just yet."

"I can't believe it. Our film accepted! What happens now?"

"The 'Argy-Bargy'. They'll want to do it their way until it's unrecognizable, so we'll have to fight our corner until we come up with a compromise. You won't have to be upset by changes."

"I'm just about acclimatised to those by now, in more ways than one! Anyway what about some champagne to celebrate?"

Sam decided to sit on the bad news for the moment so that they could really savour the heady air of success for a bit longer. Over dinner they talked casually about a celebration party for the group and close associates. Later, in the super-king-sized bed in the comfortable if characterless room, Clarissa brought up the matter of the bad news.

"I'm off to the States soon. After the film is really launched. It's to do with family business."

"For how long?"

"A few months."

Clarissa experienced the pang which was becoming all too familiar. She realised, too, that she knew very little about his family, apart from what little she'd gleaned from the photo in his flat. That simply confirmed what she had already surmised from his easy life style, that he came from a pretty well-to-do background.

"Are your parents still living?"

"My mother only. She lives on Long Island in a condominium for the elderly. She's pretty independent, but there's help at hand if she needs it. It's a lovely place. Why don't you come with me?"

"I wish, oh how I wish I could. But it's impossible. I would have to tell Jim what he already suspects and break with him. I couldn't just breeze off as if nothing was going on between you and me. I can't take that step yet for Jenny's sake."

Sam was silent, sipping his wine and then he said "It will be almost unbearable being parted from you for so long, but I suppose it will give us both time to take stock and consider seriously what our future together holds and just how committed we are to each other."

Clarissa could not, did not want to break away from her family for the foreseeable future. Of that she was certain, but the implication in Sam's last words that there might not *be* a future together struck her like a death knell which terrified her. She had to consider that word 'committed'. Where did her commitment lie? Did love and commitment necessarily go hand in hand? Was 'love' what she felt for Sam—exciting, romantic, energising, altogether delightful—or was it the pain she was feeling for her family, the concern and worry, the reluctance to abandon them? Hadn't she committed herself to Jim all those years ago, probably without much idea of what that would mean when romance faded and problems were paramount. Would it be so with Sam even though she felt what she'd never felt with Jim—a meeting of minds as well as hearts, the extra buzz that came from being not just a lover but a colleague?

CHAPTER THIRTY FIVE

Clarissa had time to consider yet more in the next month, for Sam had to go off to the States earlier than anticipated. He was in fact, among other things, trying to negotiate the setting up of a fund for the Group into which an amount from his mother's estate would be paid—in the fullness of time. Alfreda Melsonby was gradually being weaned from the idea that it would be money down the drain. In principle she supported what the group was trying to do, but was doubtful about its future as a profitable proposition. With its recent success under its belt, Sam was hoping to strike while the iron was hot and win her co-operation and that of her rich friends. He would return for the party and then go straight back to the family affairs he was currently engaged in.

Clarissa had *time* to consider but not the *opportunity*, for there were more problems to contend with. She arrived back from Birmingham in the early evening. On opening the door she heard noisy chatter and giggling coming from the kitchen. She went in to see Jim and Gillian engaged in some kind of wrestling match with Jenny attempting to snatch at something Jim was holding. The table was spread with a partly-eaten meal and the whole atmosphere was one of happy, easy familiarity. On seeing Clarissa the two adults jumped apart, almost guiltily.

"Hi Clarrie." Jim walked across and hugged her in a manner which, to Clarissa's mind, was designed to allay suspicion. "Have some food—there's plenty left."

"Thanks, but I ate on the train. I'm tired. I'll go and unpack and have an early night, a very early night, if you don't mind."

As she walked up the stairs she heard whisperings and half-stifled laughter. The episode disturbed her but her system seemed disinclined to cope with any more emotional trauma and shut down as she unpacked, showered and went to bed. Troubled as she was, she fell asleep almost immediately.

Jim woke her on his way to bed. "I thought I'd pop in to see if you were awake and ask how your trip was."

"Fine. Our film has been accepted."

"Terrific. Congratulations. You've certainly worked hard and you deserve the success. Great stuff, Clarrie," and he came and hugged her.

"Thanks, that's kind of you."

"I don't suppose I could climb in . . . . ?"

"No, sorry. There's not enough room and well, you know—things, etc."

"OK."

"You seemed to be having a good time in the kitchen, you three—when I arrived home."

"Yes we get on fine together. You were right. Gillian's good for Jenny."

"Has she gone?—Gillian I mean."

"No. She was anxious to see a TV programme which she would have missed travelling home. She's gone to bed. Is that alright?"

"Fine." After a pause, Clarissa continued "What were you hiding behind your back that Jenny was anxious to get hold of?"

"Don't know what you mean? When?"

"Earlier, in the kitchen, just as I walked in. You were all horsing about in the kitchen."

"Oh that. It was a holiday brochure as a matter of fact."

"Oh? Where are you planning on going?"

"Gillian had the idea that if you were tied up during the summer holiday, perhaps she might accompany Jenny and me for a break away somewhere. Only a thought. Nothing concrete."

That she might be able to join Sam in America instantly popped up in Clarissa's mind. She could make it look like an essential trip in connection with the film. But ought she to? She'd neglected Jenny shamefully already and she wasn't at all keen on Gillian being 'in loco parentis' with Jim as the other 'parentem'. She wouldn't yet, however, pour cold water on a plan which could be useful to her. The lure of Sam on Long Island might yet prevail!

"Mm. Well it looks very likely that we'll be busy finishing the film and revising and all that so it might be advisable to keep the idea in mind."

Jim went off to his lonely bed, though Clarissa was beginning to wonder just how lonely it was, what with the e-mail ladies and all! In spite of having already slept soundly Clarissa soon dropped off again and knew nothing more 'till morning

CHAPTER THIRTY SIX

When Clarissa got downstairs the next morning to prepare breakfast and rouse Jenny, Gillian had already gone, leaving a note to the effect that she was always available if and when she was needed. Clarissa grinned wryly to herself. Available to whom? Herself, she presumed, but in her present state of mind 'availability' was open to being construed as applicable to another adult member of the Coniscliffe family! This idea flitted in and out of her mind as she ferried Jenny and friend to school and returned for a coffee to set herself up for the morning's chores.

The 'phone rang just as she'd settled herself down with the crossword. She ran to answer it, certain that it would be Sam, only to have her hopes dashed in a catastrophic way by an impersonal voice enquiring if she were Mrs Clarissa Coniscliffe and then going on to inform her that she was ringing from the hospital into which her mother had been rushed that morning, seriously ill. It would be advisable to come at once, so bad was the old lady's condition. Clarissa had of late seen very little of her elderly mother, though she had kept up a telephone connection. In spite of the recent lack of contact (largely because of her relationship with Sam) there had always been a strong emotional bond between mother and daughter, which made the news of her mother's illness fill Clarissa with anxiety-near-panic.

She 'phoned Jim and Gillian (!), threw a few things into a case, jumped into her car and drove the fifty or so miles to the hospital where her mother was a patient. She was allowed to peep at her mother, in an intensive care ward, wired up to an array of forbidding-looking apparatus. Later she was allowed to go in and sit beside her bed holding her hand, but her mother remained unconscious and oblivious of Clarissa's presence. It was unlikely that her mother would recover and it was known to Clarissa and the medical authorities responsible for her mother's care that, in such an event as this, excessive resuscitation treatment was not to be administered.

Her mother's condition was the result of a massive stroke and there was no doubt that a life or death decision would have to be made soon. At this point, however, Clarissa was not yet convinced of the inevitability of her mother's death and requested that things be allowed to continue as they were for the present. There was precious little to keep Clarissa from dwelling on all the problems besetting her, but she concentrated on the slim possibility of her mother recovering sufficiently to leave hospital and requiring full-time care. Where? The thought of putting her into an institution filled Clarissa with horror and premature guilt as if she had already done so. Somehow she would have to care for her at home. That thought did not sit happily with the prospect of further amorous adventures with Sam. Jim would accommodate himself to the changed circumstances in his usual kindly, obliging way—however inconvenient that might prove to be—and Jenny, initially, at least, would be pleased to have a Granny, whom she saw infrequently but liked, as part of the household. But was it fair to take on an infirm old woman who would restrict their lifestyles enormously? An idea began to form in Clarissa's mind which would turn out to have nothing to do with caring for her infirm mother but was, nevertheless, engendered by that prospect.

Her reflections were interrupted by the sudden realisation that the wall mounted clock had stopped. This filled Clarissa with panic so that she was not surprised when moments later the nurse came into the room with the sombre news that her mother had died. "We did everything we could but to no avail, I'm afraid."

"May I see her?"

"Of course. Just give us a moment or two and we'll come for you. Would you like a cup of tea or coffee?"

"Not at the moment, thanks. Later, perhaps."

"Would you like us to ring anyone for you?"

"I have my mobile, thank you. I'll ring my family later. Don't worry, I'm all right."

Her mother was elderly so her death was in the nature of things, but at forty one, Clarissa felt 'orphaned', vulnerable and not up to being the head of the family as her mother had been. In the matter of generations she'd moved up a notch and suddenly she was aware of her own mortality.

The only consolation was that she had been spared the responsibility of a life and death decision on her mother. She rather suspected that those charged with the care of her mother had taken the responsibility for that decision from her and she was relieved.

Before she left she went in to see her mother. She wept as she placed her hand over the frail, old one and bent to kiss the old lady's forehead. She whispered her heartfelt thanks for all that her mother had meant to her. Then with a heavy heart she left for home.

CHAPTER THIRTY SEVEN

The funeral took place at the local church near where her mother had lived. Mrs Adams had not been a regular attender so Clarissa was surprised at the number of mourners and the genuine warmth which the female vicar injected into the tribute. She was also surprised that both her sons attended and seemed to remember their grandma with great fondness. After the guests had departed after the refreshments, which Clarissa had put on back at her mother's bungalow, the whole family was gathered in the sitting room trying to relax after the inevitable ordeal of recent events. Talk was desultory and rather forced. Jenny was the only one who added a touch of lightness to the occasion by declaring that she was glad grandma had gone off to heaven in a posh car and could anyone tell her what make it was! Jim made himself useful by making a fresh pot of tea and gradually everyone 'relaxed' into themselves, reading, snoozing and flicking through the TV channels. They were interrupted by a ring at the door bell.

"I'll go." Jenny was at the door before most of them had pulled themselves together.

"Oh Amy, hello. What a pity you've missed grandma's funeral. She went off in a lovely car, but it was rather rude of those men to put her in the boot."

Clarissa jumped from the settee to face a smiling Amy, amused by the child's comment.

"What a silly thing to say, Jenny . . ."

"I'm very glad they gave your grandma a nice car, Jenny. They didn't put her in the boot but in a special place for people just like your granny, so don't worry." Amy turned to Clarissa. "I'm so sorry, Mrs Coniscliffe. You must be feeling upset. I hope you don't mind my being here, but I'm on my way to visit mum and dad and it wasn't much of a détour to come here."

Clarissa was speechless. What on earth did that girl think she was doing here, intruding into their family affairs?

"Sit down, Amy," Jim indicated a seat. "Will you have some tea?"

"I'd love some. I'm feeling a bit tired."

Clarissa fumed inwardly. Tired indeed. And we know why! Playing the sympathy card, is she? We'll see about that.

In spite of her tiredness, Amy looked beautiful, her already sensuous appearance enhanced by her pregnancy. The men were all solicitous for her, clearly overwhelmed, not only by the mystery bestowed on her by her race, but far more by her overt femininity which her present condition lent her and which they only partially understood.

"Excuse me please. I'm very tired and I'm going to lie down. You may well have gone, Amy, when I get up, so I'll say goodbye to you." Clarissa walked out of the room.

She must have lain on the bed for over an hour, not sleeping, trying not to hear the rise and fall of the men's voices punctuated by the higher pitched tones of Amy and Jenny. She heard the front door open and close and the sounds of Jenny's chatterings receding down the street, presumably accompanied by Jim and/or Rob. This was bizarre. Tom and Amy were ensconced in her mother's sitting room, doing whatever they were doing and Clarissa was banished to the bedroom. It was quite clear that the girl was a pushy, forward type who had ensnared her son, or why would she intrude into a family where she knew she was not wholly welcome? Another half hour passed and she heard the door open and close again, this time to let out Amy accompanied by Tom who got into his father's car, opened the passenger door for Amy and then swept off in the direction of town.

Clarissa got up and went into the kitchen to make a drink but changed her mind and poured herself a large glass of wine. She went into the sitting room, taking the bottle with her. By the time Jim, Rob and Jenny returned she was a quite a way along the path to being 'well oiled'. Though it was still early evening, Jim could see what lay ahead and decided it was time to remove Jenny from the scene. He cajoled her into agreeing they all needed an early night by promising a series of his very own stories about his childhood, which he embroidered wildly and which Jenny loved. Rob, too decided to make himself scarce, which was the worst thing he could have done, for Clarissa—not realising that Tom had merely taken Amy to the station and had not taken her all the way home—thought that everyone was deliberately going out of their way to avoid her. By the time Tom came back she was ripe for a 'set to'.

"Are you two deliberately going out of your way to make trouble?"

"Please, mother, don't start."

"How dare she show her face here at a time like this? What on earth business is it of hers to present herself here when we're mourning the death of my mother?"

"Some people might consider it a kindness for someone to go out of her way to show concern at such a time."

"Come off it Tom. Can you not see her game? She's wheedling her way in to be sure of you."

"She has no need to wheedle herself in. She *is* sure of me. Just as I'm sure of her."

"Are you indeed! What about the doctor her lot have got lined up for her? When she finds out you can't keep her and her baby, what then?"

"Well it's perfectly clear that we can expect no help from you, so unless we're both fuckin' idiots we must have got some plans on our own. And by the way it's *our* baby."

Jim flung open the sitting room door. "I'm taking Jenny home. She's not listening to this."

"I'm off too." This from Rob who'd heard the raised voices and come into the room. "Surely to God, mum, you can try acting like a grown up—on this of all days."

The front door slammed shut and Jim's car was heard moving off.

"Before I do go, though, mum I've one or two things I'd like to get off my chest. I don't suppose you are aware that I know you spent some time at that sleaze pot near me with lover boy and, no, Tom didn't grass on you. I spotted a car hanging around across the road from me and it didn't take me long to work out whose belongings were scattered about on the back seat. I saw you drive off together on at least two occasions. So point number one: you aren't in any position to dictate the terms of anyone else's relationship till you've sorted out your own sordid little affair. Point number two: How is it that you can ponce about do-gooding to a little black boy—oh yes I saw it all in the local press—and behave like the nastiest kind of racist towards your own son's choice of partner? Doesn't add up does it? Sorry Tom, I should keep my nose out and all that, but there it is. It needed to be said. I'm off now. If you need me, Tom, you know where to find me."

The front door of the modest bungalow was working overtime as it opened and banged shut again.

"I'm staying Mum." Tom looked at his mother. "You're not in a fit state to be left on your own. I'm sorry things have turned out like this on your mother's funeral day. With hindsight, perhaps, Amy shouldn't have come, but hard though it is for you to believe, she meant her visit kindly."

Clarissa crumpled. She sat on the settee, shaking with silent sobs, the tears rolling down her face. Tom sat down beside her but didn't touch her. Eventually he put his hand over hers and said "I understand, mum—everything, even Sam and all that. Looks like we've both got problems."

Clarissa moved her hand to squeeze her son's but said nothing. "Tell you what, ma, why don't I make us a cup of cocoa or something, like you did when we were kids?"

Clarissa loathed the stuff, but she nodded in agreement. Tom went off into the kitchen and Clarissa made an effort to pull herself together. Tom popped his head round the door. "Looks like Gran didn't like cocoa. Will Horlicks do instead?"

"Perfectly."

CHAPTER THIRTY EIGHT

With everything that had gone on over the last few months, Clarissa had hardly noticed the maturing summer. It seemed an age since that never-to-be-forgotten visit to the Hellers' in early summer. Sam was already out in America and was planning to return for a flying visit for the celebration party. Clarissa took up the idea of Jim, Jenny and Gillian going away for a holiday. They understood that she was going to fly back to the States with Sam after the Party. She had vaguely mentioned the party to Jim and said that of course he was welcome, but it would clash with the beginning of their holiday so she assumed he would not be coming.

Nothing more was said on the subject of Tom and Amy, though relations were more cordial and Tom 'phoned her from time to time. She never rang him and had not spoken to Amy since the day of her mother's funeral. She heard nothing from Rob, though Jim was in touch with him. Not that it mattered much now, but she knew Rob would not mention the episode in Birmingham to Jim, or to anyone else for that matter. She had, however, thought long and hard over what Rob had said to her. He had been right, of course, if somewhat 'tabloidish' in the style of his saying, and she was disconcerted to realise how her relations with Sam must seem to an onlooker—though Rob was hardly a detached observer. She contrasted, with shame, her childish and spiteful behaviour with Tom's adult and forgiving manner towards herself. She had two wonderful sons but she doubted how many of their good qualities came from her.

Her mind was in a ferment but a course of action was beginning to suggest itself to her. However until after the party it was something she would simply toy with, as an idea slipping in and out of her consciousness.

Sam rang her from New York three nights before the party and invited her to stay at his flat, with Jim, of course, as he assumed he would be coming.

"No, Jim won't be coming. He's taking Jenny off on a holiday to France. The nanny's going too, to help. So, yes, please, I'd love to accept your invitation."

"Great. And you know I've booked you a return flight to the States with me. That's still OK, isn't it?"

"Of course." They chatted on about Sam's mother, the financial arrangements for the group, how things were with her after her mother's death and other topics they had in common, and ended with each declaring how much they had missed each other over the past months. Neither could wait for the weekend.

And, of course, the rest of the week crawled by, though there was much to do getting Jenny and Jim ready for their French holiday. They were taking a cottage belonging to some friends of Gillian—a situation which did not please Clarissa at all, who would have preferred 'neutral ground' to being beholden to Gillian. She felt disturbed as she bade her daughter goodbye on the Friday morning, not just because she would miss her but because this was the first time she, herself, had not been 'in' on a family holiday. If only one could have one's cake and eat it!

She desperately wanted opportunities to be with Sam but she disliked the idea of another woman (particularly one she suspected her husband 'fancied') sharing the care of her child on a 'family' holiday. She wanted Sam as a lover, indeed more than a lover, but she did not want to lose the benefits—practical and emotional—of being married to Jim. The realisation was dawning on her that a hinterland to a relationship was important, a history of shared experiences, significant and mundane.

Sitting on the early evening train to London, she was seized by nostalgia for the family holidays they used to have, the five of them together. Really, what had she shared with Sam? A number of clandestine 'trysts', a certain amount of glamour and a lot of damned hard work and hassle, all involving deception of her husband and neglect of her child. If she were to have a permanent, full-time relationship with Sam they would acquire their own 'hinterland', with memories of what they were currently going through; they would laugh and cry, be filled with remorse and joy, especially joy that they had found each other. For in spite of what should be considered the sordid details of an affair, Clarissa was convinced that without Sam she would never have become what she now was. He had believed that she had talent, without any tangible evidence of it, and had engendered in her the confidence to use it full time and with seriousness.

Jim had not done that in all their years of marriage, understandably no doubt, with the demands of rearing a family.

She almost worshipped Sam. She thrilled to him and came alive in his presence as she felt she could not do with any other being. He was the soul-mate she sought and the future with him would be complete fulfilment. Was it a crime to seize such an offering as this? For Sam was offering her this gift. But what of the hurt she would cause, the trampling underfoot of her family's needs and emotions? Dear Jim, always ready to accommodate others, always there to pick up the pieces, asking nothing in return but the opportunity to pursue his cranky hobbies and the security of being loved by his wife and children.

In this confused state of mind she reached London, where Sam was waiting at the barrier. They both wanted this evening to be magical and therefore both tried too hard to make it so. Sam laid on a delicious meal whilst Clarissa soaked in his bath, candles, gin and tonic and all. She dressed with extreme care and produced the desired effect. But somehow things didn't add up to the evening of evenings both had anticipated. Sam was full of the States, places he'd visited, people he'd met, whilst Clarissa had nothing to say which did not give away the awful time she'd had with the death of her mother and the deteriorating state of her family's affairs.

Instead of feeling fascinating, she felt domestic and provincial and could offer Sam nothing to parallel his adventures away from herself. Consequently she acted restrainedly and when she tried to contribute something interesting she felt false and brittle. They ended up gossiping in a desultory way about individuals in the group, particularly Leo who it seemed had moved in with Felicity in Dorchester.

"They're going great guns down there. Apparently they're putting on art and film shows for various societies in the area and they occasionally get Guy along and add a musical dimension. If I don't look out, my group is going to desert me just when I've twisted mother's arm to release some cash for us. C'est la vie."

"Nice for Leo, though. I'm very pleased for him."

"Oh and by the way, you'll meet the Hellers tomorrow. They're coming to our little bash."

"Sounds as though this bash isn't going to be so little. What's it going to be like when we're famous?"

"We *are* famous, especially Christian. Did you know he's made the Nationals?"

"Oh great."

"You don't actually sound too enthusiastic. He's your protégé remember!"

"I am, it's just that my sons have mixed feelings on the subject."

"Surely they're pleased for him."

"It's *me* they're not pleased with. To put it bluntly, they think I'm a hypocrite of the first order. Amy and all that."

"You still feel the same way about her? I must say I'm surprised, though of course I can understand how you feel and I don't know her."

"We had reached a bit of a truce, Tom and me, but a splash across the national papers will set it all off again. Rob was very sceptical when it reached the local news in his area."

Clarissa was dismayed that they'd got round to her family affairs which she was sure Sam would find tedious, at the very least, in spite of his assurances to the contrary. Besides, it would bring up long term issues which she didn't want to go into until after her trip to America, at the very earliest. She wanted to do the ostrich thing for as long as possible. She changed the subject: "What do we do now?"

"Bed sounds nice."

"No, darling, I mean with the film."

"We wait for orders, but my guess is that we finish the full script and hope they'll let us in on what they do with it, even to the extent of suggesting actors, locations and so on. There's masses to do but a lot of it can be done at home, now that we're sure that they like our stuff and we know how each other works and all that."

"Of course, I have had other offers," she teased.

"From young Heller, you mean?"

"Mm. Sounds interesting. Must say I'm tempted."

"You won't get the perks you've had with me!"

"Don't you be too sure, Mr Film Director. He might fancy *my* perks."

Clarissa was beginning to loosen up a bit. Sam made a dive for her and before they knew it, they were doing a chase-and-catch game round Sam's sitting room like a couple of silly teenagers. This was the prelude to a night's passion which even the unpropitious start to the evening did nothing to diminish. That she fell asleep eventually, exhausted, did not keep at bay disturbing dreams in which she was the sole mourner at Tom's funeral with Jim and Sam as pall bearers.

CHAPTER THIRTY NINE

"Oh, hi, Francesca."

Their lazy morning in bed was interrupted by the telephone. Sam answered.

That woman, again.

"Oh that's amazing. Thank you so much, my darling. Whatever would I do without you? Just ring if you have any more queries." Sam turned back to Clarissa.

"That was Francesca."

"Yes, I gathered that. The 'amazing' Francesca."

"She certainly is. She's arranging this do tonight. She's lending us their house for the occasion as none of us has a place big enough. I really ought to pop over there and lend a hand."

"Do you really have to? I was hoping we could spend the day together."

"We'll have lots of time on our own in the States. Come over with me. She'll be delighted to see you. We needn't stay long but it shows willing."

It would have been churlish to raise any further objections, so against her will, she agreed. She didn't want to stay in Sam's flat on her own. The memories of the last time weren't too pleasant!

The Mynotts' house in Swiss Cottage was spacious and elegant, set in a beautifully-maintained garden down a side road leading into a little copse. Anthony Mynott was a successful banker, a pleasant fellow, but not quite what Clarissa would have expected in a partner for the graceful Francesca, being on the short side and running to fat. Clarissa and Sam were welcomed effusively and given coffee. Everything seemed to be under perfect control, with no panic in evidence. It was clear that preparations were afoot, with a marquee already erected on the lawn and helpers wafting around arranging this and that, but Francesca was cool and relaxed. "What one can do with money to back one up", thought Clarissa, contrasting her own fraught attempts at entertaining with these effortless activities.

The day was fine and warm so they relaxed outside on the terrace at the back of the house, which looked out over a little valley with a gentle slope on the other side, displaying an array of greens from the palest shades to the densest of dark fir tree hues. Here and there magnificent houses were dotted up the hillside, sufficiently sparsely to give each of them the air of a small country mansion—the word 'idyllic' sprang to mind.

The time went lazily by, with lunch being served and afternoon tea, without Francesca seeming to raise a finger, though she saw to the ordering and acted the hostess to perfection. Clarissa was seething inwardly at the apparent infinity of 'that woman's' accomplishments. She was glad when eventually Sam decided they must fly if they were to get home and back for the party.

"I rather doubt that your concern over helping Francesca was really justified," Clarissa remarked rather sourly on the way back to Sam's. "She had an army of *paid*, I suspect, helpers."

"Lovely day, though, don't you think?"

Clarissa managed to avoid saying anything by pretending she hadn't heard. She was furious that she managed to spoil every experience for herself by emotional turmoil of one sort of another. Francesca really bugged her and always would, she suspected, even if she and Sam became a firm item.

* *

They had left themselves little time to get ready for the party and there was certainly no opportunity to relax together in bed, as Clarissa had hoped. Within no time flat they were speeding back to Swiss Cottage, where they found proceedings fairly well under way. The evenings were drawing in a little at the beginning of August and flares lit the pathway to the house and Marquee, reminiscent of the occasion at the Hellers'.

Most people were gathered in the Marquee. It was to be a very informal affair with little organised in the way of congratulatory speeches, but Sam got up on a small platform improvised for the band and after apologising for his late arrival (which elicited knowing winks, nudges and cat-calls) he thanked a few people—more of which later—especially the Mynotts for organising the evening and lending their lovely home.

The food was lavish, the wine flowing freely, and everything was in place for a superb night's enjoyment. Clarissa found herself taken over by the Hellers, Heinrich with reminders of his Festival choir, Adam urging her to think about his offer. Bella was not there. "Over in Switzerland for a festival. Dad and I are performing next week but we couldn't miss this." Leo joined their group with his usual declarations of astonishment at Clarissa's attractions. "I gather you and Felicity are an item. Haven't you brought her along?"

"Not her scene, my lovely. But she sends her best to you."

The band struck up again after a short interval and, as at the Hellers, Sam had to wait his turn to partner Clarissa on the floor. They were engaged in some smoochy number when Clarissa was aware of a couple deliberately colliding with them. She looked up impatiently from Sam's shoulder where she'd been resting her head, straight into the eyes of Jim, dancing with Gillian!

"What the hell are you doing here?"

"Exactly the same as you, it would seem!"

"But you're in France!"

"Well as you see . . ."

"Where's Jenny, for heavens sake?"

"With mum."

Sam intervened. "Looks like we need to find somewhere to talk. Let me refresh drinks. Good to see you, Jim and . . . . ?"

"Let me introduce Gillian." Sam and Gillian shook hands and Sam led them off into the house where they found a quiet corner to sit down." Clarissa was speechless. Jim, who seemed amused by her dumbfoundedness, began to offer an explanation.

"We wanted to come to see what all the fuss and carry-on has been about. I think we both deserve that, at least."

"Why all this elaborate subterfuge? *I* gave you the invitation for God's sake!"

"I knew you didn't really want me to come and would have found some excuse for me not doing so, so I outmanoeuvred you. And here we are, having a jolly good time, as I perceive you are!"

"So the French holiday was a sham all along?"

"By no means, only deferred for a couple of days." There was a silence, but only Clarissa appeared to be disturbed by it. Jim sat with his arm resting nonchalantly on the back of Gillian's chair and hummed along to the music. Gillian seemed happy to let her eyes take in the elegance of their surroundings. Clarissa was sure that the pair of them were *enjoying* her discomfiture. It seemed an age before Sam arrived with their drinks. He behaved with his customary urbanity, ignoring any tensions there inevitably were in such a mix of people.

"I thought you two, were in France—though it's delightful to see you."

"We were just telling Clarissa that I decided at the last minute that neither Gillian nor I should miss this. But we're off early next week. Congratulations, by the way, on your success with the film. Are we going to be treated to a preview?"

"Later. Francesca's arranged something in one of her palatial rooms. Have you had anything to eat yet?"

It appeared that they had. Sam sat down and looked enquiringly round. "Who's going to start?"

"What do you mean?"

"Well, my dear, I got the decided impression when were interrupted in our dancing that questions needed to be answered, possibly asked."

"Let me kick off then." Jim began the proceedings. "I think we've sorted out the question of our appearance at the feast. But what I'd like to know is how do things stand with you and my wife?"

"Jim, please . . . ."

"You've a right to know, Jim, but I'm not sure that this is the time or place to go into that just now. We wouldn't be able to keep calm and we've the other guests to think of."

"Don't worry, Sam, I'm not going to make a scene but, before Gillian and I go off on holiday, it would help to know. Gillian understands what I'm getting at."

"OK, then. I love Clarissa and I think she is not indifferent to me. Does that answer your question?"

"Perfectly. Come along, Gillian. Let's go and continue our dance." Jim led his partner off.

"Clarissa jumped to her feet. "Take me home, Sam. I can't stay here after this. I'm sure the 'amazing' Francesca will stand in for you."

"I'll try and hurry things along, get my speech over and so on. I don't suppose it matters if I'm not here for the showing. Wait here and I'll go and have a word with Fran."

The diminutive was not lost on Clarissa. Oh God, this jamboree was turning into a nightmare and she was damned if she was going to hang around to its end. She ran out to where the cars were parked. As chance would have it she had the key in her handbag, as Sam had asked her if she would drive them home in case he proved to be incapable. As she drove out of the drive she thought, "Turmoil and flight. That seems to sum up my life pretty accurately."

CHAPTER FORTY

Clarissa had no intention of repeating the last motorway episode and made for Sam's flat where she left the car, collected her belongings, left a note saying she was OK (with apologies for taking the car) and checked into a small hotel she had passed often with Sam.

A gentle alarm woke her early the next morning and a cab was waiting for her outside the main door to take her to the station to catch an early morning train north. She arrived home mid morning, had coffee, got into her own car and went straight to Jim's mother's. Before Moll had time to argue she grabbed hold of Jenny and took her, protesting loudly, back to Normington.

"But, mum," howled Jenny. "dad's picking me up from Gran's, for France."

"I know all about that darling. Don't worry. You're still going to France, but I want you here with me before you go. I'll miss you, you see, so I want to spend today with you, just the two of us."

Whilst Jenny was breakfasting and watching her favourite video, Clarissa rang Maria and, by being economical with the truth, persuaded her to come over in the evening and stay overnight until Jim returned. She then rang Sam and ordered him to contact Jim if he knew where he was staying (which, fortunately, he did) and to tell him to ring home, but in any case to collect Jenny from home *not* from his mother's the next morning.

"And what about you? You're booked on a flight to America this afternoon, or had you forgotten?"

"Cancel it. I'll pay you whatever I owe you. You go."

"I'll cancel too."

"No, emphatically no, Sam. I'm not ill or out of my mind or anything, so you need have no worries on that score. I actually *need* you to go."

"What are you going to do?"

"Think. I've booked myself into a little hotel I know by the sea and I'm going to take some work with me and I'm going to think very long and hard."

"As it happens I really should go. But please let me know where you are. Contact me at the usual. I love you, Clarrie."

"I'll be in touch, Sam. Take care. Sorry about your car. I daresay you managed with 'amazing' contacts!" She heard Sam chuckle at the other end.

The last thing on Clarissa's mind was going on holiday, but she wanted to keep her plans a secret. The rest of the day she spent with Jenny until Maria arrived in the evening.

"Tell Jim, if he doesn't ring, I've gone over to mother's on business—urgent—so I had to go over tonight for an early morning appointment." She went up to see Jenny who was quite happily reading in bed, looking forward to the jaunt to France the next day. "I'll miss you mum, but Gillian's alright and Dad likes her. They don't row 'n stuff." The child's last comment was not lost on Clarissa!

Just as she was about to leave, the 'phone rang. Clarissa insisted that Maria answer it. It was Jim. He didn't seem too convinced by Maria's tale and it was obvious that Maria was getting deeper into hot water, trying to keep up a deception of whose background she had little knowledge.

Eventually Clarissa took over. "I'm not going to the States, Jim. Something's come up to do with mother's house. It's urgent, apparently."

"Well, you're no good with things like that."

"It's time I learned, isn't it? You've got to go to France. Jenny's so looking forward to it. Anyway I could do with time on my own."

"With Him, you mean!"

"No truly. Alone. He's gone to the States."

"It all sounds very fishy to me. But OK. Plan 'A' it is then, but when we get back there's some serious talking to do."

CHAPTER FORTY ONE

Ensconced in her mother's house, Clarissa settled down to some serious thinking. An idea which had suggested itself to her when she sat in the hospital as her mother lay dying began to take more definite shape. Monday morning saw her deep in discussion with a member of staff in one of the estate agents' offices in her mother's local town.

"I'm after a quick sale, or rather a quick buy," Clarissa said. "If that's possible. I'm after a property just outside Normington, where I live. I know it sounds impossible, but I'd like to be in that property inside a fortnight. Is there any way I can do that without my mother's property being sold first to pay for it?"

"It's not usual, but not impossible. We can make arrangements in exceptional circumstances. Who is handling the Normington property?"

"One of your branches."

"That makes it a bit simpler. I'll have a word with your bank, so if you'd kindly give me your details." Clarissa gave him the information he asked for. "Bear with me." (How often Clarissa was to hear that much—used phrase during the following negotiations). He left the room. As she sat 'bearing with' the clearly-aspiring young man, she wondered if indeed, contrary to what she'd told Sam, she *had* taken leave of her senses. She was sure she would not follow the gobbledy-gook she would have thrown at her and would find herself up to her ears in debt, with two properties on her hands. She pulled herself together. She would need all her wits about her if she was to follow the business jargon but, more importantly, if she were to succeed in the plans she had for her future.

Tyrone, as she had been invited to call him, started setting out the steps that were to be taken, at a rate of about a million words a minute. Clarissa interrupted and expressed the desire that he was to regard her as a blithering idiot and to address her in words of one syllable, if they lay within the vocabulary of estate agents.

This did not get the jokey response she'd hoped for. Tyrone regarded her with a mix of superiority, pity and contempt which made Clarissa regret having laid so much emphasis on the 'blithering idiot' bit. She hoped he didn't see her too much as a target—'taking her for a ride'.

He did, however, obligingly slow down and, with painful concentration, Clarissa managed to follow what he was outlining to her. In addition to some jiggery-pokery indulged in by the estate agent and her bank, it seemed her being in possession of a bungalow was to her advantage as they appeared to sell very quickly; Clarissa could rest assured she would be in her cottage in Swaby near Normington within the fortnight.

With the good offices of a small removals firm she took away enough of her mother's furniture and household goods to make her own cottage habitable, while leaving the bungalow still pleasant enough to attract a buyer.

The cottage was near the spot where she had taken Sam. It was set in an elevated position and had superb views over the surrounding countryside towards a range of hills which separated her dale from the next. It was approached by a rough track and seemed from a distance to rise up out of meadowland. Cows and sheep grazed around it and she'd even glimpsed a couple of deer racing gracefully into a thicket at the other side of 'her' field. 'Hill Cottage' was in need of some major attention to turn it into a 'des res', but there was nothing to prevent her from moving in immediately and living there in comfort and safety.

She had a couple of days spare after the move and before Jim et al returned and she turned her attention to the next stage of her script-writing. The fine weather prompted her to take her lap-top out of doors down to the lake where she often took the dog for a walk. At first she was fully engaged with her work, but after a while her thoughts turned to Sam. What an idyll it would be to live here with him. An escape from hectic life in London, where they would spend most of their time. A hideaway where they would recharge their batteries.

But this was not why she had moved from the family home and she returned to the script. She'd reached the point in the narrative where Emma is struggling to keep herself and her child alive. She never failed to be moved by the sheer will and tenacity of this woman. Clarissa did not see such overwhelming struggles ahead for herself, but she realised that Emma had entered her subconscious as a role model for dealing with even such paltry vicissitudes as she was facing. For the rest of the time she had to herself she worked and thought and planned until she was exhausted.

CHAPTER FORTY TWO

Clarissa returned home to find a letter from the Khatiris. Before opening it she realised, to her horror, that she and Jim had not got round to arranging a meeting with them as they requested. She had decided it would be better if Jim saw them without her as she couldn't guarantee that she would stay calm, but she was certain Jim had not done anything about it. The letter was indeed an enquiry as to when they (the Khatiris) might have the pleasure of meeting with them. Clarissa was yet again conscious of the extreme courtesy of Amy's parents and felt ashamed that she and Jim had not had the manners to contact them. The postmark on the enveloped revealed that the letter had been lying in their hall for over a week and she decided to go round there and then to call on them. Mr Khatiri opened the door and indicated to Clarissa to step inside. "So you have heard the news?" he said as he showed her into the sitting room, "and that is why you have come I suppose."

"What news? I'm afraid I have no idea what you are talking about."

Mrs Khatiri was sitting on a low chair and looked very pale and strained. "It will be alright for you now. Your son can be free, but my daughter is finished."

"Look, I don't know what you mean. Has something happened?"

"But why are you here therefore?"

"I've come to apologise for not replying to your invitation for a meeting. We've been very busy, but that's no excuse, I know."

"Your son said he would let you know."

"I've been away and he hasn't my address. My husband is in France so Tom won't have been able to contact us." Clarissa was frantic to know what it was they had to tell her. "Has there been an accident? Is someone ill? For heaven's sake tell me."

"Amy has miscarried. The baby is lost."

On looking back at that moment, Clarissa was not sure what she ought to have felt, given her attitude to the Tom-Amy relationship; relief perhaps? What she did feel was an overwhelming sadness.

"I'm so sorry. How dreadful for them. They were so looking forward to it. Excuse me, I'll have to sit down. I really don't know what to say. Poor kids."

"Aren't you pleased? Surely this solves your problem for you!"

"If you mean that Tom has no obligation to stay with Amy, forget it. If he doesn't stand by her now he's not my son."

"I don't understand. My wife and I thought you would be pleased."

"Aren't *you* pleased? Amy can marry the doctor you've got lined up for her, now."

"No good Muslim man will look at her after this. She has behaved not well."

"Where are Amy and Tom? I thought I saw Amy's car outside. Is she here?"

"There are both here. They are out walking at the minute to give our daughter some fresh air. She is not well."

"Will they be long? May I stay?"

"They will be here soon. Let me offer you tea until that time." Clarissa accepted gratefully.

Once again Clarissa felt she was the only one suffering uneasiness as they waited for the young people to return. The Khatiris, though clearly upset by recent events, made conversation trying to put Clarissa at ease. They asked her about her other children, and responded warmly to word of Jenny, having been told by Amy what an engaging child she was. They showed great interest in her scriptwriting and congratulated her on the acceptance of the film. It seemed Amy had spoken well of the Coniscliffe family and thought Jim 'a fine gentleman'. Their old world courtesy had its effect on Clarissa, though they had no intention of trying to impress. They simply *were* impressive in their simple, polite way.

When the pair did come in, Clarissa was feeling much more relaxed and spontaneously ran to Amy and hugged her. Then she turned to Tom and embraced him. "I'm so sorry, my dears. You won't believe me after all I've said, but I wouldn't have had this happen for the world. But you're young and there'll be other opportunities in the future. So take heart."

Tom stared open-mouthed at his mother. "Mum? Am I hearing things?"

"Yes, my dear boy, but not voices in your head. This is your stupid old mum here, realising what an absolute idiot I've been, bigoted and horrible."

"Not altogether stupid, ma. We've decided to take some of your advice and go on with our studies and defer babies 'til we've qualified."

"But you are going to stay together?"

"Try to stop us."

There was than a welter of embraces all round, with the women weeping and laughing and good old Mr Khatiri shedding the odd tear.

"What a meeting! What a meeting! Let's have some more tea."

Clarissa would have preferred champagne, but anything would have tasted like Nectar of the Gods in such a situation.

CHAPTER FORTY THREE

The trio from France returned home brown and fit. Jenny had never had such a wonderful holiday, she declared, a little to Clarissa's chagrin! It looked as though Gillian would never go, so much there was to relate of their trip. Jim spent a longish time seeing her off—eventually—which made Clarissa more than ever convinced of a more than employer/ employee relationship!

When at last they were alone, Clarissa dropped her bombshell.

"You've done what? Have you gone mad?"

"Never felt saner in my life."

"But how the bloody hell can you afford it? Have you come into a fortune or something, or are you now the proverbial 'kept woman'?"

"Not a fortune exactly, but enough to make it work. And Sam has nothing do with this. He doesn't even know."

"Does that mean you're leaving us?"

"Not in the accepted sense of the word. It all depends on you really."

"On me? That's rich. Who's been doing all the cavorting about?"

"Put your hand on your heart and say you haven't done a bit of cavorting yourself."

"In front of a child? What do you take me for?"

"Not a teeny-weeny, very discreet, little cavort."

Jim grimaced and then grinned lopsidedly. "Well, one very teeny-weeny cavort—very discreet. More a big snog really!"

"Do you love her?"

"I *like* her, very much. But I'm married, Clarrie, in case you'd forgotten!"

"I suppose I had, a bit. Be honest, Jim, what has our marriage become—not just since I met Sam, I mean, but for a year or two?"

"Well, I thought it was alright."

"I'm afraid I didn't. Oh I'm not blaming you, not even myself and goodness knows I did plenty of whingeing. But people just grow out of each other, sometimes."

"And Sam's the right fit for you at present, is he? A spanking pair of new shoes that fit like a glove (if you'll pardon the mixed thingummyjig), whilst I'm a worn out pair of slippers, vaguely comfortable but doing the feet no good at all.

"Something like that. Not a bad simile that—for a . . . . !"

"So when do you propose to embark on this fruitful idyll with your soul-mate? I assume the love nest is for him?"

"That's where you're wrong! Listen, see how this grabs you? I move into Hill Cottage on a part-time basis, taking Jenny with me if she wants to come and I think some gentle persuasion might have to be brought into play here—since you're the full time worker and all that. We still do our parenting job, sharing the caring, going on family holidays and so on."

"Where does lover boy fit in? Remember, I'm not having Jenny on this 'uncle' at weekends lark."

"As far as I'm concerned, Sam—I presume that is to whom you are contemptuously referring—will not be part of the arrangement."

"How you two quarrelled?"

"Occasionally, but not in the way you mean. Most of our tiffs have been because I've refused to commit myself to him permanently or because I've got it into my head that, if she were free, he would marry Francesca—a jealous fantasy born of my insecurity. No, I could become a permanent item with Sam now if I chose, but I don't choose."

"Why ever not?—if that's what you want."

"Because I need to prove to myself that I can make it on my own. Be in charge of whatever destiny awaits me. Sorry if that sounds clichéd. I've had helps all along the way—doting parents, an utterly dependable husband and now a rich lover who will hand me opportunities on a plate. I've never lived in the world the majority of people inhabit. Those scenes in the courtroom with Christian and then with his mother afterwards; the visit to the Young Offenders Institution with all those young men incarcerated for dope and crime; going out to yet more dope and crime because that's all they know in their lives. OK, I know the majority of people don't live like that, but an increasing number do. I've talked social conscience all my life and what do I do when confronted with a real life situation, in my own family for God's sake? Insult the nicest people on earth, denigrate my son's choice of partner and generally reveal myself for the shallow being I am. No, I'm not going out on a crusade, and, no, I can't unlove Sam, but I can face up to the realities in my particular patch and start testing my strengths and my so-called convictions."

"You've 'unloved' me."

I haven't, Jim. But I can't live with you as I did before. Dare I hope that Gillian might come a bit more into your picture?"

"That would be convenient for you wouldn't it? She might. I don't honestly know."

"For heaven's sake don't woo her for my convenience!"

"You're bloody crazy. You know that, don't you? If you turn down Sam's offers of work what are you going to live on?"

"I've had offers from other people. I've applied for a job on the local rag and I'll do part time teaching—if I have to. And I'm going to write seriously, for myself, creatively. And . . . . I'm going to sing!"

"My God!" was all Jim could say.

CHAPTER FORTY FOUR

Clarissa and Sam were walking beside the lake near 'Hillside Cottage'. It was a grey but mellow autumn morning—the kind which forecasters describe as having no weather. She was smiling to herself.

"What's amusing you this day of our Lord Twenty Something and Something?

"Memories. It was the evening of a day such as this about a year ago that I explosively dropped a plate of sandwiches into your life!"

"Ah. The sandwiches. They have much to answer for."

"Can one be beholden to a sandwich? If so I am. 'Clarissa Coniscliffe attributes her new life to a sandwich!'"

"I was led to believe that I had more than a little to do with the new life, or was I horribly mistaken?"

"No, my love, you are not mistaken."

"And now, like the sandwich, I am no longer of any use to you."

"Not true."

"Why are you pushing me away, Clarrie?"

"In addition to everything we've discussed over and over again and still, like Jim, you consider me 'barking', I will not move on this one until Jenny is, at least, at university or the equivalent."

"How can Jim be party to such a set-up?"

"I don't know but he is. And more to the point, Jenny is perfectly contented."

"You can't be sure of that."

"No I can't. But how happy would she be if I decamped with you and left them in the lurch? As for Jim, he's not living the life of a hermit."

"Lucky old Jim. I am!"

"Oh come on now. I couldn't find the hair shirt last night! Seriously though, Sam, I can't hold you to this. I adore you and want you and if you find someone else, I'll be pole-axed. But, for me, that's the way it must be."

Clarissa took his hand and they walked on, Sam rather grim faced.

"By the way," said Clarissa, wanting to lighten the mood a little, "nobody's adequately told me what happened after I left the party. Jim grunts facts at me and ends up with 'nothing much."

"Ah. That doesn't satisfy your sense of the drama of what you imagine *ought* to have happened? Well, Christian arrived . . . . yes . . . . *devastated* not to see you there."

"Yes. I am sorry not to have seen him. But probably it was just as well with my 'clash of cultures' crisis at about that time. How was he?"

"In fine form. Leo organised his trip. Okay-ed it with the powers that be and so on. He's taking qualifying exams to go to Art College."

"I must get in touch with him."

"You could come on to see me."

"We'll see. What else happened—you know after my hasty exit?"

"We all went frantic looking for my car—and you of course—we phoned everywhere we could think of. We even thought of sending Christian after you, but he'd sold his van!"

"Oh come on, stop taking the . . . . you know I can't say that word!" How'm I going to make it as a writer without four-letter words?"

"Write for children!"

"Want to bet?"

"To cut a long story short, Jim went off with Gillian to their pad and I 'dossed down' at Francesca's in a luxurious four-poster bed."

"I knew she would come to the rescue"

"Yes, she's a Real Marvel, in fact 'amazing'. She ferried me home the next morning and the rest, as they say, is history!"

"Didn't anyone else ask for me?"

"No-one else was aware that you'd gone. Bacchus was well and truly on the throne that night!"

By the time they'd walked round the lake and sat chatting, it was drawing on towards lunchtime. They started back towards the cottage. Sunshine was appearing spasmodically through the breaking clouds and highlighting the already-turning leaves on the trees lining the far shore. The odd intrepid rabbit scurried across their path and the bird population of the area went about its business, well-used to the quiet habitat.

"I must say, Clarrie, you've chosen a wonderful spot for your new life. I could live here. No, my dear, I know that's not possible. But, at least, let me put some work your way. I want you to think of you scripting for us in this lovely old house on the hill."

"How can I refuse? I haven't gone completely barmy."

"I won't come in. Things to do and all that." Sam started to walk away when he stopped abruptly, put his hand in his pocket and pulled out a tiny parcel.

"Hey, I forgot to give you this. I'd lose my head if it were loose." He put it into her hand with a squeeze.

Clarissa opened the tiny box which revealed a little silver and sapphire broach with its clasp missing.

"Felicity sent you this with her love? She's sorry about the missing fastener. She's having one made. I'll get it from Leo. I'll hang on to it for you." He got into his car and drove down the rough track.

Clarissa went indoors, held the brooch to her heart and sobbed. After a while she dried her eyes, walked into her tiny study, which was catching the late morning sun, and opened an official-looking envelope.

The local rag had taken on a new member of staff.

WILL'S STORY (AS TOLD TO SAM)

I lived 'ere wi' me dad after me mam died. Us kept body 'n zoul together doin' this 'n that, mainly 'urdlin' and a bit of woodsman work. Us didn't make a fortin' but the 'urdlin' made a fair bit from the gentry who 'ave the land but don't know stick fro' stamote when it comes to managin' anythin'. Anyways I were a bit of a lad in those days and used to go to the odd 'op in one or t'other of the villages and that's where I met Emma. At Piddle 'op. 'Er were a com'ly zort of girl, I suppose—zome called 'er beaut'ful—but 'ansome is as 'ansome does and 'er behaviour ter me were anything but 'ansom, as yer'll zee. We did court fer 'bout four month or zo and then us were wed.

Mi dad let us stay wi' 'im 'ere for a while and then we did rent a little cottage over by Stinsford way. Us were quite 'appy and then her took to goin' to church in a big way. That Stinsford 'un you've no doubt 'eard of. Us'd been married a year and no childer on the way, which were a zadness for us both—specially 'er. I thought 'er were too impatient and that things would 'appen in time. 'Owever 'er got to arrangin' the flowers every Zat'day a'ternoon for the Zunday zervices, and I 'ave to admit 'er 'ad a rare talent for 'un. 'Er'd gather the most draggly lookin' zpecimens from the meadows and turn 'em into a work of art. 'Er loved the work. T'was about 'er only respite from the domestic. I used to call for 'er some Zat'days arter she'd afinished and we'd go on to Dorchester for the market and after mebbee to a 'op.

One Zat'day I went to pick 'er up as cutom'ry and I finds 'er deep in conversation wi' two fellahs—well, gentlemen, from their fine dress and zpeakin'. One were gettin' on in years but t'other were a 'andsome 'arry and I could see that Emma were very taken wi' 'im.

I weren't very 'appy and I made that right clear to all concerned. I asked 'er 'ow long this'd bin goin' on, but 'er 'edged about and zaid 'er didn't know what I were talkin' about.

To cut a long ztory short 'er ran off wi' this young fellah. She had 'is child and lived wi' 'im for about eighteen month—wanted for nothin', it zeems. They was often seen in the comp'ny of the older man—a very 'appy quartet, it zeems. The young fellah was an up-'n-comin' architect, studyin' church architecture and stone masonin'. The older one were a writer, but 'ad bin a stonemason in 'is young days, so was helpin' the young 'un a bit. I used to go over on a Zat'day just as usual and 'ang about to watch 'em. I 'ave to say 'er looked bloomin' and 'appy and the pair on 'em seemed very luvvy duvvy. I were upset as yer might zay and jealous as 'ell. But I just 'ad ter get on wi' me life as best I could. I'd moved back 'ere to look after me dad who was ailin' and, just after e'd passed away, I were zitting' ere on a bleak a'ternoon—misty an' all that—when a timid knock came ter the door. 'Twere the dog that heer'd it. I opened up and there were Emma standin' outside lookin' like a ghost. 'Er clothes was plain, but good as yer might say and a held 'er babby to 'er breast. The child were warmly wrapped in a rich shawl and later, on close viewin', were rare and 'ealthy. 'Er ('twere a maidie) 'ad bin well looked after. I thought first to shut the door on 'em, but the mother looked so pitiful I nodded to 'er to come in. I zat 'er down by the fire and brought a tot o'zummat ter bring life back into 'er.

We didn't speak for nigh on 'alf'n hour and then 'er whispered "Zorry". I weren't goin' ter be taken in that easily, but I listened to 'er tale of woe. Evidently 'er man were climbin' high up the ladder and was goin' round grandcircles and Emma were a 'inderance to 'im. 'Er were clever enough, but lacked polish and o' course bein' married were the real big problem. The scandal of a divorce were out o' the question. 'Er were a fall'n woman! 'Ee loved 'er apparently but wanted 'er on the zide, as folks do say. The old fellah suggested 'er lover zetting' 'er up somewhere out o' the way and takin' care of 'er, visitin' 'er when it zooted 'im like. 'Er weren't 'avin' that. Nor livin' with the old 'un as a high class servant—even for the zake of 'er little maid. That a'ternoon I'm a speakin' of, 'er went down on 'er knees and begged me to take 'er back as a servant. That zooted me. I needed some help wi' the 'ouse and me work and I reckoned 'er owed it me. So 'er moved back in wi' the child. There were gossip o' course, but it don't reach us out 'ere so I didn't take no 'eed. 'Er took the little room up in the loft, wi' the maidie and worked for me in 'change for bed 'n board (but not *my* bed I 'asten ter say). When the child were about two year old and beginnin' to get a 'old on me 'eart 'er zudd'nly up an' went. I never zaw 'er again—not alive, that is . . . .

EMMA'S STORY (FROM LETTERS AND DOCUMENTS)

Life with Will was not easy from the start. We lived with his father at first and I think he tried to please his dad rather than me. He was dominated by the old man—seemed frightened of him and his fits of temper. I pleaded with Will to find another place for us, which he eventually did after I'd threatened to run away. Life however grew worse as Will, released from his father's domination, grew dominating himself and just as moody and ill tempered. He didn't actually hit me but he was cruel and used me badly in all ways. I would have liked a child but took steps not to conceive, as I didn't want to bring a baby into such a household as ours. I loved Will, particularly at the start. He was good looking and very skilled at whatever he undertook and I coped with his funny ways as best I could to keep the peace. I was helped by going to church and getting involved with things there. I enjoyed doing the flowers of a Saturday afternoon. I used to take some paper and coloured pencils and sketch the plants before I picked them and afterwards when I'd arranged them. Will was impressed by my artistic abilities, as he called them, but I sensed he wasn't altogether easy either and didn't like me looking at them, as I sometimes did in the evenings if I had an hour spare. He grew very jealous of me talking to two gentlemen who used to come to sketch in the church. They'd seen me sketching and fiddling about and showed an interest in what I was doing and gave me some hints on how to achieve certain effects. I'd never had anyone show any interest in my talents since I left school to look after my mother, who died shortly after, so I was flattered by their attentions.

One Saturday the younger man came alone and asked if he could go with me when I went to gather my flowers and help me with my drawing. I have to confess that I thought rather too much about Justin than I should—that is, I often couldn't sleep for thinking about him, but I kept as calm as I could and regarded myself as a very privileged pupil and nothing else. Nothing improper passed between us on that occasion, but it soon became apparent that we were attracted to each other and it was difficult for me to keep his attentions at arm's length. At last the inevitable happened and I found I was with child. I didn't know what to do. I couldn't stay with Will and try to pass the child off as his, and if it hadn't been for the exceptional kindness of Mr Hardy (Justin's friend) who offered me work and a home with him, I would have ended up in the workhouse.

My duties were light with Mr Hardy. I was lady's maid to his wife, who saw to it that, as my confinement approached, I was not over-stretched at all. I joined the family in the evenings and Justin used to come round to join in our social gatherings and tutor me with my drawing and painting. Sometimes, I have to admit, he stayed longer than he should, but the master and mistress made no objections and left us to ourselves when they retired to bed. I wrote to Will and told him everything. I didn't expect a reply and I didn't get one, except that after the baby was born a mysterious envelope was pushed through the letterbox containing an exquisite silver and sapphire brooch, which I seemed to recognise. I thought I must have seen it on the dress of a friend of Mrs Hardy and, what with all there was to do after the birth, I forgot about it. Justin adored the child and was a very good father, as far as his commitments would allow. Mr Hardy set aside two rooms for us to use as our quarters and for much of those early months with the child we were very happy. Apart from Justin's necessary visits to the outside world we lived a separate existence, in a fantasy world of our own. Mr Hardy was determined to protect us from scandal and gossip, as far as he could. That's why he let us stay at his house and he hoped he could pass me off as some as some poor relation who had taken the fancy of Mr Justin Powers. For six months we played at happy families. I never looked to the future though I knew things would have to change. I shut out of my mind dark thoughts about the months and years ahead. We walked the child in the rambling garden in the afternoons and played and talked and relaxed together in the evenings. My baby was very little trouble. She was a happy child and, apart from feeds, did not disturb our nights. Those months were the happiest of my whole life.

It didn't last. Justin's visits suddenly became very erratic. He excused himself on the grounds of working for his final examinations. Mr Hardy told me as gently as he could that Justin needed to attend social gatherings to make good contacts for his future career and that I could expect to see much less of him in the future. I knew for certain that a future with Justin was out of the question when a grand young lady came to dinner one evening. I wasn't invited but was asked to attend on the ladies after supper. On this occasion I was not introduced to Miss Charlotte Swainton, as I always had been to guests. I was expected to pour the tea and coffee and hand round the sweetmeats and when the gentlemen joined the ladies I was politely but firmly told to retire. After all the guests had gone, Justin came to our quarters and let himself into what served as our bedroom. He would have proceeded as usual but I drew away from him. I answered his questioning look by telling him I realised he had just entertained the woman he intended to marry and, that being so, I would not allow him to use me as a wife. He did not contradict me but said that his marriage to Cara (his pet name for her) would make no difference to 'us'. He would set me and the child up in a small property he owned near Lulworth and would maintain us and visit us as often as he could. In other words I would be a 'kept woman'. I could not believe that the man I had come to love, who had fathered my child, could contemplate marriage, knowingly deceiving his future wife from the start. I said no more but refused any further embraces and bade him goodnight. I spent a sleepless night, worrying about what I could do. I would have to leave Mr Hardy's house—though he would try to detain me. Where could I go? How could I support myself and my child? Who would employ a fallen woman with a young child?

Eventually I fell into a troubled sleep full of feverish dreams, in one of which the sapphire brooch cropped up. Try as I would I could not put a face to the owner of this ornament. I woke up in a panic believing myself to have stolen the trinket. As I was feeding my baby and still anxiously trying to work out our future, it suddenly came to me where I had seen the brooch. Will had a photograph of his grandmother which he prized and which took pride of place on the dressing table in our bedroom. He had had it tinted and the brooch stood out in beautiful shades of blue and silver. Will must have put the envelope through the door. But why? It must mean that all was not enmity between us. I couldn't believe Will capable of generosity such as this, but having no other plans formulated, I decided to throw myself on his mercy—for the child's sake. I would wait until the Hardys took their afternoon walk and would slip off with my baby and beg Will to take me on as a servant, a drudge—anything to keep body and soul together.

It was getting dark on a bleak miserable afternoon, when we arrived at Will's and knocked on the door. He was astonished to see us, but let us in and gave me food and drink and discreetly left me alone to feed the baby. He didn't ask for details and I did not try to supply them. I had wronged him and it was no use trying to excuse myself. He agreed to take me on, but made it clear that no marital relations were to be established (much to my relief) and I could expect no privileges. I could use the space in the loft. He would keep us and I would act as his housekeeper and in any other capacity he found useful. These arrangements suited me well and if he had stuck to them life could have been tolerable

* *

For the first month or so all went well. I cleaned up his house, which he had allowed to fall into a disgraceful state, cooked his meals, mended his clothes and did all he demanded of me and more. The child flourished, spending a great deal of time in the open air, in spite of the cold, grey weather. I tried as hard as I could to stifle the feelings of rejection and disappointment I'd suffered at the hands of Justin, but I could not rid myself of the heavy stone I carried at my heart's core. Sometimes I gave vent to weeping when I thought myself alone. It was after such a bout of weeping that things grew worse. Will had come in on me suddenly. His face took on an ugly dark expression as he warned me to forget 'that' 'un' and concentrate on my work. I was to remember who was my 'saviour', as he put it.

As the spring advanced he decided he needed help outside with his hurdling. It was just at the time when my child was growing more demanding. She was trying to walk and hung onto me to aid her. Will had shown no overt interest in her, but now and again I caught him glancing at her with something resembling friendly interest. It must have been painful for him. We had not produced a child of our own, but as soon as I was with another man one comes along. He must have considered his manhood slighted. Hurdling was a strenuous job for a strong man, let alone a woman not a year past childbirth and with the Hardys I had become unused to hard work. Out of spite he used to drag me around with my child strapped to my back searching out coppices of hazel to source his work.

Without a morsel to eat or drink he made me set down the child in a pen whilst I cut down the branches, peeled them and split them ready to be used later on. Then we would break for about twenty minutes in which I had to feed and change my child, leaving only seconds for me to grab a morsel myself. I then had to trudge home to begin the actual weaving of the season's rods, which was hard on the back and rough on the hands. He kept me busy until sunset with only the shortest of breaks to make my child comfortable. Some days the child was fractious and I worked with her wailing in my ears and my heart heavy with anxiety for her. It was my job to prepare the evening meal and carry on with all the customary domestic duties. I put my child to bed but often she was too lively to settle down straight away, having been in the pen all day. I tried to play with her and stimulate her as best I could, but often I was asleep before she was, exhausted with the backbreaking labour of the day. One night I caught sight of myself in the cracked mirror and started at the sight of a stranger in the room—myself—haggard, gaunt and prematurely grey at twenty eight. How I survived those months I do not know.

The winter brought a change of occupation but no let up in hard work. I fed the livestock, chopped the logs, stoked the fires and tended my child (a delight, but ever increasing in liveliness). All this I just about bore, but one night I heard Will struggling to put his key in the lock. This was not unusual, as he was increasingly a longstaying customer at some inn or other. Always I was either asleep or feigned sleep and he never bothered me. But this night I was awake and heard him make a stumbling assault on the ladder leading to the loft. I tried to prevent him, but was afraid to push him too hard in case he fell and injured himself. He sprawled into the attic and with the most abusive curses tried to pin me down on the sacking and pallet which served as my bed. The noise woke the child who started to cry out in fear. I fought him off, caring little for his injuries now. I managed to fling him down the ladder and barricaded the entrance with whatever came to hand, mainly my so-called bed. For all I knew I could have killed him, but I had no intention of trying to find out. I stayed awake all night and then I heard faint stirrings below. I was determined to stay where I was and do nothing he might demand of me. When he went out I would gather what few things belonged to us and escape.

After a great deal of cursing and shouting up to me, Will eventually went out. It wasn't his way to ill treat me in the way I have just described. He had become dependant on drink as his means of escape from the sadness of his life and this had changed him for the worse. No doubt I could have stayed and smoothed things out between us but I could not live with him as his wife. This would mean more scenes such as the one last night and I would not risk my child being caught up in the fighting between us. I left before feeding the child which, as she was still at the breast, I could do on our way and supplement her needs from a farm or small shop we might pass on our way. With my belongings tied up in a bundle in one hand and the child bound to my back, I set off towards Dorchester, where I thought I would be far enough away from Will and where there was more chance of getting some kind of domestic work.

Because I had set off so late in the day there was little chance of reaching Dorchester before nightfall, burdened as I was. I kept off the main road in case I was spotted and word got to Will. He would want me back as I had become indispensable to him and I felt he had become almost attached to my child. Had I known that day what unbearable times lay ahead for us I would have turned back. But in the midday sun my spirits rose and a sense of self worth, which for so long had been smothered, rose in me and I was determined that no man, Will or Justin, would have power over me. I think that day was the happiest of my life. This was the first opportunity for months I had time for my little girl, Felicity. The grass was dry and firm so I took her down from my back and, after a short rest, let her toddle along at my side—very haltingly as she had only just taken her first steps. I sang to her and played the games of young children. She chuckled and gurgled and I vowed that if it lay in my power she would break free from the shackles that bound women and would learn independence from men. I would see to it that she received the education only meted out to boys at this time and she would be free to earn money that would save her from the powerlessness of women such as myself.

We whiled the afternoon away in walking, chattering and laughing until I became aware that the sun was fading and we had no shelter for the night. I kept a look out for anything that would serve as a shelter and some benevolent spirit must have been watching over us, for soon we came across a substantial barn with plenty of fresh hay and I made us comfortable for the night. The next morning I went up to the farmhouse back entrance to enquire if they were in need of any extra hands about the place. It was an impressive building with mullioned windows and tall chimneys. There clearly was no shortage of money and there was a chance that extra help might be useful and well within their means. A pleasant-faced middle-aged woman answered the door. She smiled at Felicity and answered my enquiry politely. She would see the mistress and let me know. Meanwhile I could take a seat in the kitchen. She gave me a cup of tea freshly made and a biscuit for my child and indicated that if the child needed to be fed she would give us time and space. After the treatment I'd received over the past few months I almost wept at this unexpected kindness. She returned after about twenty minutes and said that I needn't hurry, but the mistress would see me as soon as I was ready. She led us through a warren of corridors and up the back stairs to the main part of the house, which was genteely though rather shabbily furnished, as though the place had seen better days. I was shown into a small, cosy chamber which clearly acted as a lady's boudoir and I was introduced to the lady herself. She couldn't have been more than my own age, if as old. She was very pretty in a refined and sensible way and stretched out her hand to me in welcome.

"You could be just the person I'm looking for. Please sit down. Mrs Corwin, would you take the little child, while we discuss things?"

Mrs Corwin had a way with young children and Felicity allowed herself to be carried away without a murmur.

"I'm looking for a woman to organise my household and do a few household chores. My Mrs Corwin needs some extra help as she's really the cook and is overworked at present. I'm mainly occupied with the farm and am mostly out of doors. You may wonder why I am prepared to hire you without knowing any thing about you. Again I refer to my Mrs Corwin who is adept at summing people up quickly and accurately. Now tell me before I ask you if you are willing to work here, what can you offer me?"

Whilst summarising my skills and experience to Miss Winston I inwardly wondered at the polite and friendly manner of both women. People of my station in life more usually met with condescension, if not downright rudeness. Miss Winston was not in the least perturbed by my reluctance to produce references, but seemed satisfied with the enigmatic suggestion that I had encountered difficulties not altogether of my own making. In short, I became the housekeeper for Miss Ursula Winston.

* *

It was out of the ordinary run of things that a woman, and a young one at that, should own and manage a large farm. Most of the staff were used to the idea and worked well for her, though there were one or two of the menfolk who muttered and tried to best her. But she usually came out on top in any confrontation, with an astuteness beyond her years and a skilful use of her feminine charms. Speaking of which, she was not without suitors, most of whom she held at arm's length. All of this provided many evening hours of gossip for we servants as the summer months passed by and we sat out in the orchard after our work was done. As housekeeper I kept apart somewhat, but I couldn't help overhearing the giggling remarks of the maids as they speculated on who would come courting the missus next. I was very contented with my position and Felicity benefited from the attention of a doting group, while I was given a little freedom for myself. I sometimes took out my sketch pad into the fields around and couldn't help thinking of the day when I first met Justin and those happy evenings when he coached me in drawing and painting. Miss Winston often used to take Felicity for an hour or two when she could spare the time or when the child could go with her out into the fields without interfering with the work in hand. My youth gradually returned and my figure filled out. I was aware of admiring glances from the male hands but I wasn't interested. After Justin, their coarse advances repelled me. All I was concerned about was the wellbeing of the child, earning my keep in the best way I could for my kind and trusting mistress. If only life could have gone on like this, but I seemed dogged by ill fortune.

I wrote earlier of my mistress' suitors. She held the occasional dinner party for the local gentry and, whilst some handsome young beaux were always in attendance, no particular one had been singled out for her especial attention. I was returning from a walk with Felicity late one afternoon. A young gentleman on horseback passed us in the driveway. I stepped into the side and glanced up. I nearly fainted to recognise Justin and, though I couldn't be sure he recognised me, he looked straight at me. He did not stop and I hurried up to my room and prepared the child for bed. As I tended to her my mind was in confusion. He could only be in the region for one purpose—to see Miss Winston. Reason deserted me. I did not think, as I perhaps should have, that he had been here on business. As a landowner he could be seeing my mistress on quite legitimate grounds, but I decided that Justin had not recognised me and I quieted myself that

I was safe as long as he wasn't a frequent visitor. I persuaded myself that he was visiting my mistress as a fellow landowner, no more. But one evening, serving at table at one of her soirees, I was disconcerted to see him as one of her guests. His wife was not with him and he seemed to be making free with my mistress in a flirtatious manner. I was serving a guest seated straight opposite Justin and, once again, he looked directly at me without appearing to recognise me.

Life flowed on pleasantly for a few more weeks without incident. Whatever my mistress was engaged in with Justin was her affair and, though I was anxious for her, I decided it was not my business to say anything. I wanted the details of my past life to be known to as few people as possible.

I was sitting sewing in my room one summer's afternoon. Felicity was out with Miss Winston when there was a knock at my door. Thinking it would be one of the maids I bade the visitor come in. To my utter consternation, Justin stepped in ordering me not to call out as I most assuredly would have done, I was so taken by surprise.

"Mistress is out," was my first greeting.

"It's not your mistress I've come to see."

"Well, let me direct you to whoever it is you've come to see."

"Don't be silly, Emma. You know very well whom I've come to see. It's you I want, I've missed you." And he made to take me into his arms.

"Please don't touch me. I have a place here and I don't want to lose it through philandering."

"How can you call it 'philandering' after what you and I have known? And the child? As her father I have a right to see her."

"You have no rights at all over the child or me. Go to your wife and possibly, her child by now and do right by them."

"There is no child. Oh come on, Emma. My wife is merely a convenience. You were and are the one I adore." And he lunged at me again.

"Justin, if you don't go this minute, I'll make such a racket that the whole household will come running and where will your precious name be then."

"Who will take notice of a servant? I'll simply say that you flirted with me outrageously the other evening and I've come to remonstrate with you."

"Look, Justin. You have ruined my life once by taking advantage of me and I've somehow managed to piece the ruins together. I'm happy here. My child is well cared for and the only right you have over us is to leave us in peace. I beg you to."

"Emma, think of your child. Let me set you up with her, as I planned to do before you ran off. Her future will be safe as an educated, refined young lady. What can you do for her on your own?"

I covered my ears. The advantages for my child were tempting, but he was not to be trusted. No doubt his wife was living comfortably on his money, but she did not command his heart. I knew that a future based on deceit would not turn out well and knowing him now as a scoundrel had killed any affection I once had for him.

"I must go now Emma, but I'll be back for your answer. Think well about it. I'm offering you a life of comfort and prospects for *our* child. Don't choose hardship and penury."

After he'd gone I knew that, once again, I would have to escape. It would break my heart to leave this friendly, happy farm but I had to get out of Justin's clutches. I would leave a note for my mistress for she would try to prevent me from going if I told her face to face. I intended to go this very night.

Felicity came skipping into the room full of the excitements of the afternoon. She was so happy here, thriving on the love of everyone around her. My heart was heavy at the thought of dragging her away from all this into a future of uncertainty, but I could see no other feasible option. When the child was in bed and asleep, I put all our things together into the same bundle I'd brought to this house. When all was quiet for the night, I crept along to the mistress' room and left a note outside her door. I woke up Felicity and calmed her by telling her we were going on an expedition to see the owls and set off once again in flight.

Fortunately the night was mild and, when we were a safe distance from Miss Winston, I found a tumbledown outhouse where we stopped for a rest. I had pointed out several owls to the child, who at first, was excited at the nocturnal expedition, but as the night wore on became exhausted and fractious. I laid her down on a pile of old hay in a corner where she immediately fell asleep. Although physically fatigued I would not allow myself to sleep for I needed to protect the child and had to work out a plan for the next day at least. With the money I'd saved from the wage the mistress had insisted I take we could survive for a short while, but I had to find work and lodgings. I had heard that there was work to be found in Poole and there I would be well out of reach of Justin (and Will). I knew that a carrier's van left from the White Hart in Dorchester sometime in the afternoon. I would take that as far as Poole and try my luck there. I spent the rest of the night thinking about what I had rejected. Had I acted too hastily? Was I selfishly depriving Felicity of a secure future? Should I not have explained everything to Mistress and asked her to look after the child until I had secured a home for us? But I couldn't bear to be parted from my daughter. I was even more determined to do all in my power to provide the best for the child, whatever it took, without resorting to Justin's dubious charity.

****

As soon as it was light, I picked up Felicity and walked on to Dorchester. We skulked around in back streets for I did not wish to be seen and recognised. I bought some bread and milk for the child and a drink for myself. The hours dragged by. I fancied I saw people I knew and shrank back into the shadows, shushing the child. Just before three, we went to the White Hart. The carrier was just dropping his passengers from the neighbouring villages and within a few minutes we were on board. Felicity was excited with this new adventure and as we rode along she pointed out everything that caught her attention. The journey was a long one with many stops at intervening villages and long before we reached Poole, Felicity dropped off to sleep. I nodded too, in spite of striving to keep awake. At about nine o'clock the cart pulled up outside the Coaching Inn in Poole. I managed to secure a room at a small lodging house I'd been told about at the inn yard.

I trailed round the whole of the next day looking for work to no avail. The towns-folk were not as sympathetic to the idea of a woman with a child as a prospective employee as the country people would have been and we trudged back to the lodging house for a second night. The landlady was a hard-faced woman but she must have had a soft spot somewhere for she advised me of jobs going at the 'Nets' the local term for an establishment which produced all manner of tackle for the commercial fishing boats which anchored in the large harbour. She offered to look after Felicity (for a small fee) until I'd sorted myself out and I went to sleep that night with a little less anxiety. Felicity was not pleased to be left and I hated leaving her, even for a day, but I tore myself away and presented myself at the Nets. I did not mention my child and I was hired. The wage was a pittance and the conditions of hire were stringent. The hours were long and the work backbreaking and tedious, so that by the time I got 'home' at night, I was utterly exhausted. To make things worse, that summer was hot and conditions at the 'Nets' resembled those of a slave sweatshop.

Felicity's behaviour was deteriorating, too, with the constraints of being kept indoors more or less all day. She had been used to running free at the farm and she constantly asked why we could not go back there.

One stifling night, on my way back home, I called into a tavern to buy a cool drink to enable me to crawl back to the lodging house. As I sat in a semi stupor over my ginger beer, I was conscious of the chatter of a group of young women sitting at the next table. They were common working girls, judging by their language, but they were quite well dressed. They were confident, loud and worldly-wise.

"Sh! Keep yer voice down, Betsy, else we'll be in trouble."

"Well, I tell 'ee, some these fellahs'll pay anything to satisfy their 'needs' as they call 'em."

"Where's your patch then?"

"Ah that's my secret, in'it? But it sees me alright."

"Are you on tonight then?"

"You bet I am. In fact I'm off right now to get some shuteye before my shift, as you might say."

She went amidst much giggling, winking and nudging amongst those left behind. I knew exactly what they were talking about and my first, instinctive reaction was one of revulsion, but later that night, tossing in bed in my airless room, aching from my labour, my mind strayed back to the women's conversation. I desperately wanted a good life for Felicity and for that I needed money. I would never get anywhere at the 'Nets' except an early death. After all I *was* a fallen woman, so morally I had nothing to lose. I had already been a kept woman, so how much lower could I fall?

The next night, I called in at the same tavern and contrived a conversation with the women who were there again.

"You mean that's all you get for all that work? You're a fool, gel. A good lookin' woman like you. Get on the game!"

"And how do I do that?"

"'Ere, luvvie. Go and see this woman". She handed me a piece of paper with a name and address on it.

To cut a long story short, I 'got on the game'. I told my landlady that I was working nights, and if she suspected anything she kept it to herself.

In fact the hours suited me much better. I was at home all day to see to Felicity. We went out and about and went down to the harbour every day. I reined in her wild behaviour, taught her to read and write and her aptitude convinced me that efforts on my part to get her educated would not go unrewarded. My present occupation, though repellent, was not without its compensations. I attracted a 'respectable' clientele and within a year was able to take a set of rooms in a better part of town. I decided to take up drawing again and after my expenses and putting money away for Felicity, I had money left to attend a Saturday morning Art class. Felicity was looked after by one of my 'friends'. It took me two years to gain a diploma in Drawing and Fine Art which enabled me to set up a class of my own. I was asked to do some modelling for the Saturday morning class so that we were able to live quite comfortably, if frugally, on my accumulated income. My greatest wish was for my child to win a place at the school for young ladies in the town, when she was old enough.

* *

Eventually, as the years went by, I was able to give up the job which I hated. As Felicity got older I was afraid of her finding out my secret business so, though I could have done with the extra money, I decided to turn my back on this lucrative but shameful activity. Whilst deploring prostitution I cannot speak too highly of some of the friends I made among those of us who plied the oldest trade in the world. Some were in the same position as myself, working to support dependants of one sort or another—mother, child or even a disabled husband. They were among the most generous hearted individuals I'd met and could be relied on to help in difficult times. I was employed by the local College of Art to tutor only the first year students, as my qualification was not good enough for the higher levels. I was encouraged to enter my own work in various exhibitions and even managed to sell some of my pictures and sketches, which were mainly of the scenes around Poole, the areas around Dorchester, and portraits of Felicity. These latter led to others wanting portraits of their family and I became quite well known locally (under an assumed name, for obvious reasons) as a portrait painter. With Felicity's future education in mind, I hired a tutor once a week to refine the teaching she was receiving at the local area school, but I needed another source of income to provide all she would need at the girls' High School where I intended to enter her for a scholarship.

This source of money came to me in an extraordinary way. I received a letter in the post one morning from Mr Hardy's wife asking me to meet her for tea at the Grand Hotel and she named a day and time. I was astounded and somewhat apprehensive for I could not fathom how she had come by my address. Did this mean that Justin also knew where I was and would come pestering me again? However I no longer feared him as I once might have done, for being in a small way a woman of financial independence, he would not dominate me and I had acquired a new degree of confidence. So I agreed to keep the rendezvous with Mrs Hardy, leaving Felicity in the care of a friend.

Over tea, Mrs Hardy revealed that she had been to an art exhibition in the town and had taken the catalogue home to show Thomas.

He had poured over the catalogue all evening, though it was a slight affair. Eventually he held it open at a page with the portrait of a child and pushed it over to me. "Does she remind you of anybody?"

I scrutinised it for a few minutes and said that I thought that she did, but I couldn't think who.

"Emma! Don't you think?"

"Could she possibly be Emma's daughter?"

"We remembered your drawing and so on," explained Mrs Hardy "and decided it could be possible that somehow or another you were now an artist. We enquired about the portrait's artist (because of course you don't use your real name) and found out your whereabouts. Thomas wouldn't rest until I contacted you. You've no idea how he fretted when you left us. He particularly missed your little girl. As you know his regret was not having children."

I explained that I had little choice, but was sorry to have caused him such distress. She calmed my anxiety and went on "Thomas wants to know how you are and how you are supporting yourself and your child and I must admit I'm curious too, my dear."

I told her as much as I thought she could take at this stage, without deliberately trying to deceive her. She would gather that although Felicity and I were well and comfortable now, we had been through hard times. "We both want to help you in the most appropriate way we can. Please take this as a small gift." And she handed me an envelope. "Thomas would like to see you again and if we can fix on a time we can send our pony and trap for you."

"I would like that, but I must make sure there will be no danger of meeting Justin."

"Ah, yes. Justin. That was a very sad business. He was a promising young man but his marriage is not happy and he seeks solace away from home. His business is not flourishing and altogether he seems to be going from bad to worse. We do not see him. You are in no danger there."

"Are there any children?"

"No. Perhaps that is the trouble. Whether a child would keep Justin at home is open to question. I suppose you've seen nothing of him since you left?"

"Once only, when, I hope, I sent him out of my life forever." Mrs Hardy did not enquire further and we parted affectionately. With Mr Hardy's help I was able to see my daughter succeed at the High School and win a scholarship to the Slade School of Art in London.

I am approaching my fortieth birthday and my health is beginning to decline. The effort of writing this is almost beyond me but I am helped by my now good friend, Miss Winston The doctors (Mr Hardy has insisted on a London consultant seeing me as well as the local man) are agreed that the hardship of my early years has undermined my constitution and that the tuberculosis I have contracted will be terminal. My lovely Felicity is with me and I am calm and cheerful. She will not know the depths to which I sank and she will hold her own in the hard world. That is all I wish for.

Lightning Source UK Ltd.
Milton Keynes UK
UKOW051201060212

186742UK00002B/67/P

9 781456 787929